BACK FROM THE GRAVE?

"When I passed your house I saw someone on your front porch," Walter told me.

"Anyone you recognized?" I asked.

"I wish. I didn't get a very good look, but it appeared to be a young woman in her late twenties, short blonde hair, wearing a tight red dress that looked like it had been sewn on. Cut down to her knees."

"You saw all that?" I was skeptical. "My front porch is on the second story and the road is 100 yards away. Also, you were in a moving vehicle. Don't tell me you were driving too?"

Then it hit me. Marilyn?

DEADLY DIAMONDS

Pamela Troutman

Copyright © 2004 by Pamela Troutman

All rights reserved. No part of this book shall be reproduced or transmitted in any form or by any means, electronic, mechanical, magnetic, photographic including photocopying, recording or by any information storage and retrieval system, without prior written permission of the publisher. No patent liability is assumed with respect to the use of the information contained herein. Although every precaution has been taken in the preparation of this book, the publisher and author assume no responsibility for errors or omissions. Neither is any liability assumed for damages resulting from the use of the information contained herein.

This is a work of fiction. Names, characters, places, and incidents either are the product of the author's imagination or are used fictitiously. Any resemblance to actual events or locales or persons, living or dead, is entirely coincidental.

ISBN 0-7414-2103-8

Published by:

INFI∞ITY
PUBLISHING.COM

1094 New Dehaven Street, Suite 100
West Conshohocken, PA 19428-2713
Info@buybooksontheweb.com
www.buybooksontheweb.com
Toll-free (877) BUY BOOK
Local Phone (610) 520-2500
Fax (610) 519-0261

Printed in the United States of America

Printed on Recycled Paper

Published June 2004

For my semi-angelic granddogs Shiley and Ally,
and their wonderful parents, Jim and Beth

DEADLY DIAMONDS

Timing is everything. If I hadn't just spent a week in Los Angeles, if I hadn't driven past the little house on Fifth St. Helena Street where Marilyn Monroe died, if I hadn't visited her lonely crypt with sad dying flowers hanging over the edge of a tiny vase, I probably wouldn't have been so intrigued by the messages left on my answering machine while I was gone. But as I said, timing is everything.

The answering machine's red light was flashing like some winking evil eye when I returned to my office after the trip. I was hot and tired, having just driven in from the Corpus Christi airport some 40 miles away, and since my Porsche 914 doesn't have air conditioning I had spent the entire time thinking of having a large, cold, very alcoholic drink when I got home. Now I was home, or at least in my office one flight of stairs away from home, and the only thing between me and that drink was the blinking red eye.

I took a step toward the stairs, hesitated, and thought, what the hell. It'll only take a couple of minutes to play the messages, and then I won't have to come back down. I can put up my feet, relax and replay in my mind video style memories of the sights of Los Angeles, the mountains, Hollywood, the beach at Santa Monica, and the rolling Pacific Ocean. The machine was blinking six times, an indication that there were six messages. I pushed the play button and waited, hoping there was nothing pressing, nothing that would endanger the drink and a trip down memory lane.

Message number one: "Hello, this is Marilyn. I need... I want to... ask you some questions about your... services. I'll call back later." A funny, breathless little girl voice, very appealing, and definitely sexy.

Message number two: "Hello, this is Marilyn again. I just wanted to see if you're back yet... I really need to talk to you. I'll try again later."

Okay, so why didn't she leave a number?

Message number three: "Leonard Townsend? Are you the private detective? I need someone to find my dog. He's been gone an hour. My name is Henrietta Fluffle. Call me at 555-2398. You don't charge much, do you?"

Hmmmm, this one had an annoying habit of asking the answering machine questions. Did she expect it to answer? At least she left her number, although she would be disappointed. Yes, I do charge much. I don't have to, because I have a reasonably sized trust fund provided by my affectionate and financially unchallenged grandparents, but I do anyway. It's good for my ego. Plus I like getting paid a lot for sticking my neck out.

Message number four: "Oh, you're not back yet! I can't leave a number because I can't go back home.... I don't know what to do!" There was no name, but I recognized the voice all right. It was Marilyn, sounding breathless and excited, lost and unhappy. At least she explained why she hadn't left a number, sort of. I waited impatiently for the next message.

Message number five: "I found my dog. He was in the neighbor's garbage, chewing on chicken bones. You don't need to call me now. This is Henrietta Fluffle. And don't send me a bill."

A bill for what? Listening to her messages?

Message number six: "Hello, it's me, Marilyn. Oh, I wish you were there. I need help and I don't know who else to turn to. Won't you ever come back?" The last message ended in a sort of desperate wail, a combination of fear and despair that made the hair on the back of my neck stand up and head north. I wondered how soon she'd call back, or if she ever would.

I went upstairs and glanced out the front window at the beach across the street. The night sea was rolling slowly, touched softly by a large moon which was partially hidden underneath thin, wispy clouds. White sand was visible in the moonglow and I could see waves breaking unevenly onto the shore. Somewhere in this eerie night was Marilyn, the mystery woman who thought I could help her out of whatever trouble she found herself in. Funny how her voice had that little girl, breathless quality that Marilyn Monroe's had, the famous cadence and innate sexiness that has never been duplicated in the decades since her passing. Would she look anything like her famous predecessor? Or would she be a big disappointment, a 200 pound blowsy brunette with little girl squeals and big girl troubles? I sighed and went into the kitchen to fix a drink.

While I was pouring a generous helping of rum into a not so generous glass of cola the telephone rang. I reached over to the far end of the counter and picked it up, hoping to hear Marilyn's voice though it would probably mean postponing my drink. I wanted to help her even though I didn't know what her trouble was and wouldn't recognize her even if she were standing on my front porch.

A deep, masculine voice spoke grumpily when I answered. "Evening, Len. It's Walter. When did you get back?"

Walter Hughes, homicide detective for the Rockport police force, was a friend who liked to come over and socialize, particularly when he was on the outs with his sometime girlfriend, the fiery tempered Marie Fox. When I departed for the balmy Pacific shores of California, Marie and Walter were like twittering love birds and completely indifferent to my departure. However, that had been a whole week ago, and they might be mortal enemies now.

"I just got back, Walter," I replied, sipping my drink. "Reluctantly, I might add. Los Angeles is a fantastic city and Hollywood is the ultimate cheap thrill."

"Sounds great, Len," Walter said, sounding morose. "Any of those Hollywood agents discover you?" The last was said with a snicker.

"Yeah, they discovered me. They discovered me checking out some of their gorgeous young talent. There's some good looking women out there, Walter. Speaking of which, how is Marie?"

"Marie? Marie who?"

"Uh oh," I replied, wishing I hadn't asked. "What happened this time?"

"Well, you'd have to have been there," he said, gloomily.

"Try me anyway." Sometimes I really don't know just when to shut up.

"Oh, it started with Marie saying pigs are smarter than horses, and me saying it was the other way around, and it went downhill from there." Now Walter sounded embarrassed, which he probably ought to have done.

"Well, Walter, it's pretty important that a man and a woman agree on which is smarter, a pig or a horse," I said, taking another but much larger swallow of my rum and cola. "It's lucky you found out now, before you had kids and a mortgage."

"Can it, Len," Walter replied, a bit testily. "Like I said, you had to be there, and it only started with the pigs. There were a lot of other things discussed."

A change of subject seemed long overdue. "Any interesting homicides while I was away?" I asked.

"Not even any uninteresting ones. It's been real quiet. The only thing that happened was a robbery out your way. Since nothing else was going on, I rode along for the practice.... Say, that reminds me, there was something interesting."

"What was that?" I asked, taking another sip.

"When I passed your house, I saw someone on your front porch." The gloom had left his tone.

"Anyone you recognized?"

"I wish. I didn't get a real good look, but it appeared to be a young woman in her early twenties, short blonde hair, wearing a tight red dress that looked like it had been sewn own," he continued. "Cut down to her knees."

"You saw all that?" I asked incredulously. Was he putting me on? "My front porch is on the second story and the road is 100 yards away. Also, you were in a moving car. Don't tell me you were driving, too?"

"No, I wasn't driving, too," he mimicked my tone. "Listen, pal, if you'd seen her, you'd have noticed the same things. In fact, you probably would have skipped going to Los Angeles. Of course I couldn't make out her facial features, but with that hair and that body, how bad could they be? She sizzled!"

"Why didn't you stop, find out who she was and what she wanted?"

"When I'm on taxpayer time? That'd look nice in the newspapers, wouldn't it? 'Homicide detective Hughes, while joyriding on burglary investigation, takes a little detour to ogle red clad temptress.' Say, did you check your porch for scorch marks? They'd be in the shape of stiletto heels."

That's when it hit me. Marilyn? Sure sounded like a description of Marilyn in her movie Niagara, I thought, romanticizing the description a bit and letting the recent Hollywood visit influence my thinking. My wishful thinking.

"Did she look like Marilyn Monroe?" I asked, chuckling a little to pass the thing off as a joke.

Walter caught on right away. "So your mind hasn't gotten back from Los Angeles yet? Yeah, I guess you could say she did. Remember, though, I didn't get a good look at her face. For all I know, close up she might look like Michael Jackson."

The dream soured and I came back to reality. "You're probably right," I agreed reluctantly. "But while I was gone, a woman named Marilyn with a breathless, sexy voice left four messages on my answering machine that she was in trouble and needed help."

I heard a low whistle. "Could be a psycho who thinks she's the movie star and is afraid the Mafia or FBI is after her." Walter sounded half serious.

"Or it could be a sexy dame named Marilyn who just happens to have blonde hair, a good figure and an exciting voice who, with that list of assets, just naturally got herself or with help into trouble. And since I am the only private eye in this town, she looked in the phone book, got my address and phone number, and came after me to get her out. Which I may be willing to do, depending on what the trouble is. Now, what day was it you saw her here?"

"This morning."

"Okay, let's get off the phone so she can call me."

"All right. How about lunch tomorrow around noon, at Los Tres Amigos?"

"Fine, if I'm not busy taking care of Marilyn." I hung up and went back to my drink, hoping Marilyn would call again soon. I unpacked, hung up my clean clothes, put the dirty ones in the hamper and looked again at my telephone. I went through the mail that had accumulated in my absence, discarded the advertisements which was the

4

majority of it, and filed the bills. There were several inquiries from people who might need a detective, but I decided to wait until the next day to consider them. Anyone who writes a detective instead of calling can't be in much of a hurry. Right now I was intrigued by this Marilyn, whoever she was, and I managed to only glance at the telephone three or four times a minute, willing it to ring. About midnight I gave up and went to bed, only to dream of the long and fruitless pursuit of a red dressed elusive phantom, with shimmering blonde hair, beckoning arms and an unseeable face.

I awoke early the next morning to bright sunlight streaming into my room and landing on my pillow. I had forgotten to draw my blinds, which would have allowed me at least another half hour's sleep. Too late now, I thought regretfully, and got up to take a shower, hoping I wouldn't miss Marilyn's call while I was rinsing my back or soaping my hair. I hoped, like the real Marilyn, she wasn't an early riser. After I showered and dressed, I went back to my mail and considered the several potential job offers I had.

The first job offer, using the term job loosely, involved an irate farmer who wanted me to track down some night vandals who kept writing obscene graffiti on his barn while he was asleep. He had tried staying up and waiting for them himself, but he kept falling asleep on the job. After all, he wrote, he had to get up each morning at four to feed his animals. He ended with an offer of payment if I could catch the varmint. Did two chickens and three goats sound about right? I laughed out loud when I thought of my beagle hound Pokey in a fence with chickens and goats. I'd probably wind up with six animals in the canal out back of my house that I'd have to rescue within seconds of their initial meeting. So much for that job.

The second offer was from a Mrs. Charles Pomfret, whose name was vaguely familiar to me from the society columns of the local newspaper. She lived with her husband in a gigantic house on the other end of the island of Key Allegro, the same island in Aransas Bay where my home/office combo is situated. The resemblance ended there. While I had a modest two story home with an office downstairs, she had an elegant mansion overlooking a private beach in the front and a large Hatteras yacht parked in her canal space out back. Half of her boat could have eaten two of my house if it wanted. Mrs. Pomfret had a slight problem, though, and she wanted to consult me in private at my earliest convenience. Since I had seen the jovial Mr. Pomfret recently in the company of one very attractive young redhead, I was willing to bet I knew what the problem was and what Mrs. Pomfret wanted kept confidential. If I was right, it wasn't the kind of job I liked. I moved on to the next envelope.

The writing was shaky and the message was heartbreaking, if familiar. I got requests like it often from worried parents. It seemed that a

Mrs. Small had a daughter in eleventh grade who was a good student, minded her manners, helped out around the house, and in general didn't seem to have any problems out of the ordinary that a seventeen year old girl might not be expected to have. Until lately, that is, when she started dating a new senior at her school who had a fast car and an even faster reputation. The mother had noticed a change in her daughter's manner and attitude and she was afraid that drugs might be involved. Would I be able to find out? There was fear and concern written in every line and my heart went out to her. The answer was probably yes, and it would get much worse before it got better, if it ever did. I decided to give her a call, because it would be easier to help her earlier, if this still was earlier. I made an appointment to see her after lunch. This gave me the morning to devote to waiting for Marilyn to call. Not exactly fair to my dog Pokey, who must be anxiously waiting for me to pick her up at the kennels, but isn't that how the expression "a dog's life" came about?

CHAPTER TWO

Waiting for a telephone to ring is one of the hardest things I can imagine. The silence goes on and on if it doesn't ring, and minutes tick by as if they were attached to bricks. When the telephone does ring, it's your Aunt Matilda wanting to ask when you're going to visit Uncle Edgar, whose health is always on the down side, or it's a salesman for some burial company wanting you to do something morbid and foreboding called "prepurchase" or "preplan" your own funeral. Gross. Or, it's a call from the local department store wanting you to buy a service contract for an appliance they sold you six months ago. Chances are if the appliance has worked this long, it will continue working just fine over its normal life expectancy, and they know that, hence the offer. I got about four of that type of call while I was waiting for a ring from Marilyn. They did nothing to improve my mood, so when it was finally time to meet Walter for lunch, I growled menacingly at the telephone, turned on my answering machine and headed for Los Tres Amigos.

Walter was already there when I arrived, seated happily at our favorite booth and flirting with pretty dark haired Juanita, the waitress. She had fancied Walter for several months and always flashed her lovely brown eyes his way whenever he and I lunched together. I wondered if Marie Fox would quickly see the error of her ways if she knew Juanita was lurking hopefully in the background, ready to strike like a cobra if the opportunity arose.

I sat down across from Walter and gave Juanita my order. I've eaten there so often I don't ask to see the menu anymore, I can see it with my eyes closed. Juanita left reluctantly and Walter finally gave me his attention, at least part of it.

"Did you hear from the mysterious Marilyn?" he asked, his moody dark eyes still following Juanita, who hip swinging walk, admittedly, was well worth following.

"No, she didn't," I said. "I guess she probably found a way out of her trouble or maybe she left town."

"Too bad," Walter sympathized. "She appeared to be a real looker. I wonder what her problem was."

"We'll probably never know. I've got an appointment after lunch with a woman whose teenage daughter is following the wayward wind, or so it sounds. I'll know pretty soon."

"That's a shame. A lot of them are these days. You couldn't believe the calls we get from the high school. Don't know why some of these kids think it's a good idea to pack heat in a classroom. Why, there was one kid last week who took his father's samurai sword to his English

7

class! He'd had a fight with his girlfriend, for goodness sake!" Walter shook his head in wonder.

"Oh, brother," I said. "I hope the girlfriend isn't the daughter I'm supposed to help. I'm not much good at fencing."

Juanita arrived with our lunch and we began to eat. Walter had his usual non-Mexican meal, a chicken fried steak, and I had the Mexican platter. I have asked him hundreds of times how he could pass up all of the great Mexican food when he is in a Mexican restaurant, but he only shakes his head and orders American. Of course he also orders spaghetti in a seafood restaurant and hamburgers at the China Moon.

After lunch I drove over to the south side of town and looked for Mrs. Small's house on Oleander Drive. It was a small, well maintained wooden frame house, painted an off white. In front was a 1988 Chevy of some sort, washed and waxed, but faded from years under the Texas sun. I parked my Porsche under the limited shade of a palm tree and walked up to the front porch. Before I had a chance to ring the doorbell, the front door opened and a petite, brown haired woman invited me in.

Mrs. Small was in her early forties, neatly dressed in a light green skirt and a crisp, white blouse. Curly brown hair framed her oval face, and clear, intelligent blue eyes looked at me hopefully. Her skin was light and smooth, but her expression was worried. She spoke softly as she invited me to have a seat on an overstuffed blue sofa in her living room.

"Tell me what the problem is, Mrs. Small," I said, anxious to get started.

"Please call me Ruth," she said, folding her hands in her lap. "If you're going to know my family's darkest secrets and see its dirtiest laundry, you might as well call me by my first name."

"All right, Ruth," I said, giving her time to collect her thoughts and gather her courage to begin. I glanced at a table to my right. There was a picture of a teenager on it, a pretty young girl with a smiling face and laughing green eyes. "Is this your daughter?"

"Yes, it is," she answered, and for a moment her face brightened with a wide smile. Only for a moment, though, and when the smile left her face she aged 10 years in a few seconds. "At least, it was. Now she's so different, I don't feel as if it's the same girl. It's the same body, but as for the rest of her, I just don't know."

"Why don't you describe her as she was, and then tell me what happened," I suggested, becoming uncomfortable with the pain Ruth was obviously in.

"Melissa is 17 years old. She's my oldest child, born one March in a little hospital in Corpus Christi. Born during the good times, when my husband was young and strong and healthy, before he got the sickness that was to take him from us. We were both working before she was born, and we had saved up enough to put a down payment on this

8

house," she said, gesturing widely around her. "When we found out I was pregnant, it was like we'd been given the greatest gift there ever was. I can remember even now the look on Don's face when the doctor told him he had a healthy baby girl. I guess when you have so much happiness, you never think it can all go wrong someday." She paused a moment, biting her lower lip.

"We had ten good years, after that. I quit working, and took care of Melissa and the house. Don worked as the foreman for a construction company, and was paid well. Then one day he came home with a pain in his chest. It was cancer. He fought it as best he could, but he was dead within two years. He just couldn't win the long fight."

She took a tissue out of her pocket, but she didn't wipe her eyes. She just twisted the tissue in her hands, clenching and unclenching her small fingers nervously. Her expression grew hard and her eyes gazed remotely out the window at a delivery truck across the street.

"Don's medical insurance paid the bills, and he had some life insurance, so money wasn't a problem. We had enough and I was able to find a job in a boutique in Rockport. We were making out all right. I missed Don terribly, and maybe that was part of the problem. Maybe I didn't pay enough attention to Missy after Don died. A few months ago Missy began coming home late from school, without letting me know where she was. She'd never done that before. Then, on her report card, I saw she'd missed several days of school. She said she had been sick, but she'd never taken off from school without telling me before. She used to be outgoing, talkative. Now she's remote and withdrawn."

Ruth stood up, as if her pain would lessen if she were on her feet and could pace nervously about the room. I wondered if the embarrassment at her daughter's behavior made her too ashamed to face me as she spoke. She was obviously a proud woman. You could see it in her carriage and in her cool, appraising eyes.

"The worst came this week," she continued, her voice lowering as if speaking the words were almost too distasteful. "She was gone all Tuesday night. I was frantic with worry. She's been dating a young man named Harry Bascomb, and I'm afraid he's what my mother would have called a 'wrong un'. I've tried not to say too much against him, but I haven't done a very good job. When she came home early the next morning, she seemed befuddled and spaced out. I found this in her purse."

She handed me an envelope she had taken out of her pocket. I sniffed it curiously. Marijuana.

"I just didn't know what to do," she continued unhappily. "One of my friends, Marybelle Adams, said you had helped her when her son got in trouble last year. She said you can work miracles. That's what I need right now, a miracle."

9

George Adams was basically a decent kid who had gotten mixed up with the wrong crowd. He was picked up by the police for joy riding in a stolen car. His new good friends got together, said he was the one who stole the car and got the others to go for a ride. I was able to prove he wasn't even aware the car was stolen and the kid who did take it was sent to reform school. I was also able to get George a stern lecture from Walter Hughes, who can be very impressive on the subject of what happens when good kids get mixed up with bad ones. Topped off with a tour of the local jail, our George had gone straight and was now in his first semester at the University of Texas. George was a success story, but then he hadn't gotten into drugs. Drugs make things worse and usually permanently so.

"Where did your daughter say she spent the night?" I asked Ruth, who had returned to her seat and was staring morosely at a dying floral arrangement on her coffee table.

"She said they went to a drive-in movie, and fell asleep during the second feature. I'm not very sure if I believe her, even though I really want to."

"And what about the envelope?"

"She said it belongs to Harry, that he didn't have room for it in his pockets. She told me she had put it in her purse and had forgotten to give it back to him."

"Do you know what it is?"

"I believe I do," she replied hesitantly. "It's marijuana, isn't it?"

"Yes, I'm afraid it is," I answered reluctantly. "I'd advise you to get rid of it."

She nodded briefly, got up and disappeared into a room down the hall. A moment later I heard a toilet flush. When she came back, her eyes were slightly red.

"Can you help me?" she asked calmly, but her eyes were pleading.

"I'm not really sure what I can do at this point," I told her. "Let me ask you a few questions and then we'll see if we can come up with a plan." I'm always a sucker for a poor widow woman. "This Harry, is he the only 'wrong un' your daughter hangs out with?"

"Yes, I believe so. She's so infatuated with him," she replied. "I think she'd be all right, if only she weren't involved with him. I'm afraid of what he is going to get her into, what he may already have gotten her into."

"Well, it could turn out he's a drug dealer," I said. "Obviously he is a user. I could find out just what his involvement is. If he's a seller, we might be able to get him put away for awhile, long enough maybe to get your daughter over him. If he's just a user, there's probably not much that can be done."

"I'll try anything at this point," she told me hopefully.

"Okay, why don't I see what I can find out about him and we'll take it from there. Meanwhile, play it cool with Melissa. Be there for her, if she needs you, and talk to her if you can. Don't put her down, just listen. Offer advice if she asks. Don't tell her you got me into it. I'll report back to you in a day or two."

Ruth smiled and held out her hand. When she asked me what the fee would be, I knew she would have given everything she owned to get her daughter back on the yellow brick road, but I named my minimum fee. As I said, I'm a sucker for pretty widows.

CHAPTER THREE

It was about time for the Rockport high school to let out. I hustled over to the local after school hangout where I was fairly certain to run into a kid named Roy Owens. He helps out when I'm on a case involving someone in his school. Roy is a sharp senior, an all A student, captain of the football team and probable winner of a scholarship to the University of Texas by the end of the school year, but his heart isn't in it. He wants in the worst way to be a private detective and I know someday, after he gets his college behind him, he'll make a good one. He is nice looking, with wavy dark hair and clean cut features, intelligent and quick witted, with an active sense of adventure. I wish him well, but I know someday he'll be awesome competition if he decides to settle in Rockport.

The local hangout is a Dairy Queen near the high school which welcomes the kids as long as they behave and confine their youthful antics to something harmless like shooting straws or making limp paper airplanes out of napkins. If they get too rowdy Big Martha, who runs the place, will banish them from her malt and milkshake kingdom until enough time has passed for the miscreants to repent and kiss up. The last time I saw her throw someone out it was because he had put sugar in several of the salt shakers and before it was discovered about six customers had sweetened their fries. The custom caught on, and now it is not unusual to see kids sugar their fries. Ugh.

I pulled up in front of the Dairy Queen and looked at my watch. I was a few minutes early, so I went in and asked Big Martha to fix me a large Heath Blizzard. Big Martha is about six feet tall, and she always looks like she has just bitten into a lemon. She has straggly hair which she over perms and dyes a strange orange color, resulting in a rather unusual look, like her hair is made out of lots of tiny electrical wires. Managing the Dairy Queen suits her, even though boredom during the slow times has tempted her to try out all her ice cream offerings. She has steadily gained weight during her 12 years there to where I'd guess she probably weighs around 250 pounds. In spite of her sour look, she is friendly, easy going and remarkably intelligent. I always enjoy a visit with Big Martha.

"How've you been, Martha?" I asked her, realizing it had been awhile since I had seen her.

"Pretty busy, Len," she replied, scooping a generous helping of Heath pieces into my Blizzard. "Lots of new families moving into the area, with bunches of new kids stopping by after school. I've had to hire extra help. I may even have to delay my vacation until I'm sure things are running smoothly."

"Where are you going this year?"

"Paris, I think. I haven't been to the Louvre in five years. Want to come?" The last was said with a flirtatious wink.

"I just got back," I replied quickly. "Not from Paris. From Los Angeles."

"Oh, yes, Los Angeles. I love Los Angeles," she gushed. "Like to shop on Rodeo Drive!"

As I said, she's very intelligent and she uses her smarts investing her earnings in the stock market. She travels as often as she can get away. I wondered what she bought on Rodeo Drive. I didn't see any evidence of it or the Louvre in the Dairy Queen. All I saw was pictures of cows and hamburgers.

The big glass door in front of the restaurant opened and some high school kids came in, laughing and talking. I took my Blizzard and went to a small table. Before long I spotted Roy coming in with his arm around a tall, skinny redhead. I caught his eye and after he got a milkshake he unfastened himself and came over to my table. He sat down, but his long, slender legs seemed not to fit under the small table. He shifted them several times in a futile effort to get comfortable. Roy was way over six feet tall, built slim, and he could run like a rabbit. He moved his legs from under the table and stuck them in the aisle.

"What's up, boss?" he asked, stirring his milkshake. His dark blue eyes expressed curiosity and extreme interest. The redhead had taken a seat at another table with some other girls, but she glanced at us from time to time.

"I need some information on a senior named Harry Bascomb," I told Roy after the usual greetings were exchanged. "Do you know him?"

Roy's lip curled in distaste. "Yeah, I know him. He's new this year. Thinks he's hot stuff, and a lot of the kids agree with him. Actually, he's a real punk. Full of bravado, but in reality he is a bully with a definite lack of self esteem." Roy was interested in psychology this term. He figured it would help him psyche people out when he was a detective. He was probably right.

"Is he into drugs?" I asked, although I pretty much already knew the answer.

"I don't know for sure. I don't get close enough to him to know what he's up to. It wouldn't surprise me though. He hangs out with users. Do you want me to find out?"

I hesitated. "Maybe. What do you know about Melissa Small?" Roy always kept my questions to himself, which was wise, because I wouldn't ask them if he didn't.

"Missy? She's a good kid, a little shy. Is she mixed up with him?"

"Just starting to be, I think," I told him. "Doesn't sound like a hot idea. Why don't you look around a little bit, see what you can find out on your end. He mustn't know we're curious about him though, and she can't know either."

"Sure, boss," Roy said enthusiastically. "Starting now."

"Let me know what you find out, and I'll pay the usual rates," I said. The usual rates ranged from cash to credit to the loan of the Porsche 914 for something really special. I hated loaning it out, though. Especially to a teenager, even if this one was trustworthy. His parents approved, but I'd still not want to see either one of them damaged in some stupid teenage wreck.

Roy nodded, picked up his shake and went over to claim the redhead. I watched them for a moment as they chatted noisily with the other girls at their table and then I got up and walked out, remembering what it was to be young and all knowing. Wonder how I managed to forget so much, so soon, I thought with amusement.

I decided to go back and check my answering machine, although I wasn't really hopeful that there would be a message from Marilyn. She had not called during the morning hours, so why would she call during the afternoon? A telephone or a cell phone is always within reach. However, if she hadn't called because she was working, she might call after work in the evening. I decided to stay in, hoping to hear from her before I turned in for the night. First, though, I had to go pick up my beagle hound Pokey at the kennels.

Green Pine Kennels is on the outskirts of town, but why it's called Green Pine I don't know. Not even one blade of grass grows out in the dirt filled weed infested acres that house the kennels, and there isn't a pine tree for dozens of miles around, unless you count the ones imported for sale at grocery stores for Christmas. Now, there is some fake wooden paneling inside the kennel's offices, but it isn't green and I'm not real sure it is meant to be pine.

Bob Rattlesnake, named after a fighting Cherokee in his distant past, owns the kennels, and even he doesn't know why they are called Green Pine. That was the name when he bought them and he is too lazy to change the name. Besides, he can't think of a better name anyway, other than to call them after himself, he says, and to call them Rattlesnake Kennels would put a lot of folks off. Unimaginative and crotchety, his curt manner deters many potential customers, but he has an enthusiastic love of animals which led me to choose him to watch Pokey when I'm out of town. He is second to none in providing good care for his charges and spares no expense in providing good food and clean surroundings. His rates were a little high, but so are mine.

Bob led me to Pokey's stall, limping a little as he walked.

"Did you hurt your leg?" I asked.

"Naw," he replied, spitting tobacco out of the side of his mouth. "That German Shepherd bitch Marlena Dogtrick took a piece out of my ankle this morning. Nasty dog, that one."

"Has Pokey behaved?"

Bob gave me a skeptical look. "Well, you asked. That dog howled every day you were gone. First she howls at all the other dogs. Then, when she's tired of that, she howls at my helpers. Then she barks at passersby. When she runs out of everything else, she'll bark at the moon. Here she is, and you're welcome to her."

We had reached Pokey's run and the little darlin' started barking in her enthusiasm to see me. Pokey is a four year old purebred beagle who guards my back yard against dangerous intruders, such as cats and birds. She once scared off a would be burglar who wasn't smart enough to recognize a friendly bark when he heard it. Pokey almost knocked me over in her enthusiasm to get out of her run and into my Porsche. She jumped up on me a couple of times, trying to lick my face but hitting my belt buckle. Finally she gave up and took off for the Porsche, sitting down beside it and licking a tire.

"Good dog," I complimented her, having been afraid she'd take off down the road after an imaginary rabbit. Pokey couldn't make up her mind whether to be upset with me for leaving her for a week or just glad to see me because I'd finally come back. She chose the latter course when she saw I had saved her the last of my Heath Blizzard. We were buddies again.

I drove back home, allowing Pokey the rare privilege of hanging her head out the window to sniff the enticing smells in the brisk sea breeze. Every now and then she spotted a cat or dog in the street and growled, but other than that she behaved herself surprisingly well.

When we got home I put Pokey in the back yard where she immediately dug up a small mound of dirt, uncovering a weathered bone. I hurried inside to check my answering machine and sure enough, there were two blinks. I held my breath hopefully as I pushed the replay button.

The first message was from a tired sounding woman, who unenthusiastically informed me that I had just won a fabulous vacation to Rio de Janeiro, if I would only call her number and claim my prize. I'd heard that one before.

The second message was Marilyn, sounding more breathless than ever. "Oh, you're still not home! I'll try again tonight. This is Marilyn. Please be there, please!"

At least now we had a definite time. Well, sort of a definite time, anyway. What did she consider tonight? Did her tonight start at 5:00 or 9? I sighed, as I realized I was going to be chaining myself to the telephone for however long it took for her to call. My curiosity was ravenous now and must be satisfied before long, or I might be inclined to search house to house for this woman.

Unfortunately, however, I had already made plans for the evening. I was going to go find my contact in the drug underworld for information on Harry Bascomb. Paul Boggins, a semi-shady character who owned a bicycle in the middle of Rockport, was a renegade type of guy whose shop was a hangout for tough guys who were into drugs and other vices. I had once done him a favor, and from time to time when I needed information he would supply it, if it didn't involve anyone close to him. I wouldn't doubt Harry Bascomb had already found his way to Paul's shop, even if he was new to town.

Paul has never been caught selling drugs or using them, and I don't believe he is guilty of either. It's just that his shop is the gathering place of those who do, and he is privy to their secrets. Their dirty, sordid little secrets. Well, I could put off seeing Paul tonight and go after him tomorrow. Tomorrow morning might be better anyway, because there wouldn't be as much chance of running into Bascomb, if indeed he was one of those questionable characters who hung out at Paul's. Hopefully he wouldn't be skipping school in the morning.

At five o'clock the telephone rang and I caught it on the second bell. It was Walter, wanting to know if I had heard from Marilyn.

"Yes and no," I answered impatiently. "Yes I heard from her, but no I haven't talked with her. I got another message on my machine. She's supposed to call back tonight. Unfortunately she didn't think to give a specific time so I wouldn't have to hang around and wait."

"At least she didn't say soon," Walter said helpfully.

"At least she's still calling," I added. "Want to come over and wait with me? There's a game on tv."

"I might as well. Marie is still being hardheaded."

"Well, I can sure understand that, after the high tone argument you had," I commented unsympathetically.

"Stuff it, Len," Walter replied testily. "You know what she's like. How would you like to argue with her?"

"I'll pass," I told him hastily. "Sometimes I get into trouble with her when I just say hello."

"It's the way you say it," he replied, taking her side for the moment.

"We can talk about it when you come over," I said, trying to change the subject. Marie was always a no win topic.

"Not a chance. I don't want to hear her name tonight and maybe not any other night," Walter told me. "I'll be over about seven and we can talk about the game or the weather or even about Marilyn. Maybe she'll come over. I'd like to see her if it's the same woman I saw yesterday on your front porch."

"If it's the same woman, you're welcome to leave when she gets here."

"We'll see about that." He hung up without saying goodbye, a disconcerting habit he's picked up from Marie.

I fixed an early dinner with a steak from the freezer and a baked potato. I added a salad. As usual, I was off on my timing and had to eat the potato first, then the salad, then the steak. I can't ever seem to get things in the kitchen ready at the same time. For dessert I had some peach ice cream I had bought before my trip to Los Angeles. It still tasted good. The meal took an hour from start to finish and the telephone hadn't rung once. I resisted the temptation to pick it up to see if it was still working.

At 6:30 p.m. I turned on the television and caught the local news. It was the same old replay of shootings and car wrecks, with new names and new faces. Here and there the cameraman had seen fit to give a full color close-up of a bloody head or mangled torso, so I gave up and went over by the window to watch the ocean across the street. Whitecaps were forming and I could see shrimp boats hurrying to get back into port before the night hours overtook them. Marilyn, where are you? I wondered fitfully.

I let myself fantasize about her. Would she look like her famous predecessor, with the inimitable look of innocence, starry eyed and luminous? Would she have the shape that men have killed for, and than funny, fluid way of moving her lips that no one since has ever been able to duplicate? Would she look lost and out of place, as if she were thinking of something long ago and far away, something sad and indescribable? Or would she turn out to be a pimply faced adolescent, a gum smacking, sassy mouthed, smart aleck of a little chit whose big problem was she had been caught stealing lingerie from the department store and could I please fix it for her?

The doorbell rang and I could see Walter on my front porch, glancing across the water at a Wellcraft Scarab in the distance. I could almost read his mind. It was a good thing we weren't going to talk about Marie, because the fellow who owned the Scarab was always after Marie to go for a ride with him, and doggoned if it didn't look like a familiar shapely brunette seated beside him. Luckily the boat was too far away to tell for sure, and getting farther away all the time, but I saw a look of absolute thunder pass briefly on Walter's face.

I opened the door and he marched in, looking at me to see if I had seen him looking at the Scarab.

"Did you see the Scarab?" he asked in a low, growly voice.

"I thought we weren't going to talk about her," I answered.

"We aren't talking about her," he replied childishly. "We're talking about a boat. Did you see it?"

"Yeah, I saw the boat... Now where are we?"

"Could you tell who was on it?" he continued, the growl lowering.

"No, it was too far away."

The telephone rang, and with much relief that we weren't going to get to continue that pointless conversation, I hurried over to answer it.

17

Predictably, it was for Walter. He always leaves a number where he can be reached by the men at the station.

"Yeah?" he murmured into the receiver. "Where? Any names?"

After a minute he hung up. He shook his head and turned back towards the front door. "I won't be able to keep you company after all. There's been a killing."

"Who?" I asked curiously.

"Girl by the name of Melissa Small. Over by the high school. She was stabbed and strangled, just to make sure," Walter said.

My heart turned over. "Wait for me, I'm going with you."

Walter turned to me in surprise. "What about Marilyn?"

"Melissa Small is the daughter of my new client. Was the daughter," I corrected. "I'll help you tell her mother, if she doesn't already know."

Walter nodded and we left, each taking his own car. I'd need transportation to get to Mrs. Small's house, if Walter couldn't get loose to come along. Some people just get bad breaks, and it looked like Ruth Small was one of them.

CHAPTER FOUR

There were already three black and whites at the scene when we arrived. Their rooftop lights were flashing blue and red, giving the area a gaudy carnival look. A crowd of local neighbors and teenagers from the high school had gathered, whispering among themselves in an effort to get more information, and one television news van had just pulled up. It began unloading camera equipment.

The police had roped off a large area in the woods behind the high school and several patrolmen were searching in the weeds for possible clues. In the middle of the area were the remains of Melissa Small. I followed Walter over for a look.

Missy lay on her back, wearing a blood spattered pink tee shirt and tight fitting blue jeans. She was a tiny girl, probably not much more than five feet tall. I doubt she weighed as much as 100 pounds. She had long, brown hair and it was spread out like seaweed on the ground beneath her. Her facial features were swollen and unrecognizable, at least to me from the picture I had seen in her mother's house earlier that day. There was a belt wrapped tightly around her neck, obviously used to strangle her. She was not wearing a belt, and the one around her neck was so tiny that it seemed likely her own belt had been used to kill her. She had also been stabbed several times in the chest. Someone had been very thorough. There was no sign of the weapon which had been used. Walter stepped back a short distance and grimaced.

"I wonder what in the world made someone think he had to kill this child?" Walter mused aloud.

"You already know the probable answer to that," I commented bitterly. "Maybe nothing. It may be that some drug freak killed her for the fun of it. His kind of fun. He might not even have known her. Or thought, in his drug induced stupor, she was the devil, or a dog, or a witch. Or it could be she did know her killer, and wanted to break up with him, and he wouldn't let her. Whatever the reason, it wasn't enough. It never is. Now I'm going to go tell her mother."

"Go ahead. I better stick around here and find out what information has been gathered so far. Tell her I'll be along in awhile."

I went back to my car and drove over to the Small house. There was a light on in the front room, and as I shut off the Porsche's engine, I could see Ruth's silhouette in the window. Perhaps she was waiting for Missy to come home.

I walked up to the house and was greeted at the front door by Mrs. Small. Her face was ashen.

"Something's wrong, isn't it? Something's dreadfully wrong!" Her eyes were wide with alarm and she clutched at my arm like a drowning man at a lifejacket. I wasn't certain I could ever make her let go.

"Let's talk here in the living room, Ruth," I told her gently. "Come with me and sit down, and I'll tell you."

I guided her to the sofa. Her gait was stiff and uncomprehending. Her eyes never left my face and she never loosened her tight grip. I unwrapped her fingers, took hold of her hand and began.

"I was with Walter Hughes, the police detective, when he received a telephone call tonight," I explained carefully, knowing she was probably too frightened to assimilate many details. I'd probably have to tell her again later. "The call was about Missy. She's been found near the high school."

"Found? She was found?" she said, her eyes pleading. "Oh, Len, is she…dead?"

"Yes, she is. I'm sorry," I answered, waiting to see if she wanted to hear more. Her eyes left my face and went to Missy's picture. A single tear ran down her cheek and disappeared.

"I knew it! I knew it a few hours before you came. She was late again, but I wasn't worried. I thought you'd be able to work a miracle for me like you did for George Adams and his family," she told me. "But all of a sudden, I felt this pain. It was like nothing I'd ever known before. A pain in my chest. Somehow I knew Missy was gone. I can't tell you what it was I felt, but I knew she was gone. How did it happen?"

"Are you sure you want to hear all this now?"

"Yes, I'm sure. I've already heard the worse. Now, tell me what happened. I have a right to know, don't I?"

"You have a right to know," I began. "Missy was found in the woods in back of the high school. She was strangled and stabbed. The police don't know who is responsible yet, but they're working on it."

Ruth got up and went into the kitchen. When she came back she was wearing a sweater over her light green cotton dress and carrying a white purse. "I want to go to her," she said evenly. "Please take me now."

I hesitated, remembering the blood on Missy's sweater and her swollen face. "I don't think that's a good idea," I told her. "Wait until later. Why don't I fix you a strong drink? It may make things easier for now."

"I don't want things easier," she said between tight lips. "Things aren't ever going to be easy again. I want to be with my daughter. Do you think I can't stand the sight of my daughter, that the blood and carnage will make her any less my daughter? Well, you're wrong. Take me to her, or I'll go by myself."

I opened the front door and let her out first. It had gotten dark while we were inside. Thousands of stars hung over us, indifferent to our sad mission. Ruth got in the car and stared straight ahead, folding her hands in her lap. We drove over to the high school in silence, with me wondering if I was doing the right thing under the circumstances. Well, Ruth hadn't given me much choice. I wondered what Walter would say when we arrived.

The police photographer had almost finished taking pictures of the dead girl when we got to her. I heard Ruth gasp, and I took her arm to steady her. She gently removed my arm and knelt down beside Missy. Walter came over to me and asked softly, "The girl's mother?"

"Yes, that's Ruth Small," I replied quietly as she cradled Missy's head in her lap. "Have you learned anything?"

"If you count the minuses, yes we have. We have learned that nobody saw her after 5:30 p.m., that nobody saw anyone in the area where she was killed and nobody knows why someone would do this to her. That's what we've learned. Pretty impressive, isn't it?"

"It's early, Walter. You can't expect to solve them all in ten minutes."

"I could if I could just get people to cooperate with us even 50 per cent of the time. You know it is likely somebody knows something about what happened here, but they don't want to get involved. Either they're afraid it will happen to them, or they don't want to get mixed up with the police, or they just don't feel like it's their business. What they don't think of is it could happen to another girl if whoever did this doesn't get caught this time."

The mortuary assistants had arrived and were getting their stretcher ready to take the dead girl to the county morgue. Ruth stood up and moved aside to let them do their work. She wasn't quite crying but her expression was one of unspeakable sadness. She came over to me as the attendants loaded Missy gently onto their stretcher.

"Please, could you take me where she's going?" she asked.

"Of course," I replied, "but are you sure you want to go there now? There are certain things that have to be done..."

"I don't care. I want to go."

I led her back to my car and we got in. I made a brief stop at the local hamburger stand. She started to protest but I shut her off.

"Look, Ruth. I bet you haven't eaten since lunch."

Her silence confirmed my guess.

I continued. "I know you probably don't feel like eating now and you probably won't for quite awhile. But you need to keep your strength up. I'm going to get you a hamburger and coffee and you're going to try to eat. Then we'll go."

The order came and I handed it to her. She chewed slowly, staring out of the window. She asked for more coffee. Finally she was through, although she had eaten less than two bites, but even so a little color had come back in her face.

"Still want to go?" I asked.

Her eyes widened and she replied, "Yes, of course. Please."

I drove over to the county morgue, which was behind the police station. Walter's car was just arriving so I pulled in next to his space. He came over and reintroduced himself to Mrs. Small, who obviously did not remember him, adding, "When you're up to it, I want to ask you some questions."

"To help you find out who did this?" she questioned.

"Yes, you might be able to help."

"I'll answer you now," she said, giving the morgue a hard look.

We followed Walter back to his office, giving up temporarily on the morgue, an idea which I wholly approved. We wound through the busy police station where the night's arrests were being processed for their day in court. Several very happy and somewhat lewd drunks spotted Ruth and gave an appreciative whistle, but a hard look from Walter shut them up quickly. Ruth hadn't noticed. She was still in a daze, lost in sad thoughts and old memories.

We finally got to Walter's cubicle. He offered Ruth a cup of coffee, which she quickly accepted. I wondered if she wasn't trying to wire herself up on the caffeine.

"How much have you learned so far about what happened to my daughter?" Ruth asked in a shaky voice.

Walter hesitated. He didn't like to come out and say he hadn't learned much of anything. He didn't want to make it worse for her than it already was. He chose his words carefully.

"We have our best men working on it, Mrs. Small," he began. "The crime lab went over the scene thoroughly and we have men in the area questioning--"

"You haven't learned anything," Ruth interrupted accusingly. "Why don't you just come out and say it? You don't know who did this. You may never know who did this." She sounded near despair now.

"Wait one moment, Mrs. Small," Walter said comfortingly "You're absolutely right that we don't know much now. It's early on. But you're not right that we won't ever know what happened. That could happen, but it's only an extremely remote possibility. As I said, we have our best people working on it. We will cover all areas. I will work day and night until we have this person, this unspeakable animal, behind bars. You have my word. Sure, there's a chance we won't catch him, but the odds are so great against it they aren't worth calling."

Ruth seemed reassured by Walter's vehemence. Her expression hardened and she spoke again. "Well, you don't have to look far. I know who did it. It's that boy she's been dating. His name is Harry Bascomb, and he's the one who did this."

"We have somebody out looking for him right now," Walter assured her. "If he's the one, we'll get him."

"He's the one she was with this afternoon," Ruth told him unhappily. "He was always the one she was with, when she came home late. She's been with him almost every afternoon for the past week. It was him all right, you can bet on it."

"Had she any enemies?" Walter asked.

"No, she didn't," Ruth asserted, her voice quavering. "Until she met this character, she was a normal teenager. She had only gone on a few dates with decent, honorable young men. She made good grades, helped out around the house and was respectful to me. Then, after she met him, she started staying out late and then she skipped school. I don't know why he thought he had to kill her, but that's what happened."

"You might be right, but don't close your mind yet to other possibilities," Walter warned her. "It could be that a stranger did this. She may have been waiting for this young man, and someone else came along. We want to get the one who did this. Did Harry Bascomb ever threaten her? Was she afraid of him? Did he ever hurt her in any way?"

"If he had, would I be sitting here talking to you now instead of having taken care of him then?" Ruth asked. "I admit, I've never seen him hurt her. He always treated her all right in front of me. I wouldn't have allowed otherwise. She didn't seem to be afraid of him. I wish she had been."

"Did you know where she was today after school?"

"No, she was supposed to be home," Ruth said regretfully, her head bowed as if she were embarrassed to tell us. "Before, when she wasn't where she was supposed to be, I'd find out she was with him. When she didn't come home today, that's where I though she was. I still think it."

"Let me have the names of those other fellows she dated, before Harry came along," Walter said, getting out his notebook.

Ruth frowned for a moment. "Let's see, there was that Adams boy, George. She went to the movies with him once, about six months ago. Then there was Tony Merritt, who took her on his sailboat several times, about five months ago. She went to a school dance with John West, but none of these dates were anything serious. Just fun."

"Who were her girlfriends?"

"She's been friends with Kathy Graham since first grade. That's her best friend. She has lots of other girl friends, but Kathy can tell you more about that than I can." It was obvious that the strain was beginning to wear on Mrs. Small. She looked about three times more tired than she did when she walked in half an hour earlier.

"I think you've helped us all you can for now, Mrs. Small," Walter said, apparently coming to the same opinion about her condition that I had. "Why don't you go on back home and get someone to stay with you for awhile? Do you have a relative or a close friend I can call for you?"

"No, thank you," she replied. "I'm not going home. I'm going to Missy. I want to be with her while I still can."

Walter looked at me accusingly. I shook my head. I had nothing to do with this.

"That's not a good idea right now, Mrs. Small," Walter told her gently. "There are things that have to be done, police procedures... It would be better if you came back in the morning. She can be released then. You can see her at the funeral home. A good night's sleep will help you deal with this."

"No, I'm going across the street to be with her," Ruth said firmly. "I know you mean well, but no. You just go ahead and find out who did this, and let me worry about how to deal with it. Thank you for your advice, but I'll be doing this my way." She got up and started for the door.

I followed her out, even though she seemed unaware of my presence. She weaved her way through the cluttered desks of the police department, past the recently arrested and the newly drunk semblance of humanity who lined the barren green walls. She went out the door into the night's cool, fresh air, crossed the street and made her way into the main office of the morgue, where an overweight, middle aged attendant sat chewing on a piece of cherry pie. He looked up as she came in and reluctantly put his fork down as he got to his feet.

"Can I help you, ma'am?" he asked her, seeming a bit uneasy at the presence of two live visitors.

"Yes, I've come to see my daughter, Melissa Small. Please take me to her."

"Oh, I'm sorry, I can't do that," the man said apologetically, running nervous fingers through his thinning hair.

"Why not?' she asked sharply, sounding impatient.

"Well, ma'am, they've just started...uh...working on her. Nobody can go in while she is being worked on."

"Nonsense. I'm her mother."

The man's wide brown eyes glanced appealingly to me. "Can you explain it to her?"

"I'll try," I replied, taking Ruth's arm and leading her to a sofa. We sat down as my mind searched for appropriate euphemisms. There weren't very many. "Ruth, your daughter was involved in a crime of violence. A death such as that requires an autopsy, which will determine the cause of death and help convict the one who is responsible. You don't want to interrupt this process and undermine the investigation. Let's go back to your house and tomorrow you can see your daughter and make the arrangements."

Ruth's shoulders sagged. Her exhaustion had finally caught up with her, and stark reality undermined her resolve to be with her daughter, at least for the present. She nodded her head reluctantly and let me lead her to my car after signing some forms given to her by the attendant. We drove back to her home without speaking. It seemed as if there were no words to say.

When we were inside her house, Ruth told me I should go home, that she would be all right. I was able to persuade her to call a neighbor to keep her company during the long night ahead. When a tall, gaunt woman with worried eyes arrived, I left. I hadn't thought of Marilyn all evening, which was just as well, because when I got home there were no messages waiting. I wondered if she had given up and called Joe DiMaggio instead.

I arose early the next morning and went outside. Across the street the bay seemed to be awakening early like me as the sun touched it. A gentle breeze was making tiny ripples across the calm, reflecting waters of Aransas Bay, which was almost colorless this early in the morning. Later, when the wind blew harder and clouds filled the sky, the water would turn a bright emerald green or a soft blue, according to its mood and the ratio of sun to clouds. I've never seen the same color twice, and I've lived there most of my life. I hoped wherever Missy Small was now she was enjoying the view and had found a peace she didn't have here. I said a prayer for her soul.

Back inside, I started the coffee pot and put some sort of breakfast sandwich in the microwave. It was a new kind of frozen sausage/egg/biscuit combo. If it was good, or even semi-good, I'd eat it. If it was garbage, I'd give it to Pokey, whose culinary standards were quite a bit lower than mine. After I heated the sandwich the required 90 seconds I took a bite and then went out back to give the rest to Pokey. She sniffed it for a nanosecond and then almost swallowed it whole. Of course she also likes to eat rotten fish. Bon appetite, Pokey!

After I finished a delicious breakfast of pecan pie and coffee, I gave Walter a call. I had guessed correctly. Whenever there is a homicide, particularly one as heinous as the Missy Small murder, Walter drags a small folding cot into his office and remains there, at least during the early days. Walter answered his phone promptly, sounding a bit disappointed when he heard my voice.

"I was calling to find out the status of the Small case," I told him.

"I figured you would be," Walter replied. "Well, we aren't any further along now than when you left last night. How is the mother?"

"We went to the morgue. They were about to start the autopsy, so I got her to leave and left her with a neighbor."

"Poor woman."

"What about Harry Bascomb?" I asked. "Is he a suspect?"

"You might say so," Walter answered. "We haven't been able to locate him. His parents don't know where he is and he didn't come home all night. Could be he killed her, panicked, and is somewhere in Mexico by now, stoned on cheap grass."

"If he did it, that wouldn't be a bad place for him. Not from our viewpoint, anyway, considering the likelihood of him getting picked up for using drugs and the quality of Mexican jails."

"Did you get your call from Marilyn?"

"No, I sure didn't," I confessed reluctantly. "Not even a sexy, breathless, little girl squeal mysterious message. Guess she's given up."

"Too bad. It might have been interesting to find out what she looked like and what she wanted."

"It might have been interesting like the great San Francisco earthquake or Mount Vesuvius or any other natural disaster you might care to name."

Walter chuckled, promised to get back to me later and hung up. I showered, got dressed and decided to run over to Ruth Small's house to see how she was doing. She wasn't there when I arrived, so I drove over to the morgue. I had just missed her.

"Mrs. Small made arrangements for her daughter to be transferred to the funeral home," the attendant told me helpfully. He didn't need to say which one because a town the size of Rockport usually only has one. I thanked him and left.

Ruth Small was seated in the lobby of the Morgan funeral home when I arrived. She was dressed in a simple black dress, wearing black shoes and carrying a black purse. Her hair was partially hidden by a black hat. A thin veil covered her eyes, but not enough to hide their red rims and puffiness. It didn't look as if she'd had a very good night, but then I didn't really expect that she would.

"Hello, Ruth," I greeted her, taking her hand. "How are you doing?"

"I'm glad you came," she replied, seeming somewhat relieved. "I've got to make arrangements for Melissa, and I don't seem to be able to make decisions right now. Would you help?"

"Certainly, I'll be glad to do whatever I can," I told her.

Edgar Hamilton, director of the funeral home, came out of his office and walked over to Mrs. Small. I had never liked Edgar, who was pompous, overweight and balding, and he wore a self-satisfied smile like it was the Bronze Star. As his was the only funeral home in town, he thought he could charge about what he wanted, particularly since his services weren't the kind you normally shopped around for. On more than one occasion I had persuaded him to offer a more reasonable price to someone who couldn't afford his rip-off rates. It looked like I was going to have that privilege again. His smile, which rested on Ruth Small, quickly disappeared when he saw me standing beside her. Maybe I wouldn't have to have that talk after all.

"Hello, Mrs. Small, I'm Edgar Hamilton," he announced in melodious and patronizing tones as he held out his soft, plump hand. "Please accept my sincerest condolences on your terrible loss."

He eyed me warily as he took her hand and I returned his glance with a hard look and a curling of my upper lip. I hoped it looked like a snarl, because that's how I felt. I followed them into Hamilton's office, not taking my eyes off the old lecher. He belatedly acknowledged my presence with a curt nod.

"Would you like for me to describe the services we offer?" he asked Ruth in a steady tone, but the nervousness was coming through loud and clear. I could hear it, I could feel it. I could even smell it. I was itching to say something to him, but had to hold myself back out of respect for Ruth's loss. She was just the kind of client he liked. Confused, overcome by grief, sentimental, and looking to him for guidance in what to choose for that long and final goodbye she was about to make. But, here I was, in his face and all ready to cut his profit and deflate his greedy expectations. Ah, the defender of sweet grace from wicked intentions, that's me!

Ruth simply nodded her head and twisted her handkerchief nervously. I curled my lip a little more and narrowed my eyes. Hamilton took note and began.

"We have three types of services, any one of which would be appropriate for your daughter--"

Ruth stood up unexpectedly, nostrils flaring. "No service, no funeral service, is appropriate for my daughter. What would be appropriate, as you say, would be for her to be in her English class this morning, studying Chaucer. What is not appropriate is for me, her mother, to be making arrangements for a 17 year old girl, who should have her whole life ahead of her, to be buried in some dreary cemetery by your dreary company. Len, will you take over for me? I can't stand to deal with this puffed up and pompous old fool right now."

She didn't wait for an answer. She walked right out and took a seat in the lobby. She didn't even close the door. I turned back to Hamilton with an unpleasant grin. I hadn't realized that Ruth had it in her.

"You were saying?" I taunted.

"I'll give her the cheap service for $100 and the minimum casket arrangement," he said, resignedly.

"Just so it's a decent show," I told him. "Get the Rev. Hopkins, he's pretty good. Use Lyla on the organ. Have lots of flowers. If nobody sends any, order some and bill me. Remember, I'll be checking the tab. Have two nights visitation, and services Thursday morning. Ruth already has a dress for Melissa, don't try to sell her one. She also has a plot. I'll be going over your bill with her. I guess that's all."

I got up and walked out, closing the door behind me. Ruth gave me a weak smile.

"Sorry I lost my temper," she said. "I shouldn't let people like that get to me, but I knew what was coming and just didn't want to handle it."

"I'm delighted you said what you said to him," I replied. "He had it coming and more. I give it to him whenever I get the chance. Are you ready to leave? Visitation will be this evening."

"No, I'm staying here with Missy. As soon as she is ready, I'm going to sit with her. I won't be able to do that much longer and then never again. Not in this life." Her face assumed an air of sadness.

"I'll see you later then," I said, heading for the door.

"Len, let me know if the police find anything," she requested.

"Sure, I'll be looking too."

I went out into the parking lot, glad to escape the oppressive air of the funeral home. The sky was now overcast and it looked as if Rockport would get some rain. The weather seemed appropriate for the mood I was in. I headed back to the police station to speak with Walter. I wanted to know if they had found Harry. If he was guilty, chances are he would have already confessed. The case would be over and I could get back to concentrating on the mysterious Marilyn.

Walter was seated at his desk with his ear pressed against the receiver of his telephone. He winked at me as I walked in and motioned for me to take a seat. He gestured obscenely at the telephone, which told me that it was probably the city commissioner calling and he was taking some heat about the Melissa Small case. I shrugged my shoulders in reply and Walter continued listening to the commissioner without comment. Finally he had heard enough.

"Look, boss, if you want fast results you're going to have to give me more people," he said impatiently. "I've got two patrolmen, when they aren't busy working on something else, and a couple of snot nosed kid assistants. I'm doing the best I can with what I have, but when a guy disappears, he disappears. He could be in Mexico, for all we know. It's not so far from here. He could have been in Mexico before we even found her. If he's guilty and he's in Mexico, what can I do? I'll tell you what I can do, nothing. Not right now."

Walter was getting wound up. He continued, "Either he turns up or he doesn't. We're making our inquiries, but until you give me enough manpower, you're going to have to let me handle it my way. I have to go now because I have someone in my office waiting to talk to me."

He paused, got a reply, and hung up. "That old idiot," he said derisively. "Thinks we can run the shop on peanuts and then perform like monkeys whenever there's work to do."

"Let's do lunch," I said, getting up. "I'm hungry, unless you are so busy you have to skip it."

"Now you're talking like Los Angeles," Walter said, and mimicked, " 'Let's do lunch.' What you really want to do is avoid another 20 minutes of me putting down the commissioner."

"That, too," I confessed. "I also want to catch up on what you've found about Missy Small."

On the way over to the Los Tres Amigos restaurant Walter told me the Bascomb boy still hadn't been found, a no-brainer after I'd overheard his conversation with the commissioner. The boy's parents were sick with worry. Walter had spent the morning at the high school interviewing weepy girls and shocked boys but learning nothing more than Missy Small was well liked and considered a nice girl. Of course any student, no matter how previous opinion ran, was always considered to have had angelic qualities after a sudden, violent death. In short, Walter had learned nothing.

"Do you really think it's this Bascomb kid?" I asked.

"Who knows? Maybe yes, maybe no. Could be he was supposed to meet her there and found her like that and got scared. Maybe he thought he knew who did it or saw something. He could have made a run for it. His parents said he wasn't carrying much money, but sometimes the parents don't know. They didn't know about the marijuana he gave Missy either. Nice old couple, worried out of their minds. Better off, though, than Ruth Small, at least for now."

We went into the restaurant and ordered lunch. It was Juanita's day off, much to Walter's disappointment. She had a way of lifting his ego, and his needed lifting right now, with Marie still sulking and an unsolved murder case in front of him. Walter ordered his usual chicken fried steak and I splurged with the Mexican platter, which was actually two plates full of enchiladas, tostadas, tacos, rice, beans and tortillas. We both asked for large iced teas, immediately, because it had been a hot ride over in my Porsche.

"What is your gut feeling on where Bascomb is?" I asked, taking a bite out of a tortilla chip loaded with picante sauce.

"I haven't got one," Walter answered. "None of the kids he hangs around with would admit to knowing anything about where he is. They say they haven't seen him since yesterday. Of course they don't know anything about any marijuana Missy got from him. He seems to have been pretty secretive about himself, from what I could gather."

"I'm going over to talk to Roy Owens after lunch," I said, looking around for my iced tea. My tongue was on fire. "Maybe he'll have heard something they didn't want to tell you. I guess this Bascomb is probably the one who did it. If he headed for Mexico, we may never hear from him again. Wouldn't that been something for Ruth Small to deal with?"

"Not to mention his own parents," Walter commented. "If he did go to Mexico, and if he doesn't get killed in some drug deal, we'll probably hear from him again when he calls his parents for help, whether it's because he ran out of money or he ran into jail. We'll hear, and then we'll know. Too late to do Missy any good, of course."

"But suppose it isn't Bascomb?" I asked. "Any other leads?"

"Not even a hint of one. But it could be someone else. We aren't ruling that out. Whoever did it didn't leave many clues."

We had exhausted the subject of Melissa Small's murder. Walter asked if I had heard any more from Marilyn, and that was another negative. We talked about the weather and sports, local politics and fishing, but the subject still uppermost in our minds was Missy Small and the monster who killed her. After lunch I dropped Walter off at the police station and turned towards the high school.

Roy Owens was in study hall, so I asked the principal if I could meet with the aspiring detective in the conference room. He said it would be all right and put in a call for Roy over his intercom. Five minutes later Roy was sitting in front of me, sipping on a cola he had bought on the walk over.

"Hi, Len," he said, looking glum. "Pretty awful about Missy, isn't it?"

"Yes, Roy, it is. She's going to be buried on Thursday."

"I can't believe it," Roy continued, shaking his head. "I just saw her yesterday and now she's going to be buried. Unbelievable."

"It's always hard to believe when a person her age dies a violent death," I told him. "About all we can do is try to find the one who did it and see that it doesn't happen to anyone else."

"Do you think it's Harry Bascomb?" he asked, his narrowed blue eyes giving his face an angry look. "That's the gossip going around school."

"I don't know," I replied. "Bascomb has disappeared. What are the kids saying?"

"Nobody has seen him since school let out yesterday. Nobody wants to talk about him right now, especially with the police asking questions. Kids using drugs who hung around him are scared stiff. It'll probably be awhile before I learn anything."

"Well, let me know if you do," I said. We got up and left, with Roy finishing what remained of the soda in one big gulp and crushing the can manfully in his left hand. Macho, high school style.

I went back to my Porsche, undecided about what to do or where to go. I finally drove over to Rockport Beach to watch the waves come in, but my mood was too restless to stay idle for long. I decided to go over to the cemetery where Melissa would be buried and talk a walk through the tombstones. That seemed to suit my mood just fine and I could use the silence to think about the case. I parked under a large weeping willow and felt like crying myself when I thought of Ruth's daughter being buried here soon.

The old cemetery had tombstones dating back to the mid-1800s for people who had been dead for over a century. Dead and mostly forgotten. I began to glance idly at the inscriptions. Some relatives had seen fit to have poems or scriptures chiseled under the names of the dead. I did a double take when I read the words on one tombstone for "Husband". It said, "You've got him now, you can keep him forever." Probably not a happy marriage there.

I saw where a new grave had already been dug, probably for Melissa. I wandered over in that direction. The narrow grave was at the top of a small hill and overlooked the water. It had a spectacular view, but Missy wouldn't care now. I walked closer to the grave, feeling sad and a little morbid. The workmen were probably going to return before too long because they hadn't covered the open hole. Someone could easily fall in. I leaned over and peered in. Too late. Someone already had fallen in.

Sprawling at an awkward angle on his stomach was a young man who appeared to be in his late teens. He wasn't moving. I hesitated, looking around but not seeing anyone, and then crouched down. I steadied myself with one hand and jumped in, just managing to avoid landing on the boy. I knelt down to find out if he was still breathing, but he was already cold and stiff. I didn't know who it was, but from his size and appearance, I was willing to bet I had found Harry Bascomb. The late Harry Bascomb. He hadn't gone to Mexico after all.

CHAPTER FIVE

Luckily for me the gravediggers came back just then, because getting out of Missy's grave would have been a lot more difficult than getting in. They had a large ladder which they lowered to enable me to climb out. The two men stayed on guard by the grave while I went to the Porsche for my cell phone to call Walter. He was surprised to hear from me so soon.

"Aren't you a little early?" he asked peevishly when he heard my voice. "We only had lunch an hour ago and I said I'd call if I heard anything."

"Not a little early," I advised him. "A little late. If I had been a little earlier, I would have seen who put a body in Melissa Small's grave."

"What are you talking about?" he snapped.

"I'm over at the Rockport cemetery. I was walking through the tombstones and I came across Melissa's grave, at least I think it's hers. There's a body of a young man, looks like a teenager, in it. Face down. I didn't touch him, except to see if he's still alive. I bet it's Harry Bascomb. Want to cover?"

The homicide detective pronounced a word it is illegal to use on the telephone. "Stay where you are, Len. I'll be right there. Is anyone with the body?"

"A couple of gravediggers. I had to jump down in the grave to check for a pulse, and luckily they came along, or I'd still be trying to climb out."

"You've been in worse situations."

"Not today," I said.

He hung up, and in about five minutes I saw his car coming up the road, followed by two black and whites. It was getting to be a very busy week for the police department. Walter parked his car, an ancient Pontiac, next to mine, and got out. When he spotted me, he stalked over and demanded, "Where is he?"

"Up there," I pointed, and started walking through the graves to the top of the hill. Walter followed, handing me a picture.

"Is that him?" he asked.

I looked at the picture of a young man with long blonde hair and blue eyes. He wore an innocent look, much as someone would wear a tie or a suit. Something you could put on or take off.

"I can't tell," I replied. "He's lying on his stomach. I couldn't see his face. The hair is right and so is the shape of his head."

"How did he die?"

"I don't know. Nothing obvious, like with Missy."

"Suicide, maybe, especially with the location of the body?" Walter asked hopefully. "Maybe he killed the girl, was overcome with remorse and came up here to kill himself because he thought it was poetic justice, or some other nonsense."

"I don't think so, Walter," I told him. "It would be a pretty solution to this case, but the body was cold when I touched it. Since the grave was only dug today, probably an hour or two ago at most, he couldn't have waited for the workmen to take a break, killed himself, and then gotten cold before they got back, unless he brought a supply of ice with him."

"That sounds logical," Walter conceded as we approached the grave. The gravediggers were staring down at the body and probably wondering if they'd have to dig another grave. Walter stepped gingerly onto the ladder and then climbed down beside the boy. He looked at him from as many angles as he could without actually touching the body. Finally he seemed satisfied and got back out of the grave.

"I'm next to certain this is the boy," he told me. "He looks to be the right height, weight, has the right hair color, age and build from what I've already learned about him. I wish that photographer would get here so we could get some pictures and turn him over."

"Might learn what killed him," I added.

"Yeah, that too," Walter agreed. "Want to bet it's the same knife that got Missy?"

"Probably. If this is Bascomb, it sure reverses the direction of what we were thinking before. To start with, Bascomb isn't the killer. Maybe he and Missy were killed together, or he died before Missy in another location. Maybe a drug deal went bad. I'm almost afraid to guess, seeing how far off I was before. If I guess that far off again, it'll turn out that the city commissioner did it."

"That doesn't sound so far out to me," Walter commented. "He's a nasty little man who would kill his grandmother if it'd bring him a vote."

The police photographer arrived then and began unpacking his equipment, taking measurements and making sure he had film in his three cameras. Finally he had his equipment ready and he began taking shots. He complained bitterly about the lack of space for maneuvering inside the grave but managed to angle around in several ways and get the photos he wanted. After he shot several rolls of film from each camera he nodded to Walter. He got out of the grave.

Walter got back in the grave with the medical examiner who had arrived just after the police photographer and together the two men rolled the body onto its back. The face of the corpse was a close match to the picture Walter had brought. It was a virtual certainly that it was Bascomb, unless he had a twin or a double.

Another mystery was solved when the corpse was turned around, the question of how did he die. Bascomb had an enormous quantity of dried blood on his shirt and pants, and his shirt had large tears down the front, indicating some sort of puncture wounds probably made by a sharp knife. There was no noticeable blood on the ground where he had lain. Obviously he had been killed elsewhere and brought here, but why? Was it some sicko who got a perverse pleasure out of tossing him into Missy's grave, or was it simply a convenient place to leave a body? No, I couldn't buy that. There were just too many other places, and this was not a good one in broad daylight. There was a message here, if we could just figure it out.

A crowd had begun to collect, attracted by the presence of the two black and whites and other official vehicles. The lab was in full operation and two technicians were searching the area for clues. I did not think they would find much to go on. The photographer was taking more pictures. I saw Roy Owens on the outskirts of the crowd and motioned him over.

"Walter, here's someone who can tell us for sure if this is Bascomb," I said.

"Hi, Roy, how's it going?" Walter greeted the newcomer. "Are you sure you're up to this? It's not a pretty sight."

Roy gulped and replied, "Yeah, I'm sure. If I want to be a detective, I'll need to get used to this anyway." He went to the edge of the grave and looked down. Then he backed away, his face paling. "Yeah, that's Bascomb. What happened to him?"

"We don't know yet, Roy," I replied. "Nothing good, that's for sure. Have you heard anything about what he's been up to lately?"

"Not yet, but I'm keeping my eyes open," Roy said, paler still. I thanked him for his help and he left quickly, perhaps reconsidering his fervent desire to become a private eye. If the sight of one body could back him off, I was glad he was finding out early. Of course it was his first one, and someone he knew, so that would be pretty shocking.

Meanwhile the crowd was growing in size and becoming noisier. Luckily the on-site investigation was over and morgue attendants were loading the body onto a stretcher to take it off to the morgue for an autopsy.

"I guess I better go tell the family," Walter said wearily. "Want to come along?"

"Yeah, I'll come," I replied. "Where did he live?"

"Well, his father works over at the hardware store and that's where we'll go first. I think we'll get a positive identification from him. Maybe we better let him tell the mother. Leave your car here and we'll get it later."

Gosh, it helps being a good friend of the homicide detective. In addition to being fast on the scene, I also save money on gas. One of the benefits of living in a small town, and nobody makes any objections to my presence. They probably think I'm his partner or a live-in relative.

We rode over to the hardware store, managing somehow to beat all of the rumors which were surely spreading across the little town about the body found in Melissa's grave. I hoped Bascomb's mother hadn't heard yet. She might put two and two together and get Harry. The news would probably be on the radio within the hour. There wouldn't be any names until a positive identification had been made. Now there were two families touched by a common grief and we were just as far from a solution as we were when Melissa was found. Further, maybe.

The hardware store was almost empty when we got there, which was lucky under the circumstances. We found Harry's father, Amos Bascomb, behind a counter dusting the cash register. He was a tired looking older man with a slight stoop and a medium size paunch hanging over his belt. He wore large black glasses and carried a pencil over one ear, and he had a mole on one cheek. Just an average man, about to have his life split wide open by the worst news a parent can have.

"Good afternoon, Amos," Walter said politely. "I'm afraid I may have some bad news for you."

Bascomb stopped his dusting and gave Walter his full attention, a worried look on his face. "Did you find Harry? Did he kill that girl?"

"I don't know about that, Amos," Walter told him. "However, we have found a body which fits the description of your son. I'm sorry. I'd like you to come with me to identify him."

Bascomb took hold of the counter to steady himself and sat down heavily on a wicker chair behind the counter. His face turned an eerie white and for several moments he was completely motionless. I went to get him a glass of water. Sometimes that helps. Sometimes brandy helps. I didn't have any brandy.

"Amos, we need to go tell your wife before she hears this from someone else," Walter told him. "Do you think you can tell her, or would you rather one of us do it?"

Amos got to his feet, although he still didn't seem very steady. "I'll have to tell her," he said, "but I'd appreciate a ride."

Walter went over to Bascomb's boss and explained where we were going. The boss looked shocked and told Bascomb to take as much time off as he needed until he was ready to return. Bascomb simply nodded, picked up an old weather beaten hat, and preceded us out the door.

We all got into Walter's car and drove over to Bascomb's house, a nice little A frame out in Copano Cove. The house was well kept and painted an off white, making it appear larger than it really was. There was a small rose garden off to one side of the porch, and several different varieties of roses bloomed in the late afternoon heat. We could hear an air conditioner humming somewhere on one side of the house and I assumed this meant Mrs. Bascomb was home.

Amos Bascomb got out his key and let us in the front door. The living room was small but well furnished with a comfortable, homey look. Fresh flowers graced the coffee table and family portraits hung on the walls. An overstuffed green sofa was surrounded on two sides by deep cushioned recliners. Amos' wife came into the room and he introduced us.

Anne Bascomb was a middle aged woman with thin brown hair and dark lines under her brown eyes. Apparently the worry over Harry was affecting her badly and it was about to get worse. She was wearing a shapeless brown dress and white sandals and her eyes wore an expression of hopelessness.

"Is it Harry?" she asked nervously, looking at Walter. "Have you found Harry?"

"Let's sit down and then we'll talk, Anne," Bascomb said, seating himself beside Anne on the sofa and taking her hand. Walter and I each took a recliner. Mine made a groaning noise and I hoped it wouldn't collapse. "These men have come to us with very bad news and you're going to have to be strong, dear."

Anne covered her face and her shoulders started shaking. She began making sobbing noises. Walter and I looked at each other, wondering what she would do when she heard the news, if this was how she acted before she heard it.

"A boy has been found dead in the cemetery," Amos told her. "These men think that boy is Harry. I've got to go with them and see. Would you like to come too?"

The sobbing increased and the shoulders shook harder. Her face was still covered by her hands, but she moved her head from side to side in the universal negative gesture. Walter and I were relieved she wasn't coming.

"Is there anyone who can stay with Mrs. Bascomb until you return?" Walter asked.

"I'll go next door and get a neighbor," Amos said, getting up. "I'll be right back, Anne."

Amos left and Walter and I sat silently, neither one of us knowing anything we could do to help. I was about to murmur something to comfort her when suddenly the sobbing ceased and she blew her nose loudly into a handkerchief. She looked up at us with red rimmed eyes and decided to speak.

"How certain are you that this boy is Harry?" she asked, although she had no hope in her tone.

"Fairly certain," Walter replied. "One of his schoolmates, who is reliable, identified him."

"How did he die?"

Walter hesitated and looked at me. He hates this. Maybe it's why he brings me. The sympathy factor. I nodded. He began, "It appears as if he was stabbed by a sharp instrument of some kind, possibly a knife."

She took a deep breath and stood up. "Would you gentlemen like some tea? I think I'd better make some for myself, anyway." On her way to the kitchen she reached into a cupboard and withdrew a bottle of rum. Caribbean tea, I guess.

We declined the offer, wondering at her quick regaining of control. Perhaps the shock wasn't as great as we had imagined. After all, Harry had been missing for over a day. She had known there was trouble of some sort. Maybe with Harry's erratic behavior, she had known it was coming for a long time.

Amos came back into the house, followed by an overweight, matronly woman with sympathetic eyes.

"Mrs. Droll is going to stay with you awhile, dear," Amos told his wife. "She's brought you some nice biscuits, fresh out of the oven."

Mrs. Droll went over to Anne Bascomb and put her arm around her shoulders. She was wearing a plaid dress which hung modestly below her knees and fit a little too snugly under her arms and around her hips. Her grey hair was wrapped around her head in a loose bun. She murmured softly to Mrs. Bascomb, but I couldn't catch any of what she was saying. The two women went into the kitchen and we followed Amos Bascomb out the door.

The crowd was still milling around at the graveyard. A large area around the open grave was roped off. The photographer had already left and the lab unit was packing its equipment, almost ready to leave. All that remained was for Bascomb to identify his son and for the body to be loaded up and transported to the morgue.

A hush came over the crowd as word spread that the boy's father had arrived. All eyes were on Amos, but he was oblivious to them. Harry had already been taken out of the grave and was lying on a stretcher, covered by a white sheet. Walter knelt down and lowered the covering so Harry's face was visible. Amos nodded briefly before covering his own face with a large handkerchief. After several moments he blew his nose loudly, but did not look back at his son. The stretcher was loaded into an ambulance and began its journey.

"Are you ready to go back home?" Walter asked Bascomb. "We'll ask you some questions after you speak with your wife."

"Let me rest here a minute," Bascomb replied. His face was very pale and his breathing somewhat labored. He was seated on a bench, gazing vacantly down the road at Little Bay, a small body of water bordering Key Allegro.

Walter and I walked over to the far side of the cemetery, giving the man time to adjust to the shock of the situation. After several

37

moments we went back. Bascomb's breathing had become more labored and he looked unwell. By now all of the official cars had left and most of the crowd had followed, figuring the excitement was over. Undoubtedly they were headed for their televisions to pick up the local news.

I was becoming concerned about Bascomb. So apparently was Walter. He kneeled down beside Amos and took his pulse. Then he looked at me and shook his head doubtfully.

"Mr. Bascomb, I think we'll just stop by the hospital and see if we can't have a doctor take a look at you. You've had a great shock..."

Amos Bascomb didn't get to hear the rest of what Walter was saying. He had pitched over in a dead faint.

CHAPTER SIX

Several hours later Amos had been taken by ambulance to the emergency room of the hospital and had been diagnosed as having come perilously close to having a heart attack. We had to break two kinds of bad news to Mrs. Bascomb but at least it appeared as if Amos would recover fully. We called it a day and stopped at the local tavern for some liquid comfort and solid nourishment.

"What a day!" Walter exclaimed, and studied the menu after ordering a scotch on the rocks. "I'll probably be at the station to all hours tonight trying to make sense of it."

"I just hope Bascomb is okay," I commented, remembering how badly he looked when the ambulance attendants took him away. I wondered if it was the same one his son rode in earlier. "I guess after we finish eating I better run over to see how Ruth Small is getting along. I'll give her the news about Bascomb, if she hasn't already heard. There goes our number one suspect for the Melissa Small murder."

"One and only suspect, you might have said," Walter pointed out morosely. He put his menu down and stared out the window at the traffic driving past. "The murderer might be any one of those people going by out there and we'd never know it, sitting here. That green car there, it may contain the murderer, or that blue one."

"Not the blue one, Walter," I told him confidently. "The man in the blue car is the pastor of the Lutheran Church. I'd bet the farm it's not him."

"Well, he's probably the only one who has passed tonight you could count out, with the information I have available," Walter replied, unwilling to concede a point.

The waitress, a sultry looking brunette wearing heavy makeup and light clothing, brought our drinks. I had ordered a Bloody Mary with extra hot sauce which tasted excellent especially after the day I'd just put in. We both ordered the chicken fried steak special for supper while the waitress was still at our table, and then we went back to talking about the case.

"What about the drug angle?" I asked Walter.

"Still there. Could be some drug deal went bad," he said thoughtfully. "Maybe Bascomb cheated somebody who didn't like being swindled. Possibly the girl was caught in the middle, or perhaps she was part of the problem. Do you think she could have been dealing?"

"I would guess no," I replied, "but that's just going by what I've heard from her mother, who might be the very last person to have any idea of what was going on. I've asked Roy Owens to look around. Maybe we'll hear something from him."

"Probably not for awhile," Walter said. "I doubt anyone will start talking until this calms down. That may take some time, a lot of time."

"Or it may scare someone enough to talk," I pointed out. "If I could apply some pressure to the right person..."

"Who would that person be?"

"I don't know yet," I admitted, stirring my drink thoughtfully. "I'll have to think about it, or wait for Owens to come up with a name."

"Can you think of anything other than drugs that this could involve?"

"Well, a maniac, of course. Or someone who didn't like Harry's looks. Or someone who caught Harry and Missy watching something they weren't supposed to or--"

"I get your point," Walter broke in. "Anyone and everyone. The field's wide open and we're trying to catch a gnat with a butterfly net."

"Something like that, only harder," I said. The waitress came up to our table, balancing a tray precariously. When she was almost ready to start putting dishes down, her foot slipped on a wet spot and she dropped the tray. Our meal was instantly transformed into a sodden mess of broken crockery and tumbled food and clattering noise.

"Very fitting," Walter commented to me. "That's just about how the whole day has gone." He ordered another scotch, a double.

CHAPTER SEVEN

After we had received a helping of what we had missed on the first go round, we paid the check and left, Walter to get back to the station and me to go see how Ruth Small was getting on. After Walter dropped me by the Porsche, I took off for the funeral home, where I assumed she'd be. She was, surrounded by a number of people who had come to pay their respects to Melissa Small. Mrs. Small had taken a chair and placed it beside the closed casket which contained the daughter she had lost so suddenly.

Her face was pale and drawn and her eyes had a vacant look. They were staring somewhere past her daughter's coffin and she didn't appear to be paying much attention to any of the conversation going on around her. She didn't look over when I approached and I had to speak several times before she glanced my way.

"Ruth, I'd like to talk with you for a moment," I told her, kneeling down to her level. It was hard on my knees, but it looked like the only way I'd be able to get her attention without shouting or whistling.

"Len? Oh, sorry, I didn't see you come up. Yes, of course we can talk."

"Good. Why don't you come outside with me for a moment, where we can have some privacy?" I said, taking her by the arm and leading her through the room. She didn't protest. Several people spoke sympathetically to her as she passed but she did not reply. When we got outside, I found a small bench under some olive trees and we sat down.

"I have some news about Harry Bascomb," I began, watching her closely to see if there was any indication she had already heard. It had been awhile since he'd been found and people were surely talking. She seemed interested, but unaware of the news, so I continued. "He was found dead this afternoon. He may have died about the same time your daughter did."

She drew a sharp breath and her hand covered her mouth. "But I thought--"

"You thought he killed Missy. It doesn't look that way now. Can you think of anyone who might have done this, someone who had it in for one or both of them?"

"Well, no," she said, looking shocked. "Not for Missy. She certainly didn't have any enemies. It'd have to be someone who was after Harry. Missy must have been with him and that's why--" Her voice broke and tears formed.

"At this point we can't be sure of anything," I told her. I was unable to think of a comforting platitude or soothing verbal balm, so I sat quietly with my arm around her shoulder until she was cried out.

"Where did they find him?" she asked disinterestedly, wiping at a tear on her cheek.

"I found him in the Rockport cemetery earlier this afternoon," I replied, hoping she wouldn't ask for details. "He had been dead for some time."

"Where in the cemetery?"

I sighed. She had asked for details. "There was an open grave. I found him in it."

"Missy's grave?" she asked incredulously.

"Yes, I'm afraid so."

"What kind of a monster is it who would do something like that? Kill two children and leave one in the other's grave?"

"I don't know, but we'll find out and he'll pay," I told her firmly. "He'll pay and we'll see to it the price is high." Empty words, actually. What could we do to make the price high? The judge and jury would be in charge of that, and they might set him free. I didn't feel like pointing that out to Ruth Small though. The first thing was to catch the killer. Then we'd worry about how to get justice.

We went back into the funeral home, back into the dreary little room where Melissa lay hidden under the gold colored metal lid of the forever box awaiting that last short journey to the final place where her boyfriend was found earlier.

Ruth acknowledged greetings from people who had come in while we were outside. Several teenage girls were huddled in a corner and two were weeping quietly. The third, a tall girl with a long, brown pony tail and a dark dress, was staring ahead, her thin face expressionless. I stayed with Ruth until visiting hours were over and the crowd began to leave. I offered her a ride home, but she had come with her neighbor. I went out to the parking lot, surprised to see it was already dark. The hours had passed more quickly than I realized and it was almost time for bed. I took the long road home, driving along the beach and watching the waves come to shore in soft moonlight. I wanted to put some distance between the depressing atmosphere of the funeral home and my cheerful island retreat. I refused to bring the sadness inside with me. I wanted to shake it off somewhere, like a dog shakes water off his coat. Unfortunately, though, sadness can't be shaken off. Sometimes, with enough time and distance, it will wear off. Sometimes not.

When I got back home I went into my office and saw there was a message on my answering machine.

"I'm still trying to reach you," said a breathless, little girl voice. Marilyn! "I need help. I may be able to call tomorrow. Bye."

Perfect, I thought to myself. This is just perfect. I wondered bitterly if the woman lived across the street and only made calls when I wasn't home to harass me. Or could Walter have gone mad and be doing this as a practical joke? I called it a day and went to bed.

CHAPTER EIGHT

The morning news on the radio was full of the gory details of the two teenage murders. So was the Rockport paper. Speculation was rampant as to when the murderer or murderers would be caught and whether anyone else would be killed first. There was even an editorial in the newspaper on the need for more police protection and an extra patrol for the high school area. Walter's picture was featured near the bottom of the front page. His mouth was open and he looked as if he had just spit out a wad of chewing tobacco. I tore it out to show him in case he missed it. He hated having his picture in the paper, and this one would really get him.

The first item on my agenda was to go talk to Paul Boggins, who had the bicycle shop where the druggies hung out. He had rapport with all the kids, but it seemed he had a special level of communication with the ones who had fallen into the drug scene. I suspected he was the one who had gotten some of them to go straight even though I had no proof of this. I didn't know him very well yet but I suspected I was about to get to know him much better.

Boggins was working on a motorcycle in front of his shop when I drove up. He was a muscular, large chested man in his early thirties with a heavy, handle bar moustache and thick, wavy brown hair. His oval shaped head featured deep set brown eyes and he habitually wore a quizzical look, probably due to his thick, arched eyebrows. He looked up briefly as I got out of my car and then went back to working on the Harley.

"Morning, Len," he said, leaning over the cycle. "What can I do for you today?"

"Hello, Paul. I'm looking for information on Harry Bascomb, one of the teenagers who was killed in the past couple of days here in Rockport."

"Yeah, I heard about him today. Pretty dirty business. What do you want to know?"

"Did you know him?"

"Yeah, I knew him," Paul replied, setting down his wrench. He gave me his full attention. "I knew him better than I wanted to. In my opinion, that boy was headed for trouble. Well, I guess he found it."

"In what way was he heading for trouble?"

He frowned briefly in concentration and replied, "He was a rough talker. Always hinted at big deals he was going to pull off or had pulled off. Sometimes he flashed thick rolls of money to back up his stories, but they looked like all dollar bills to me. He implied he was heavy into the drug scene and could supply anything you wanted. A bully type. Liked to make fun of smaller and weaker kids. A thoroughly nasty punk. Pretty soon I was going to have to run him off and I wasn't looking forward to it. That kind is vicious and unpredictable when crossed."

"Did he mention anything special he was involved in lately, like the past couple of weeks?"

Paul rubbed his head and his owlish eyes stared ahead. He leaned against the wall of his shop. "Now that you mention it, there was a hint of something," he told me thoughtfully. "About a week ago he came into the shop with a brown haired kid, a pimply faced youth who wore dirty jeans and an insolent look. The two of them whispered and sniggered a lot. I didn't recognize the brown haired kid. He hadn't been in here before. After they had been here awhile, another kid came in. They started talking to him, and I overheard some talk that sounded like they were setting up a big deal. Finally I had heard enough and advised them to carry on their conversation elsewhere. I can't let kids make deals in here. I attract enough misery working on bikes without letting other kinds of trouble in. They took off pretty quick."

"Did you recognize the third kid?"

"Sure. It was John West."

That name rang a bell. Mrs. Small had named West as a boy who had once taken Melissa to a dance. I didn't trust coincidences in a murder case, and here might be a great big one staring me right in the face. Could John West be involved somehow? It could be mighty interesting to have a talk with him.

I was unable to get any more useful information out of Paul, so I bid him a quick farewell and took off. The sun was shining bright and hot, making little diamonds dance across the waves of Aransas Bay. I put my sunglasses on which made the water appear a deeper emerald and the diamonds a bit dimmer, but still plentiful. I wouldn't be able to speak with John West yet because he was still in school, so I decided to run by Walter's office. Maybe something had happened during the night.

Walter was sitting in his chair with his feet propped up on his desk. He was smoking a cigarette and reading the newspaper. He was concentrating so deeply he didn't hear me come in.

"Good morning, Walter," I said. "I guess the case must be solved. The detective has his feet propped up and he is reading the newspaper. By the way, that's a smashing picture of you on the front page. Are you going to buy extra copies?"

"Stuff it, Len," he replied, taking a deep drag on his cigarette and continuing to read the paper. "What do you want me to do? I've got three men out interviewing everybody in Rockport who ever heard of the Small girl and Bascomb. I've got inquiries pending in the NCIC, the FBI and every place I can think of. I've got word out on the street, all the usual suspects, you name it. I've also got the commissioner on my back. What more can I do?"

I decided to let it pass. "Any results?"

"Not yet," he replied, turning a page. Walter has an uncanny ability to read the newspaper and carry on a conversation at the same time. I've tried questioning him later about what he was reading to see if he fakes it, but he always seems to know exactly what he has read. A two track mind, he calls it. "I'd like to know where Bascomb was getting his drugs, but so far we don't know. I have somebody over at his house going through his room right now. Maybe they'll come up with something, if the kid was careless, but usually kids don't leave too much around the house. Mothers have a tendency to snoop. Remember, he gave Missy a packet of marijuana to keep for him. Can't imagine that was his main stash though."

"Why don't we go over to Bascomb's house and see what they've found?" I asked. "Or haven't you read the comics yet?"

"Why would I read the funny papers," Walter retorted, giving me a cold look. "I've got you to keep me amused. Oh, all right. Let's go. I was going to suggest it myself if you haven't beat me to it."

Walter got out of his chair, picked up his pack of cigarettes and put his newspaper in the wastebasket. We went out to the parking lot, flipped a coin to see who would drive and got into my Porsche. On the way over Walter told me the commissioner had called him three times already that morning, some kind of record.

"Wonder who calls him?" I mused.

"Probably everybody who reads the newspaper and has a son or daughter in high school," Walter replied, lighting a match by striking it on the No Smoking sign on my dashboard. He put a cigarette in his mouth and lit it, inhaling deeply. "What do you want to bet these murders will be the subject of today's radio talk show?"

"Probably will," I agreed, adding, "and then he'll really get some calls. Look out then."

There was a police car parked in front of the Bascomb's house and a small crowd of slack jawed onlookers stood around it, waiting for something to happen. Several people turned to watch us as we drove up and parked in back of the police car. We got out and walked up to the front door, ignoring the inquiring stares of the watchers. The door opened before we had time to ring the bell and Mrs. Bascomb motioned us in. I was surprised to see her looking as fit as she did. She must have been a lot stronger than I had imagined.

"Good morning, gentlemen," she greeted us soberly, closing the door quickly after we stepped in. She was wearing a simple black dress and had smoothed her thin brown hair into a bun. She had applied makeup since we last had seen her, but she still looked tired and unhappy. We returned her greeting and accepted her offer of tea. While she went to the kitchen, we found our way into Harry's room where

David Jenkins, one of Walter's finest, was searching through a small oak desk.

"Find anything yet?" Walter asked, glancing around disapprovingly at the heavy metal posters hung haphazardly on the walls.

"No drugs so far," Jenkins replied, glancing up. He was a new member of the Rockport police, a youngish twenty-something who looked more like he was in his late teens. He was over six feet tall and built lean, with wavy brown hair and clear, blue eyes. A popular addition to the force, especially with the town's meter maids. "Nothing out of the ordinary. The usual things you would find in any kid's room, like cassettes, CDs, magazines, a boom box, television and school books. Lots of clothes. Dirty clothes in the bottom of the closet. Pictures of girls. So far, nothing of interest to us."

Walter scowled. "Have you found any letters or money?"

"No money. There's some letters in the top drawer of this desk," Jenkins replied. "I haven't read them completely through yet, but I skimmed through several. They're from some girl named Mary."

Walter walked over to the desk and opened the top drawer. He took out a small packed of letters and handed me several. We started to read. Evidentially a girl from Corpus Christi missed our boy and wanted to keep in touch. Some of the passages were a little steamy, but none shed a light on a motive for his murder, other than teenage jealously over Missy. She signed the name Mary in great big letters at the end, as if writing her name large would make her loom large in his mind. After we finished reading, we put the letters back in Harry's desk. Walter took out his notebook, made an entry and put it back in his pocket.

I looked around the room, surveying Harry's possessions. There was a dark brown guitar case leaning against a wall by the closet. I wondered if he played well and if he had liked music. Walter started going through bureau drawers. Underclothes were stacked neatly in piles in each drawer. Walter lifted up each stack and replaced items one by one, looking for anything Harry might have hidden away. Underneath the underwear on the bottom of the pile was a folded piece of paper. Walter picked it up, unfolded it, and read aloud, "Meet me tonight at 8 on the beach, same place as usual."

"That's certainly helpful," I said. "No date, signature or purpose of meeting. No name. Could be a note someone gave him last year."

"Maybe, but why would he have saved it?" Walter asked. "This isn't the kind of note you would normally save, unless it has sentimental value. Or maybe he hid it here when his mother came into the room and then forgot about it." Walter put the note in his pocket.

We continued going through Harry's possessions, but could find nothing else of any interest. I even opened the guitar case and looked inside the guitar, but it was all clean. We left Jenkins to finish up. Mrs.

Bascomb had finished making the tea, and we sat briefly with her and chatted. We learned nothing new.

We went back outside and stared up at the sun. It was in the lunch time position. I asked Walter if he wanted to go for a leisurely Mexican lunch with some frosty cold margaritas, an idea he instantly found appealing. We drove over to the restaurant in silence, mulling over the case. Walter lit up another cigarette and carefully blew the smoke out the window. I gave him a very disapproving look. My tolerance of cigarette smoke is next to zero.

"What's your gut feeling about these murders?" Walter asked. "Do you think there is a connection with drugs or that something else is behind those two teenagers getting killed?"

"I'm not sure what to think at this point," I replied, carefully guiding the Porsche around a small red Honda which had pulled into my lane. "If it's drugs, why kill Missy? She obviously knew he was using marijuana, because she was keeping some of it for him. So if she saw something involving a deal, why would anyone get excited? If he were going to meet his supplier, he would probably go alone. Or if he did take her, they probably would have been killed together. We would have found them in the same place. There was no evidence at the location where Melissa was found that Harry was murdered there too. None of his blood, no signs of a struggle, nothing of that nature. Right?"

"Right."

"So why kill Missy? And why the fancy trick of putting Harry in Missy's grave?"

"It's your dime. Keep talking."

"It looks to me as like this is something personal," I said. "Going to the trouble of carting Harry's dead body all the way into the cemetery, past the tombstone obstacle course, and heaving it into an open grave, Missy's open grave, was a whole lot of unnecessary extra effort. It seems to me as if there is a bit of personal motive here, although who knows what. Revenge, maybe."

Walter thought for a moment. "I think you're right. If so, maybe what needs to be done is to question all the kids who knew these two, possibly turn up some new motives we haven't come across yet. I think I'll assign some men to that."

"That'll work just fine," I said sarcastically. "High school kids just love to open up to the cops. You'll be lucky if they tell you the names of the deceased."

"Well, what do you suggest?"

"Let me work with Roy Owens. Don't let the kids know you're interested just yet. Give me a day or two. If I don't turn up anything, then send your coppers in."

"All right, Len, you've got two days. I have enough other things for them to work on for that amount of time anyway," Walter said, tossing his cigarette out the window. I hate when he does that. I'm always afraid he'll start a big grass fire and burn the town down. He swears he crushes the lit part with his fingers. "If you find out anything, I want to know immediately, like before you take another breath."

"Sure thing," I agreed. In a pig's eye, or whenever I'm good and ready, whichever comes first, I thought to myself.

The restaurant, an aging stucco building which had been repainted a dusky red the previous year, was surrounded by cars, trucks and motorcycles. I drove past and parked at the first available spot, about a block away. We walked back to the restaurant and in the few minutes it took us we were already drenched in perspiration from the mid-day rays of the hot Texas sun.

I ordered a margarita and so did Walter, although he usually prefers to abstain during working hours. It looked like the case was getting him down, or the sun was. We studied our menus while we sipped our drinks and dipped tortilla chips into the spicy salsa. Neither of us was in a hurry to order. Finally we each settled on the Mexican platter, which was a big change for Walter, as he normally orders chicken with margaritas.

A scuffle broke out in one corner of the restaurant. Two men had apparently gotten into an argument over who was going to pay the check. The smaller of the two, a thin, short, ruddy complexioned man who was balding on top, had just taken his best swing at his luncheon companion, a large, dark paunchy man with a heavy moustache. His companion had easily caught the swing in his left hand which ended the trouble. He studied the man with a puzzled look. Walter, who had risen and taken a step towards the two, reclaimed his seat and spoke.

"See what things are coming to in Rockport?" he asked bitterly. "You can't even go to lunch without running into people behaving like animals. No wonder we're finding kids murdered and dumped into graves."

I raised an eyebrow, gave him a look, and finished my margarita.

CHAPTER NINE

It was time for me to locate John West, the kid who had been overheard talking with Harry Bascomb about a drug deal. Naturally he wouldn't want to discuss it with me, but perhaps I could play the tough guy act I occasionally put on for the benefit of young, impressionable kids. Sometimes it works and sometimes it doesn't. Some kids are so tough they can stare naked death in the eye and spit it back at you, with a grin. I hoped West wasn't this kind.

I drove over to the high school and went into the office. The high school was about seven years old and built entirely of brick, a rather attractive building as far as high schools go. Lots of windows, lots of doors. Benches all around the campus for students to mingle or eat lunch on. All seats were empty now, it was class time.

Mrs. Karlyle, the school secretary, was sitting at her desk and punching keys on a computer. Kathy Karlyle was a middle aged brunette with an overripe body which she had poured into a youthful skirt and blouse. She had used a little too much makeup in an attempt to recapture the fresh vitality look of youth and her cheeks were an unnatural red blush. She frowned as her computer made a beeping sound.

"Howdy, Kathy," I said, watching her frantically push buttons.

"No, no, no!" she protested vigorously, staring at the CRT display. "Len, I just erased an entire file. It took me two days to type it!"

"Sorry about that, Kathy," I sympathized. "Didn't you make a duplicate copy?"

"No, I was in a hurry. I thought I'd do that after I was finished. So when I pushed the delete key instead of the save key... well, that's all she wrote, so to speak." She turned away from the keyboard and looked up at me, her brown eyes flashing. "How can I help you, Len? I hope it doesn't involve this darn computer."

"No, it doesn't involve the darn computer," I reassured her hastily. "It involves the darn schedule. Can you consult it and tell me how to get ahold of John West?"

"That is too the computer, Len," Kathy said. "All the schedules are on computer now. In fact, all of everything is on computer. That's how come it gets so screwed up all the time. Let's see, John West's schedule." Kathy punched some keys for a moment and suddenly there was a long, rasping sound from across the room. The printer, of course. Kathy got up, walked over to the printer, and removed a sheet of paper.

"Thanks, Kathy," I said gratefully. Thank goodness small towns had not yet adopted the privacy rules of big cities. I'd never have gotten West's schedule in a big city. I glanced at the paper and saw that West was in physical education. This would be perfect. I could hustle over to the gym, talk to Coach Myer, an old buddy, and within minutes I could be interviewing West. If he were in school today, that is. The way this case was shaping up, who could tell?

The boys' physical education class was running laps around the track. I saw the coaches standing by the grandstand huddled together, no doubt discussing important matters like what game was on TV tonight or whether the new teacher would be fun to take out on Saturday night. I hated to interrupt such intellectual patter.

"Hi, guys," I called, smiling at Coaches Myers and Hartford. They turned to me, each giving a disinterested stare.

"Afternoon, Len," Hartford conceded. Myers nodded briefly and went back to watching his class show its stuff.

"What can we do for you, Len?" Myers asked, managing to talk and spit a great wad of tobacco at the same time. Nice example for his kids, but at least he managed to miss my shoe.

"I'd sure like a word with John West, if I might," I said. "I won't keep him long."

Myers nodded while Hartford cupped his hands to his mouth and bellowed, "Hey, West! Yeah, you. Get over here, on the double!"

A tall, skinny figure broke away from the running masses and headed in our direction. He stumbled briefly, caught himself, and increased his pace. Soon we were looking at a pale complexioned young man with fair colored eyes, light brown hair and an unnaturally thin frame. This was John West, a speed freak if I had to guess, and I don't mean the kind of speed you find on the track.

"West, this guy here is Mr. Townsend," Myers said by way of an introduction. "Answer his questions if you can please."

I motioned West to follow me and we went to a secluded area not far from the track. West looked at me curiously but didn't appear concerned. He scratched his leg and waited patiently for me to begin.

"I apologize for interrupting your run, but I'm working with the Rockport police on the Melissa Small murder case," I told him. "I'd like to ask you some questions."

"Why me?" he asked belligerently. "I don't know nothing."

"I hope you don't," I assured him in a tone I hoped sounded like the low growl of a wolf. "If you do know something, you could wind up like Missy Small or Harry Bascomb. We have reason to believe that drugs might fit into this thing somehow. Does that refresh your memory?"

"Naw, sir, it doesn't," he said, still belligerent, looking me straight in the eye. Oh, good. A tough guy.

"Did you know either Missy or Harry?"

"Nope," West said disinterestedly. He glanced down at his foot. I looked at his foot too. I didn't see anything worth watching there.

"Ever talk to one of them?" I continued.

"Nope."

"Ever buy drugs from them?"

"Still nope, and more nope to any more questions you have. Can I go now?"

"Sure you can go back. Harry went back. He went all the way back. We got somebody here who is killing kids and we don't know why. The only thing we can figure so far for a motive is drugs. We think Harry sold them. Now, where you figure in is here. You were overheard talking to Harry about a deal. You also dated Melissa Small. That doesn't sound much like a nope to me. You think about it kid. Either you tell me now what you know, or you go home and think about it. Two people dead aren't good odds, unless you killed them. Then, of course, the only thing you can say to me is nope, and you better say it again and again and hope I believe it. If I don't and I find out you've been lying to me I'll come after you like wet on the Gulf and you won't have a chance of coming out of this thing with any kind of good odds."

For good measure, after the last sentence, I spat. Luckily I also missed my foot. At least West had the good sense to look a little scared. He glanced uncertainly at me, turned, and ran slowly back to the track. Soon he had vanished into the pack. I waved at the two coaches, who probably didn't see me, and went back to my car. I hoped I would hear from West, but you never know.

Back at my office, that infernal answering machine was blinking again. I suspected it would be Walter but I pushed the play button anyway.

"Hello, Mr. Townsend?" I had almost taken a seat at my desk, but the voice made me stand upright. It was Marilyn. "I keep missing you...if you're there. I've called so many times...Gosh, you're sure busy. Don't you ever stay home?" Oh, good, now she was wasting time discussing my work habits. If she didn't hurry up and leave her message the machine would cut her off. "I guess I better hurry and leave my message or the machine will cut me off. I'll call you back tonight around eight. No, I can't call then. I'll call at ten. Is that okay? Oh, of course you can't answer. Well, I'll just take a chance." With a final breathless sigh that made me want to gnaw the telephone line, she hung up. Nothing new there.

What to do next? Well, Missy had dated two other young swains in addition to John West. So far I wasn't much liking her taste in young men. The next two were George Adams and Tony Merritt. Both of these lads lived in the same subdivision and were almost neighbors. I could probably get ahold of Tony Merrit after dinner if I made the effort. George Adams was away at the University of Texas unless he was home on break. Since it wasn't dinner time yet, I decided to take a drive along the beach, remembering the note in Harry's room which sought a meeting at 8 pm on the beach, same old place. Maybe if I cruised the beach I might have an inspiration as to what the same old place might be.

I started with the Rockport beach. Oh, the memories that beach had for me. The memories of the soft moonglow and softer ladies. The memories of a night spent out in a boat on the bay, watching the sun set on Rockport beach with a willing young lady in my arms, as we watched the sun quickly disappear beneath the horizon. It was a time for holding without speaking. It was a long time after that before I could watch the sun set without thinking back to the boat and the young lady and feeling sad. If the best moments could only be the ones that lasted.

A drive down the beach did not do what I had hoped to enlighten me on secret meeting places. Everything was pretty much out in the open, sand and sea and people. Pretty much all of the beach looked like pretty much any part of it. It would be hard to say I'll meet you here or there without plunking down a beach umbrella or picnic table to mark the spot. It didn't seem likely that the meeting place was in Rockport. Too public.

I flipped an imaginary coin to see which beach I'd go to next. Heads, I'd go to Fulton Beach and tails I'd go to Port Aransas. It was tails, heads down.

CHAPTER TEN

Late afternoon shadows were beginning to fall as I drove my car onto the ferry boat which would take me to Port Aransas, an island on the Gulf of Mexico about 17 miles from Rockport, whether you went by car or boat. In the summer months on the weekends I might have had to wait an hour or two to board the ferry, but in the fall I usually got to drive right on. The ride was only about half a mile long, across a deep channel, and very pleasant. Gentle swells rocked the ferry boat softly while several sailboats moved toward the channel which led to the Gulf. Often porpoises frolicked alongside the boat in a merry teasing game they had invented and only they understood. Many tourists mistook the big fish for shark because of their large dorsal fin, so for the tourists it was quite an exciting ride. I didn't see any porpoises today.

Once the ferry landed, I headed the Porsche down the island road which would eventually take me to the Port Aransas Beach. The island was pretty much a tourist haven, with its t-shirt shops, sleazy bars, seafood restaurants and numerous fishing for hire boats in the marinas. Still, it was a good place for teenagers to meet for beach activities and probably the best bet for the location mentioned in the note we had found in Harry's drawers.

On the far end of the beach were jetties, one on either side of the deep water channel. The jetties were constructed of enormous rocks, with a sidewalk on top that led about a quarter mile out into the Gulf. People found the jetties to be excellent fishing spots. I could see fishermen lined up all along both jetties, casting rods and glancing hopefully into the deep, swirling emerald green waters. I parked the Porsche next to a jetty, got out and climbed over the rocks to the sidewalk. A man about 10 yards away had locked onto a fish and was reeling it in, his rod bent over almost double. A small crowd had gathered and was shouting encouragement. From time to time the fish would come near the surface of the water and a gleam of silver would be visible. Then the fish would panic and dive for the deep, pulling out yards of line. The fisherman laughed excitedly and reeled harder. The crowd roared its approval and then, suddenly, the line snapped. After his initial surprise at losing the fish, the fisherman angrily threw down his rod and the crowd suddenly became interested in other activities and quietly dispersed. The big one that got away.

I walked all the way to the end of the jetty. Waves to the right of me pounded powerfully on the rocks and sent tingly sea spray in my direction. To my left, the rolling waves of the channel gently kissed the rocks and pulled back, only to return again and again. The jetties were one of my favorite places to hang out, particularly on the end, where boats passed on their way to open sea.

There were no obvious clues here. I was just out for the ride. It would be an excellent place for a meeting, but there was nothing here to prove that any meeting between Harry and anyone else had ever taken place. Another good prospect was the pier located several blocks to the south of the jetty. However, there was an admission fee, which would make it slightly less likely to be used by the teenagers. I decided to go back home.

There were no messages waiting for me in my office, so I threw together a salad for dinner and mixed a cocktail. As I sipped my daiquiri I reviewed the case as I knew it. So far I hadn't a clue as to motive, other than drug sale or use. The most unusual aspect of the case was the bizarre placement of Harry's body in Melissa's open grave. That sounded like revenge, or spite, or any emotion in between. It took nerve to place a body in an open grave in broad daylight, considering the high risk of discovery. It seemed very unusual to take such an unnecessary risk. Somebody was proving a point.

My thoughts were interrupted by the insistent ringing of my telephone. I picked up my cocktail and walked over to the counter, taking a large swallow before I answered. After all, it could be just about anybody.

"Good evening," I said, waiting for the reply.

"Leonard Townsend?" said a soft, breathless, incredibly sexy voice. "Finally, you're home!"

Marilyn?

CHAPTER ELEVEN

Marilyn! I had managed to be at the right place at the right time.

"Yes, Marilyn, it's me," I said quickly. "Not the answering machine this time. Don't hang up. I want to help you. I want to see you!" Okay, so I shouldn't have said that last sentence. But I was so curious!

A sigh, then a giggle. "I want to see you, too. Right now. Can I come over?" The breathless voice was half-way coaxing, half-way pleading and fully attractive.

"Right now is fine. Come on over. I'll be waiting," I answered, unable to keep the eagerness out of my voice. The heck with dinner. I could eat anytime.

"I just have to get dressed," she said, "and then I'll come. Bye." She hung up before I could ask how long that would take.

A quick glance at my watch revealed the time to be 6:30 pm. Surely she would arrive no later than 8 or 8:30. Of course, she hadn't said where she was coming from. She could be an hour away. Two hours. Three hours. It could take her an hour to dress. Two hours, or like the real Marilyn, three hours. Why hadn't I asked for her telephone number, or an address? Some professional I was. Now I was stuck waiting for Marilyn to show up, without any idea of how long that would be.

In case she meant half an hour, I chewed my way through my dinner salad in about 10 minutes. I didn't taste a thing, not even the feta cheese, or black olives, or spicy cold cuts I had added. Not even the fancy wine and vinegar salad dressing.

I poured myself a wine cooler and tried to watch a program on television. My mind kept thinking of a shapely blonde in a tight red dress and stiletto heels and I couldn't follow the plot for more than about seven seconds. Curiosity was eating my lunch. My eyes kept glancing at the front door and my ears strained for the sound of footsteps on my outside stairs. Once I thought I heard her coming and got up, hurried over to the door and went outside. I had heard only the wind. The street was dark and empty, the sky full of moon and stars. I wished on the first one I saw and went back into the house.

An hour went by, then two. A wine cooler went down, then two. Then the wine coolers went down faster than the hours. Well, that's not as bad as it sounds. I mixed them with ginger ale. Mostly it was more ginger ale than wine cooler. The telephone rang and I jumped as if I had been shot. Wrong number. Finally, at around midnight, as I was about to give up, pour a nightcap and go to bed, a car turned into my driveway. I was standing on my front porch watching the moon caress the bay water, and at first assumed the car was going to turn around and drive back the way it had come. But no, the headlights went off and receded into the fenders. It was a solid white Corvette, about a 1975 model, I guessed. The driver's door opened, and in the moonlight, I could see a shapely blonde slide off the front seat, look around, and close the door nervously. Then she glanced up, saw me watching, and grinned.

"Are you Leonard Townsend?" she called, the moonlight making her hair glow like phosphorus in the dark.

"Call me Len," I replied, motioning for her to come up.

She walked over to my steps and started climbing. Her dress was white, a sleeveless sundress carefully cut tight around her upper body and full below the waist, ending just below her knees. It revealed shapely legs as she climbed my steps, but her face was still in the shadows.

Finally she reached the top of the steps and walked onto my porch. She had not hurried, and I guessed that hurrying was not in her nature. She glanced at me closely, her eyes narrowing, and then she stared at my outstretched hand.

"I don't get to know a man by shaking his hand," she said huskily. "I find out what I need to know when I kiss him." She put her arms around my neck, closed her eyes, and raised her head. I was only too happy to oblige.

CHAPTER TWELVE

After a long moment, she broke away. For a moment we were both silent, and then I ushered her into my home. I had never been kissed quite like that before, lips so firm and responsive and right. It temporarily took my breath away.

Seeing her for the first time under adequate lighting, I was awed by her resemblance to Marilyn Monroe. Of course some of it was deliberate. The hair was cut the same way, dyed the same color and teased and curled into the familiar shape seen in her earlier movies. The makeup was good, eyebrows curved and arched, lips wide and dark, complexion peaches and cream, and absolutely flawless, except for that one mole on her cheek. I wasn't close enough to tell if the mole was real or drawn on. It was that good, because I was close. I glanced at her from the top of her blonde hair to the bottom of her stiletto heels, and she was so close to the Marilyn I'd seen in the movies it was unreal. Her skin was almost luminous and I could swear she even glowed, like she'd been touched by a magic wand. And yet, there was more. There was another side, an indescribable side, that made her more than the actress, that gave her a whole other dimension. I hoped she'd be around long enough for me to study it.

"Have a seat," I said, motioning her to the couch. "Can I get you a drink?"

"I'd really like some champagne," she replied, sitting down on my sofa, crossing her legs, and pulling her skirt modestly over her knees. "Then we'll talk. I've been wanting to talk with you for a long time."

I went over to the refrigerator, thanking my lucky stars that I always kept several bottles of champagne on ice. I took one out, worked at the cork and poured each of us a glass. It was pink champagne, very appropriate for tonight's guest, I thought. I walked over to the couch and handed Marilyn her glass.

"So, what brings you here?" I began, after I sat down, but stopped when I saw her shake her head.

"Never drink champagne without a toast first," she said, closing her eyes and sniffing the champagne delicately. "How about this? To an end of trouble?"

"Sounds good to me," I replied, clinking glasses and managing not to spill any. "What trouble are we talking about? And what's your last name?"

"Not yet," she said quickly, gazing dreamily at the bubbles in the champagne. "My last name is Miller, but I want to get to know you a little better before I tell you all my troubles. I want to make sure you're the right one to get me out of this mess."

"What about the kiss test?" I asked.

"Oh, you passed that okay," Marilyn replied, smiling. Her teeth were snow white, even and close together. It was a good thing because almost all of them showed when she laughed.

"Okay. How do you get to know me better?"

"We talk. You tell me things like where you were born, what you do on Sunday mornings, where you like to eat. That kind of thing."

"Austin, Texas. Reading the newspaper, go swimming, take my dog for a walk. Los Tres Amigos. Like that?"

"Like that, only more and longer."

"Look, Marilyn, any other time I'd be willing to play this game, or any other game you could think up," I told her gently. "But it's after midnight, I've had a long day, and I'm going to have a longer day tomorrow, or rather, today. Can't you just tell me what kind of trouble you're in, and we'll see if I can help?" I was beginning to be a little impatient, even though I sat across from the most incredible vision of loveliness I had even seen. That's what long hours and lots of wine coolers will do for you.

A repentant look crossed her face briefly, to be replaced by a laugh. "Sorry, I'm used to long hours," she said contritely. "Okay, I'll get down to business."

She took a deep breath, stood up and smoothed her dress. She picked up her champagne glass, took a deep swallow, and sat it back down. Finally she faced me with a look of fear.

"Somebody's trying to kill me," she said, her voice quavering.

CHAPTER THIRTEEN

"Trying to kill you?" I repeated dully. Of all the things I would have guessed, this wouldn't have been it. Kidnap her, yes. Follow her, yes. Stalk her, sure. But kill her, destroy all the beauty and promise she offered? Unbelievable. Perhaps a jealous lover, or an angry wife?

"Who is trying to kill you?" I asked, trying to keep the doubt out of my voice.

"I don't know. I haven't got the slightest idea," she said miserably. "I've been to the police and they don't believe me. I'm so afraid and I don't know what to do. Can you help me?"

I looked at her closely. Could she be a nut case? A paranoid beauty with imaginary followers out to do her imaginary harm? Or could she simply be over imaginative or over stressed, seeing shadows where there were none and enemies where they didn't exist? Or maybe she was right. Could someone be trying to kill her?

"Oh, I can see you don't believe me either," she cried, shaking her head and covering her eyes. "Why won't anyone believe me?"

"Hold on, here," I advised her. "I don't even know what makes you think someone is trying to kill you, so how could I either believe you or not believe you?"

She removed her hands from her eyes and sat back down, facing me. "I'm sorry. It's just that, well, when the police didn't believe me, it really shook me. I've never been in any trouble before, and I'm so frightened that I could die of that and then someone wouldn't have to go to the bother of killing me."

"Let's start at the beginning," I encouraged her, taking a sip of my champagne. "Tell me a little about yourself, and when you first thought somebody was trying to kill you. Take it slow and don't leave out anything. We've got all night, if need be. That is, what's left of it."

A look of hope came into those enticing blue eyes, lighting her entire countenance. "Well, let's see. I live in Corpus Christi, in a small apartment near Ocean Drive. I just moved in there six months ago. I got a job modeling dresses at Staples Mall. I'm trying to save enough money to go to Hollywood to be an actress. When I save enough to last a year, I'm going."

So far, so good. This was certainly believable.

"A couple of weeks ago I was driving along Ocean Drive, near the beach. All of a sudden, my brakes went out. One moment they were there, the next they weren't. I couldn't stop, and I was going down a hill. My handbrake hasn't ever worked, so it wasn't any help. Luckily I wasn't going very fast, so I headed over a curb and onto a small, grass covered hill. It stopped my car and there was no damage. But anything could have happened. The mechanic who fixed it said the brakes had a leak. All the brake fluid had leaked out. He couldn't tell if they had been tampered with."

"Is there more?" I asked, thinking that so far I had to vote with the police.

"Of course there's more!" she said, allowing a hint of resentment to influence her tone of voice. "There's a lot more. Just listen."

Marilyn took a sip of champagne, twirled her glass and gazed sadly into the bottom of it. Then she looked up at me and continued.

"Late one night when I was coming home from the shopping center I noticed a car with one headlight out seemed to be following me. There weren't any other cars around. When we got to a narrow place the car went around the side of my car and tried to force me off the road where there was a steep embankment. I held to the road even though I was terrified. He came within inches of hitting my car. Finally some other traffic appeared and the car sped off. I went straight home and couldn't stop shaking for two hours."

"Did you call the police about this?" I asked.

"Yes, I did. They were sympathetic, but they said they couldn't do anything. I didn't get the license number and I couldn't tell them what kind of car it was, or even what color. It was so dark all I could tell was that it was a small car. I don't even know how many people were in it."

"Anything else?"

"I'm getting to what else," she continued. "So far, I was only wondering. But what happened next convinced me. The next few nights I took a different road home. I parked my car in the lot next to my apartment building and walked up the sidewalk. One night when I passed some bushes someone stepped out and called my name. Remembering what had happened on the road before, I didn't answer. I ran to the building. As I was opening the door, I heard a funny sound. I looked back and saw him running off. He had a gun in his hand. He had shot at me, using a silencer to cover the sound."

"Did you call the police?"

"Of course I did!" she answered indignantly. "My fingers were shaking so badly I could hardly dial the numbers. They came right over. They searched all around the apartment building but couldn't find any marks where the bullet had hit. There are a lot of trees and bushes, so there's no surprise there. Then they said they were sorry, but they couldn't help me. I could tell that they still didn't believe me. They think I'm some kind of nut, that I want publicity."

Her face became sad. She took another sip of champagne and looked at me expectantly, probably wondering what I was thinking.

"What happened next?" I asked.

"Later that night my telephone rang. When I answered, someone hung up. That's when I made up my mind to get out, and I did. I packed a suitcase in less than five minutes, grabbed my purse and checkbook and ran out to my car. I drove to Rockport, moved in with a friend of mine, and I've been trying to get ahold of you ever since. That was several days ago. Now, here I am. What do you think?"

"I think I'm glad you're here," I replied, pouring some more champagne into our glasses.

CHAPTER FOURTEEN

"Why would someone want to kill you?" I asked her.

"I don't know," she said, shrugging her shoulders expressively. "I don't have any enemies. I haven't been in town long enough to make enemies."

Lady, I thought to myself, with your looks you can make a room full of enemies just by walking into it. I didn't say so, however.

"How about someone who followed you from wherever it was you were before?"

"I came from a little town in Louisiana. Nobody there had enough money to follow me. I didn't have any enemies there anyway, not that I know of, and in that town, as small as it is, if I had an enemy I'd have known it and so would everyone else."

"How about a psycho, some nut who admired you when you modeled at the shopping center? Did you get any fan letters, or have anyone hanging around your dressing room?"

She wrinkled her nose. "Nobody like that. Really, everyone I worked with, and all the customers, were all very good to me. Mostly they were women."

"How about boyfriends?" I countered. "Any jealous types?"

"I haven't been dating anyone long enough to have him get jealous," Marilyn said, smiling at me. "I don't want to get serious about anyone, not now. I want to go to Hollywood."

"Perhaps somebody got serious and you didn't know it."

She thought for a moment. Then she got up and walked around the room. "Maybe so," she conceded, "but if that's true, I sure missed it."

"Well, it's as good a place as any to start," I told her. "How about telling me who you've been dating and I'll check them out. Also give me the name of your employer and your address."

"Well, let's see. I've dated a lot of men. To be honest, it saves me from having to buy groceries. There's Tom, Bill, Sid, Harry, Manny, Frank, Ted, Sheldon--"

"Sheldon?"

"Not like he sounds. Barry, Jesse, Marvin, Joe--"

"Whoa, girl," I said, turning another page of my black book. "Let's confine this to, say, the last two weeks."

"This is the last two weeks. I told you I didn't want to get serious about anyone, and if I see a different man every night, I sure won't get serious. Some of these are lunch dates and some are just friends."

"Okay, give me some addresses and phone numbers and descriptions." I handed her the Corpus phone book and settled back on the sofa to await results. She thumbed through the pages and came up with some numbers and addresses, adding comments for each name, such as cheap date but good conversationalist; fancy food and fancy ideas; good food and good behavior. It got pretty tiresome after awhile and I could imagine what fun it would be to check these guys out. A lot of work with not many results, probably, but where else to start?

We drank some more champagne and talked about this and that and the other, and laughed a lot, considering the fact that this captivating woman was in fear for her life, hiding out and probably already replaced at work. I was trying to get to know her better to see if my first impression was correct. I believed that she thought someone was trying to kill her, that she really did believe someone had tampered with her brakes, tried to run her off the road, and taken a pot shot at her outside her apartment. I believed that she was telling the truth as she saw it, but I wanted to find out if she was the hysterical type who saw a man hiding behind every bush, a shadow in every corner, something sinister in every shadow. Could she be mentally unbalanced? I figured if I could just get her to talk about herself long enough, I'd be able to tell. Meanwhile, it was an enjoyable experience just to watch her shine in between sips of champagne.

"Tell me about that little town you come from," I requested, shifting my position so as to be more comfortable. "Why did you leave?"

"Oh, I already told you why I left," she said, eyebrows arched. "I want to get to Hollywood, and you can't get there from that town. You have to go someplace in between where you can get a good job and make some traveling money. The town I came from is called Runge and it has a population of about 200. It has one grocery store, one bar and one restaurant. One gas station. They all close about 7 pm. A good crowd at any of them is 10 people. A good job in Runge is picking up aluminum cans by the side of the road."

I grinned at her. "So, how did you get out?"

"After I finished high school, I hopped tables for awhile, and then hitch hiked my way out. I caught a ride with a trucker who was going to Corpus. It looked like as good a place as any to start and I got a job right away. I had saved some money from tips and wages, so here I am."

"A girl who looks like you hitchhiking? Did the trucker give you any trouble?"

"Oh, no," she said, smiling. "He was a real nice guy. He treated me like a daughter. Said he was on his way home to celebrate his 40th wedding anniversary. I know, Len, I was lucky. Now that I've got a car and some money put away, I'd never hitchhike again. But you have to understand. I was desperate. I had to get away. So I took my chances."

I got up and went over to my refrigerator. I selected cheese, pickled okra, olives, celery and other such fine delicacies. I made us a tray, added some dip and chips and set it on the cocktail table. I figured what with all the champagne we'd had, we could use a little snack. Then I opened another bottle of champagne, filled our glasses and sat back down. Marilyn hadn't moved.

"How did you get your job?" I asked.

"That was the easy part," she said enthusiastically. "I was walking around the mall, looking at all the wonderful clothes, and a lady came up to me and asked me if I wanted to be a model. Did I? Oh, did I ever! She took me into a store, and I filled out an application. I tried on some clothes. She showed me how to walk, and the next day, I was a model!"

"That was a lucky break," I conceded. "Did you enjoy your job?"

"Oh, yes, more than I ever imagined. I got to wear pretty clothes, lots of makeup, and the store paid to have my hair done. All I had to do was walk through the store and show off the clothes. The customers were always so nice to me and they were really interested in what I was wearing. I told them what the clothes were made of and how much they cost. It was a wonderful job, but I don't know if I'll ever get it back. I've been gone three days and they've probably found someone else by now because I didn't tell them I was leaving." The last was said with a small but very pretty pout and a sigh.

"Look at the bright side, Marilyn," I told her. "You're still alive."

"But for how long?" she asked.

CHAPTER FIFTEEN

I was getting sleepy and starting to use yawns instead of punctuation in my sentences. My eyelids were beginning to droop and I hoped I didn't look as if I were trying to wink. Marilyn, on the other hand, looked as fresh as if she had just stepped out of a shower, as cool and alive as a field of daisies.

"Look, Marilyn, I'm beat," I said, yawning. "I'm going to bed. If you want to use the guest room, it's down the hall. We can talk some more in the morning... well, later this morning, actually."

"No, I better not stay," she said, getting up. "I'm going back to my friend's house. I know I'm safe there. I keep my car hidden and I stay indoors." She picked up her purse and started for the door.

"At least give me your telephone number," I said.

"There is no phone where I am," she replied.

"Then the address."

"It's a post office box."

"How about directions?"

She turned and faced me, her eyes widening in surprise or amusement, I could not tell which. "Oh, Len, I'm no good at directions. I'll just call you later." She stepped out of the door and was gone, almost without making a sound. I heard a car start, back up, and roar down the street. I thought about getting in my car and following, but I was too tired and there was plenty of time for finding out where she was staying. Right then the thing I wanted most was a good morning's sleep.

Several hours later, I awoke with early morning sunlight marching across my pillow and up into my face. I rubbed my eyes with the back of my hand and glared at my alarm clock, which hadn't gone off. Of course I hadn't set it. Details, details.

The telephone started ringing and I hurried to answer it. If it was Marilyn, I sure didn't want to risk missing her, especially after I met her. I wanted to find out more about her and help her if she really needed help. It sounded to me like she did.

It wasn't Marilyn. It was a gruff Walter, before he'd had his morning coffee, if I had to guess.

"Well, Len, have you found out anything from the high school kids?" he asked impatiently. "I'm getting heat from all directions and I've got nothing to show."

"Nothing on the Small case yet, hoss," I told him, "but wait til you hear. I had a visit from Marilyn last night, or rather, early this morning."

"You did? Well, I'll be!! What's she like?"

"I'll have to get you a picture because it'd take a thousand words to tell you," I replied, getting ready for a long ribbing session.

"Does she look like Marilyn Monroe?"

"Does Pokey look like a beagle?"

"Come on, man, tell me! Don't keep leading me on!"

"Tell you what, Walter. "Let's meet for breakfast at the Sandollar Restaurant in about half an hour and I'll give you the whole works. You buy."

"It's a deal," he agreed, probably eager to get out of his office, and hung up.

The early morning bay waters were beginning to ripple with a light breeze as I drove down the beach road to the restaurant. Seagulls were swooping down to pick up careless fish which had come too close to the surface of the water. Not much of a breakfast, a live, wiggling fish, but there had been days when I'd had worse.

Walter had arrived at the restaurant ahead of me and was already inside, studying the menu. He glanced up at me as I sat down, and raised his heavy dark eyebrows questioningly.

"What looks good today, Walter?" I asked, picking up a menu and glancing at the a la carte items.

"Everything on the menu," he replied briskly, lighting a cigarette. "Skip the theatrics. Tell me about Marilyn."

"Okay, pal, I'll tell," I said, putting the menu down. "She called me last night about 6:30 and said she'd be over shortly. She got to my place about 12:30 am. No explanation."

"You didn't ask for one?"

"Let's just say I was distracted," I told him, grinning a little. I decided against mentioning the get acquainted kiss. "She's the sexiest thing I've ever seen, and that includes Brittney, Carmen and Mary Beth, and she does look quite a lot like Marilyn. But there's another dimension to her that I haven't got figured out yet."

"So what's her big trouble?"

"She thinks somebody is trying to kill her."

The waitress came up to take our order. She was dressed in a rumpled blue cotton skirt and blouse and she was chewing gum. Her teenage face was free of makeup, her large blue eyes almost empty of expression. The coast attracts lots of girls like this, the vacant minded, easy living beach bunnies who change men and towns as frequently as they change hairdos. She was new at the Sandollar, and I would bet the next time Walter and I ate there she'd be gone.

It took her three tries to get the order right and much erasing and shuffling of papers before she finally sighed, glanced crossly at Walter and walked off. I bet it would be awhile before we'd see breakfast, and it was very likely the order would be wrong somewhere. Walter looked at me expectantly so I began my story.

"Marilyn works in Corpus, or at least she did until last week. Her last name is Miller. She's a model at a Staples Mall department store and has been for the past six months. She's saving her money to go to Hollywood and be a star and she's going to make it, believe me. She thinks someone tampered with the brakes on her car, which went out while she was driving. She wasn't hurt. Then someone tried to run her off the road, she said, again no injuries. Car wasn't damaged either. Finally someone took a shot at her outside her apartment building. The Corpus police don't believe her, she said. Couldn't find a bullet. Not too much to go on. She got scared and ran, and wound up with a friend here in Rockport. She says she doesn't know why anyone wants to kill her."

"Some story," Walter commented, lighting another cigarette. "Do you believe it?"

"I believe she believes it," I said, hedging and waving smoke away. "She seems to have her head on straight. She has the kind of looks that can cause trouble. She doesn't have a steady boyfriend but she does have a lot of dates."

"Why don't I call Corpus and see what I can find out?" Walter asked. He knows a lot of the police there and several are close friends.

"I'd really appreciate that," I told him. "I said I'd talk to some of her dates, but that's like looking for a small shell on a large beach. I've got more names to call than the Fulton telephone directory has in it."

The waitress came up and placed a plate of scrambled eggs and toast in front of me. I pushed it over to Walter. She gave me an exasperated look. Then she sat down another plate in front of me which had pancakes swimming in butter and syrup. I had ordered eggs and hash brown potatoes. I grinned and thanked her. Walter and I went back to our discussion about Marilyn.

"Describe what she looks like," Walter commanded, spearing his eggs with a fork.

"Think back to the film Niagara," I said wistfully. "Marilyn Monroe had dark red lips and short blonde hair which curled over to one side of her forehead. Her skin was luminous and she glowed with some inner light nobody else has ever had. Now, take that description, add a third dimension and some unknown charismic power and you now have our Marilyn. She's in her early twenties and she likes champagne. She doesn't move; she pours. When she looks at you your skin tingles and your knees get weak. You forget all your training and your intelligence retreats somewhere in the back of your head and all you can do is watch her with your tongue hanging out, trying not to pant. At least that's how she affects me."

Walter downed more egg, then some toast. "Humph," he said. "When are you going to introduce me?"

"That's the thing," I said sheepishly. "I don't know. She's supposed to call me today, but if she doesn't, or if she does and I miss her, well, I don't know where she's staying. I don't even have her phone number."

"What?"

"Well, she says there is no telephone where she is staying and the address is a post office box. She said she couldn't give me directions because she isn't good at giving directions. She said."

Walter threw a big horse laugh in my direction. "Haw, haw," he continued. "You bought all that?"

"You'd have to have seen the salesman."

We finished our breakfast and left. I headed over to the high school to see if I could catch Roy Owens between classes. I hoped Walter could check Marilyn's story before the day was over. I was beginning to feel a little foolish for not getting at least the name of the friend with whom she was staying. I wondered if she was just a little careless about keeping in touch or if she was deliberately keeping me in the dark. If she called again, and I wasn't entirely sure she would, I would be certain to get her address, post office box or not.

Luck was with me. As I neared the high school, I could see Roy Owens out front sitting on a retaining wall and talking to that same gorgeous redhead I had seen him with at the Dairy Queen. He spotted the Porsche driving up and came over to talk with me in the parking lot. The redhead disappeared back into the high school with some other girls who had been sitting peacefully under a tree.

"Howdy, Roy," I said and offered a hand. High school kids around here are big on shaking hands.

"Morning, Len," he replied, gripping my hand firmly. Maybe a little too firmly. I almost winced.

"Have you heard any talk around school I might be interested in?" I asked hopefully.

"I've heard that Harry was definitely dealing, and that he was tight with some out of town talent, his supplier," Roy told me, his eyes bright with excitement. "I heard his main supplier was a dude from Corpus, heavy money."

"That's interesting," I said encouragingly. "Anything else?"

"I'm still working on it," he said. "Right now it's pretty hard to get kids to talk. They're still scared."

"Have you heard anything about a girl Harry used to date, a girl named Mary?"

"No, I haven't, but I'll check. He went out with several local girls before he started an exclusive with Missy."

"What he had going with Mary was probably pretty heavy," I told Roy. "Also, the police found a note in his room setting up a meeting on the beach. We don't know when or with whom. Keep that to yourself, but see if you can find out if anyone saw him on any of the local beaches with someone."

"Will do," Roy said. "Got to go now or I'll be late for class." He took off at a fast clip for the front door of the school building and waved as he went inside. A minute later I heard a bell.

A new group of kids came out the door and started forming little circles around the front steps. I was about to get back into the Porsche when I saw the slender figure of John Watts come out. I watched him closely as he walked down the steps and looked around the school grounds. Then he spotted me and stared. He took a step towards me, hesitated, and then came forward.

I waited patiently until he walked up to where I was standing. He walked slowly, uncertainly, and I got the feeling that the slightest breath of wind would tip the scales in the other direction and send him scurrying back into the building. Finally he was right in front of me, wearing a look of uncertainly almost like a painted mask across his lean, youthful face.

"I want to talk to you but not here or now," he said, skipping the customary hello, how are you routine.

I went straight to the point myself. "When and where?"

"After school. On the beach. No, that's too public. At the roadside park on route 35. Okay?"

"You bet. I'll be there," I said, heading towards my car. I got in and drove off without a backward look, wondering what little nugget of information John Watts would deliver at the roadside park and why everything was so hush-hush.

Since it was still early morning I decided to drive to Corpus and check out some names on Marilyn's list. It would take about three quarters of an hour to get to Corpus but it was a lovely morning for a drive. I eased the speedometer needle up to 70, flipped the switch on my radar detector and settled back in my seat for the short drive. When I arrived in Corpus I drove to the Nelly Real Estate Company where one of Marilyn's admirers worked.

Inside the reception area of the small brick building sat a woman wearing a frown and a yellow polka dot dress. She glanced up as I walked in, stared at me curiously for a moment and finally asked if she could help me. Not too sharp for a sales office.

"My name is Leonard Townsend and I'd like to talk with Frank Howard if he's here," I told her.

"He's here," she replied without interest. "I'll page him." She pushed a button on her desk and spoke softly into a white plastic speaker. "Someone here to see you, Frank."

Down the hall an office door opened and a tall, thin man with dark wavy hair stepped out. He came forward, offered me a firm handshake, and introduced himself. After I gave him my name we walked back to his office, went inside and took a seat.

I had decided to say I was with a collection agency and indicate that Marilyn had left town without paying her debts. Better this story than one which would give someone the idea that by following me he could find Marilyn. After presenting my tale, I asked Frank if he knew where Marilyn was.

"No, man, I haven't seen her in a couple of weeks," he replied regretfully. "How much does she owe? I might pay it for her."

"I'm not sure," I said. "I'm just supposed to locate her. I'll pass that on to the company. Meanwhile, although I've never seen her, I've heard she's a real looker. What's she like?" I gave him an encouraging smile, somewhere between a leer and a wink.

He looked at me doubtfully for a moment. "Hey, she's not that kind. She's a beauty alright, but an innocent beauty. You ought to see her, a dead ringer for the Hollywood movie actress named Marilyn Monroe but with something extra. Of course you will see her someday, just as soon as she gets to Hollywood."

"Doesn't sound like the kind to skip on a debt," I commented.

"No, she's not. I took her out to dinner, then dancing, and would you believe I took her home and didn't make a move on her? She's sexy, but she's not the kind you want to offend by coming on too strong. Trouble is, she wants to play the field, not get serious. She has stars in her eyes."

"Wonder if there could be a mix up about this debt she is supposed to have run out on?" I questioned. "Do you know of anyone who might have something against her? Somebody who wanted to cause her trouble? Maybe someone she rejected or a jealous girlfriend?"

"I know a few of the fellows she went out with, I also know one or two that tried to get closer, but there weren't any hard feelings. There's just too many women out there who are available. Marilyn is such good company and a real boost to the ego to be seen with that nobody holds it against her that she's set her sights on the big time. At least nobody I know of."

I believed him. He was big and he was likeable and he seemed genuinely concerned about Marilyn. We talked for awhile but I didn't learn anything worth repeating here and I finally moved on to the next name on my list.

Andre Trois was an artist with a studio located high on a cliff overlooking the bay. I admired the view from his parking lot as I very carefully set the brake on the Porsche. I could see miles of waves and whitecaps and lots of sailboats heading out to sea for some sun and adventure. For a moment I wished I was out there in my Hunter 22, raising the spinnaker and uncorking some pink blush to celebrate the wind.

Coming reluctantly back to the here and now, I worked my way over to the entrance of the studio and obeyed the sign which said "Enter without knocking. Artist at work." Andre Trois was seated at an easel, staring intently at a gorgeous red headed model in an emerald green evening gown. She was puffing impatiently on a cigarette and swearing mildly.

"How long do I have to pose, Andre?" she asked, running a hand through her long red hair and knocking some ashes off her cigarette. "I've been posing two hours already."

"Two hours is nothing, dear," he replied calmly, his eyes following the path of ashes from her cigarette to his deep white carpet. "Where else could you make this much money for looking lovely, doing nothing, and complaining to your heart's content?"

"Where else would I have so much reason to complain? This is boring. I'm taking a break." She put out her cigarette, gave me an exasperated look, and hurried out the front door.

Andre stood up, shrugged his shoulders and said philosophically, "Well, what have you? Beauty is so often spoiled and we must put up with it. What can I do for you?"

I hesitated before speaking. Andre was in his early thirties, about 5 feet 5 inches tall, with a slight build. His light brown hair was thinning on top, long on the sides, and graying all over. His face was thin and serious, his large brown eyes almost too big for his small face. I didn't think my debt collection story would go over with him, so I made up a new one.

"I'm a friend of Marilyn Miller's mother," I improvised, "and she hasn't been about to get ahold of Marilyn for about a week. She gave me your name as someone Marilyn knew. Do you know where to reach her?"

"No, I don't," he said, his eyes reflecting concern. "I haven't seen her for awhile. Let's see, it's been about two weeks, I guess. Have you tried her employer?"

"She hasn't been there and they don't know where she is. She doesn't answer her telephone." I didn't need to speak to her employer to know that. Marilyn had told me.

Andre frowned. "That's very odd. She seemed to be a most dependable girl. Full of fun, but reliable. Not the type to pull a disappearing act. I wonder if she could be in any trouble."

"Do you have any reason to suspect she's in trouble?"

"Absolutely none," he replied. "I took her out to lunch once. She was delightful. I was certainly captivated, as much as one can be captivated in a single afternoon. She didn't tell me very much about herself and I didn't catch a hint that she might be in any trouble of any sort. She seemed quite carefree."

"Did you ever paint her?"

"Why, no, I certainly didn't. As much as she resembles Marilyn Monroe, I felt she would not be a suitable subject for me to paint. Too

72

many people would think I was taking advantage of the commercial attraction of a dead movie star."

We talked a little more about Marilyn and then a phone rang in a back room. He hurried to answer it, leaving me alone in his gallery. I looked at his paintings, most of which were lovely young women in woods or sea settings. There was a large stack of paintings hidden behind an island in the center of the room. I absentmindedly flipped through them, my eyes finally coming to rest on a familiar pair of blue eyes and white blonde hair. Marilyn!

CHAPTER SIXTEEN

I stood up and moved across the studio as I heard Andre's footsteps approaching. He entered the room quickly, apologizing for his absence. I saw him glance over to the island, but evidently he didn't suspect I had seen the painting of Marilyn. Why would he lie? I would have to ask Marilyn what she thought of Andre and his mysterious painting. After a few innocuous remarks, I left.

I stood for a moment looking over the Corpus Christi bay and thinking. A lie always commands attention in a murder case, or an attempted murder case, particularly on something as insignificant as this.

Andre might be hiding some powerful feelings or obsession for Marilyn by denying he had painted her picture. Perhaps it was only because he didn't consider it my business. Maybe he hadn't asked her permission. It could be any of a dozen reasons, harmless insignificant reasons, or it could be something sinister. Time would tell, maybe. I started to turn towards my car, but my glance was arrested by the sight of Andre staring out his window at me, a surprisingly malevolent glare on his face. What could I have done to provoke that look? When he saw me spot him, he hurriedly withdrew from the window. I got into my car and left.

I decided to interview Marilyn's employer next, a Jane Baird who ran the women's apparel part of the Staples Mall department store where Marilyn worked. Luck was with me and I found her, a middle aged brunette fighting unsuccessfully the battle of the bulge, and hidden somewhat behind a large pile of paperwork on her desk.

"Come in, please," she greeted me cheerfully, motioning for me to be seated on a large wooden chair directly in front of her desk. "Move those papers off the chair and put them on the floor."

I did as she instructed, noticing that the top of her desk was covered with what appeared to be cat fur. I wondered where the cat was. Jane Baird was dressed in a navy blue suit, severely cut and at odds with the cheerful expression on her cherub like face. She had pale skin and light blue eyes, made to appear even lighter by her dark red lipstick. She had used too much blusher and it made her look as if she had been hit in the face with a clown's powder puff.

"How can I help you?" she asked, after we had introduced ourselves. Her large hands displayed four rings, costume type with fake emeralds, diamonds, rubies and sapphires. At least, I assumed they weren't real.

I debated briefly on which story to use, eventually settling on the one concerning the debt Marilyn had failed to repay. I reasoned that Mrs. Baird probably had Marilyn's home address in her files and might have already spoken with her family in an attempt to find her.

"I am attempting to locate Marilyn Miller for a client of my company," I told Mrs. Baird, handling her one of the cards I have had printed up which gives the name of an obscure company and my home phone number. It isn't much in the way of identification, but then no one usually asks for anything more. I've often wondered if I should cut out an advertisement from the phone book and use that for identification. I'm certain it would be accepted by some people.

"What does this client want with Marilyn?" Mrs. Baird asked, the friendly look leaving her face.

"I'm not sure, but I believe it involves nonpayment of debt," I said cautiously, watching her expression. I wanted to say enough to be believable, but I didn't want to say anything that would put her off or put her on the defensive. I could tell she liked Marilyn.

"Marilyn works for me, but I haven't seen her in several days," she told me, her eyes narrowing in concern. "I've been worried about her, because she is a very dependable girl. Not like some I'm used to. I called her family, which I probably shouldn't have done because now they're worried about her too, and they hadn't heard from her for a couple of weeks. I've been thinking of going to the police, but I'm sure they'll tell me that a young woman has the right to go off if she wants to and that will be that."

"Does Marilyn have any enemies that you know of?"

"Not enemies," she replied, emphasizing the word enemies. "There were a few other models who might have been a little, shall we say, jealous. After all, Marilyn is a natural at modeling. Perhaps there is a bit too much innate sexiness to allow her to go to the top as a model but she could certainly make it in the movies. The work is easy for her, too. She can work all day, modeling different clothes, and then be as fresh as when she started when the session is over. The other girls would be dog tired and limp."

"Was there anyone in particular who was jealous of, or resented, Marilyn?"

"Let me see," Mrs. Baird said, playing with a pencil on her desk. "I really can't think of anyone special. She has a sweet personality, and it would be very hard for anyone to get mad at her or stay mad at her."

I got up, intending to give the usual closing spiel of "If you think of anything else, call me". Before I could begin, my attention was caught by a large picture frame containing dozens of candid shots of young women who apparently modeled for Mrs. Baird. Near the bottom, in only one picture, was a very familiar face. Not the expected familiar face of Marilyn Miller, but an entirely unexpected face. The poor, lost countenance of Melissa Small returned my glance through the cold glass, held hostage in space and time by the small 5 x 7 inch photographic print.

CHAPTER SEVENTEEN

"Isn't this Melissa Small?" I asked Mrs. Baird.

"Why, yes it is," she replied, a note of sadness coming into her voice. "Another sweet girl, murdered recently in Rockport. Poor dear, she only modeled for me for about two months before she died. I haven't even sent her family her final paycheck yet."

I was curious. Mrs. Small never told me that Missy modeled at Staples. Rather an odd omission I'd have to ask her about. This was certainly a strange coincidence in a case involving murder, and I was never one to believe much in coincidences.

"Have you met her mother?" I asked.

"No, but I did send her a note of sympathy," she said, somewhat guiltily. "I was very surprised her mother never came to see her model. Usually family members are eager to see the girls model, especially the mothers."

I agreed with her, particularly in Mrs. Small's case. Mrs. Small had seemed very much attached to her daughter and I couldn't imagine her not attending an event which featured Missy as a model. Could she have disapproved? It didn't seem likely. I decided to head on back to Rockport and find out. I had just enough time to talk with Mrs. Small before meeting John Watts at the roadside park, if he was still interested in meeting me. With a kid like that you never know how long he'll stick to his original intent.

I hurried back to Rockport, hoping to catch Mrs. Small at home. I was in luck, because when I arrived her car was just parking in the driveway. She had been to the grocery store and when she got out, she carried a small bag of groceries to her front door.

"Ruth, wait for me," I called, hurrying up to her front porch. "If you have time, I want to talk to you."

She turned, looked at me wearily, and said, "I've got time. Right now, Len, time is all I have. You're welcome to as much of it as you want."

We went into the house and I sat down in the living room while she put her groceries away. When she came back, she carried two large glasses of iced tea and handed me one. She looked as if she'd lost five pounds since I'd seen her last, and her face had assumed a hollow, gaunt look. It was the look of grief.

"I was in Corpus today, talking with a woman named Jane Baird. She works with the Staples department store," I began, watching Ruth's eyes carefully to see if there was any flicker of recognition. There was none I could detect. "In Mrs. Baird's office there is a large composite of pictures of girls who model for her. Missy's picture was among them."

Ruth smiled. "You're mistaken, Len. Missy hasn't ever modeled for that woman or any other. She didn't even know how. It had to be a girl who looked like Missy."

I took a deep breath. "I don't think there is any mistake, Ruth. She knew Missy's name, knew she'd been murdered, and she said she had sent you a sympathy card."

A look of confusion crossed Ruth's face. "I don't know about the sympathy card. Actually, I haven't had the heart to open any of the sympathy cards I've received yet. But I don't know anything about any modeling. Wouldn't I know if she had done something like that?"

I shrugged my shoulders. "I don't know Ruth, but it sure looked like Missy in the picture, and Mrs. Baird said it was. Why don't we drive up to Corpus tomorrow and talk with her. Would you be up to that?"

"Certainly I would," she said. "What time do you want to go?"

I called Mrs. Baird and set up an appointment for 11 am. I explained my connection with Ruth Small. When we finished with Mrs. Baird, I could buy Ruth lunch and maybe help put back some of the weight she'd lost. I took my leave and headed over to the roadside park, hoping John Watts would show up as promised.

It was a few minutes before our appointment when I arrived, so I got out of the Porsche and sat down on a picnic table. I had brought a biography on Dorothy Parker to read while I waited. As time passed I found myself becoming completely absorbed in the antics of Ms. Parker, so much so that I was unaware of anyone besides myself in the woody little park. Blissfully unaware until I heard a footstep behind me, and as I started to turn, too late, I felt a horrendous pain in the back of my head and saw a thousand stars in a deep black sky, or was it the penultimate of exploding fireworks on the fourth of July?

.

CHAPTER EIGHTEEN

What could have been 15 minutes or 15 hours passed as I lay beside the picnic table somewhere way out in lala land. Consciousness came back in little bits and pieces with a trace of blue sky here, a smell of sea air there. Finally I heard voices, echoing voices, saying something I couldn't understand but in a tone I could comprehend: surprise and shock, dismay and revulsion. I figured they must be talking about me.

I felt a tender, tentative touch on my shoulder, followed by a quick sucking in of breath as I let out a few of my favorite curses when the pain in my head intensified. However, the conversation around me suddenly became clearer.

"Looks pretty bad. Better call an ambulance." Male voice.

"Sure he's not just drunk?" Female voice.

"Don't smell any liquor. But look at his head. Got a bump the size of a six pack." Male.

"A six pack? Doesn't look like a six pack to me." Not bright female.

"I didn't say it looked like one. I said it was the size of one." Frustration.

"There you go, exaggerating again." Whine.

The conversation degenerated into a quarrel, with all thought of calling an ambulance apparently forgotten, at least for the moment. In the ecstasy of marital conflict, I and my injuries had ceased to exist for them, and until they had exchanged the usual number of insults, I was out of luck.

I struggled to move to an upright position, an apparent mistake from the throbbing it induced in my head. I was successful, however, in that I attracted the attention of my would be rescuers and one of them headed off to find a telephone. Soon the high pitched siren of an ambulance headed our way, the noise bringing the ache in my head to new and interesting heights.

About three hours later, after all of the paperwork had been filled out, all the tests had been run and I had been comfortably settled into a hospital room, I was able to call Walter and ask him to feed Pokey.

"Why don't you feed Pokey yourself? Are you hot on the trail of a suspect?" Walter sounded out of sorts, not unexpected considering he was knee deep in homicides and fresh out of suspects.

"Not unless the trail leads to the Aransas County Hospital," I replied, looking morosely out the window at the visitors parking lot.

"The hospital!" Walter exclaimed. "What are you doing in the hospital?"

"Oh, somebody clunked me over the head with a refrigerator, or at least, that's what it feels like," I replied. "It's nothing serious, a mild concussion, but they want to keep me overnight for observation."

"Where did this happen?"

"Over at the roadside park on Highway 35. I was waiting to talk with John Watts. I was reading a book and I didn't see whoever it was sneak up behind me. Could have been John Watts or an alien from another planet, for all I know. I just sat there and let them have at it."

"Humph. Then we don't know if it's connected with Missy Small, or Marilyn, or just your average mugging, which doesn't happen very often in Rockport. Well, I think I'll run over the park and look around."

"Good idea. Don't for get to feed Miss Pokey."

"No problem. Take care of yourself." He hung up before I had a chance to tell him the name of Pokey's favorite brand of dog food.

About an hour later the door to my room opened and in came Walter carrying several sailing magazines and a couple of chocolate bars.

"Just thought I'd stop by and see how you're doing for myself. I brought you reading material and candy," he said, setting the magazines down on my bed and unwrapping a candy bar.

"Have you fed my dog?" I asked.

"Almost," he replied, taking a bite out of the candy bar. "I'll get that done on the way home."

"Did you stop by the roadside park?"

"I sure did, but there wasn't anything doing at the scene of the crime. Couldn't even find a suitable stick or anything else that might have been, shall we say, the assault weapon." Walter finished the candy bar and tossed the wrapper towards the trash can, missing by a mile.

"Well then, we don't know why I was attacked, except that I wasn't robbed."

"Maybe somebody scared him off before he got the chance."

"Maybe somebody was trying to kill me so I wouldn't talk to John Watts, or somebody else I've been talking to."

"Do you want me to go speak to Watts, see where he was when he was supposed to be talking with you?" Walter asked.

"No, I don't think that would be a good idea," I replied thoughtfully. "He's scared enough already and if he knows I've been talking with you that would probably put an end to any chance of him telling me what he knows."

"That's what I thought," Walter said, giving into temptation and unwrapping the second chocolate bar he brought me.

"I may have come up with something interesting however," I told him, and described what I had found out about Melissa's secret modeling at Staples.

"That is pretty odd," Walter commented, getting out a package of cigarettes and looking for an ashtray.

"This is a hospital, Walter. You can't smoke here."

"Name a better place," Walter pointed out illogically.

We talked about the case for awhile. Walter hadn't been able to reach his friend in Corpus to ask about Marilyn. I asked him to check my answering machine to see if she had been trying to reach me. Walter has a spare key to my place.

The door to my room opened and a large, matronly woman in a crisp white nurse's uniform hurried in, carrying a small tray in front of her. She looked disapprovingly at me, then at Walter and next at the two candy bar wrappers near the trash can. Her curly brown hair tumbled around her shoulders while a frown sat comfortably on her forehead.

"Visiting hours were over three minutes ago, sir," she said firmly and meaningfully to Walter, adding, "You'll have to leave."

Walter, who hates bossy women, jumped up out of his seat, winked at me, and left without a further word. I could picture him chuckling as he walked down the hall and picture me being left alone to the tender mercies of this militant nurse.

"It's time for your sleeping pill," she told me, setting her tray down and handing me a capsule.

"I don't need—"

"Doctor's orders," she insisted, the frown widening and deepening. She handed me the pill and a glass of water. I took it, hoping she would leave. She did, but only after she had taken my temperature, blood pressure and pulse, and had given me several more sour, disapproving looks.

Early the next morning the doctor came around again and pronounced me fit. He signed the papers necessary for my release, wished me luck and left. My headache had slowed to a dull, hardly noticeable hurting and I was more than ready to leave. The police had brought over my Porsche and parked it in the hospital lot, so I had wheels.

First stop on my agenda for the morning was a brief trip home. I wanted to reassure Pokey I was still in the land of the living (and feeding) and see if I had any messages, particularly from Marilyn. Pokey was glad to see me, but it seemed Marilyn could do without my cheerful countenance because there were no messages from her. I glanced through my mail, saw nothing of any use, not a big surprise. I don't know why mail order companies send out advertisements for products you can buy cheaper at the grocery store but they do and they must make enough money on them because the advertisements keep coming.

Ruth Small was standing by her front window looking forlorn and unhappy when I arrived to take her to meet her daughter's former employer. She was wearing a blue linen dress and tiny high heels which added at least three inches to her height. She opened her front door before I had a chance to shut off the Porsche's engine, indicating to me she was tired of sitting around her house, confronting her grief.

She climbed into the passenger seat and smiled bravely at me.

"I like your little car," she said, running her hand across the leather seat. "It's more my size than the one I drive."

Little car? Hmmph.

We drove off in the direction of Corpus Christi. The day was fine, the sky a rare, incredibly light blue and the sun a glowing yellow ball providing enough heat to make the outside temperature comfortably warm, not unbearably hot as it sometimes does in Texas. Ruth's facial features softened during the ride and I assumed the beauty of the day and the lulling vibrations of the car combined to make her relax. I hoped this day would be a good one for her in spite of the probability that she would learn her daughter was carrying on a secret life.

We passed a number of sea gulls, flying inland in search of edible handouts. I gave Ruth a bag of popcorn at a traffic light and she tossed a handful to the gulls, who suddenly swooped down and surrounded the Porsche, begging for more. We obliged until the light changed color, and then a last toss of popcorn high into the air sent them climbing while we made our getaway into the mid-morning traffic. I looked over at Ruth and found she was actually laughing, something I hadn't seen her do before. It suited her.

Jane Baird was waiting for us in her office. She had found several more shots of Missy modeling clothes for Staples. I introduced the two women and they regarded one another warily. We took our seats and Mrs. Baird handed me the photographs. In one, Missy was posing in a two piece bathing suit on the beach, tossing a beach ball. In another, she was dressed in an evening gown holding a single red rose and looking incredibly young and innocent. In the third, she was in school clothes, a skirt and a sweater, holding a notebook. She was smiling a sweet, mysterious smile.

Ruth looked at each picture for several seconds without saying a word. Her face paled and her breathing quickened. She bit her lower lip.

"Yes, that's Missy," Ruth said finally. "I thought I knew her, but now I just don't know. I can't imagine why she wouldn't have told me about all this. How long did she work for you?"

"She worked off and on for six weeks during the summer and a few Saturdays since school started," Mrs. Baird replied gently. Her large blue eyes were sympathetic. "I thought she was a very nice girl. She only worked one or two days a week during the summer, that's all we needed her."

"I guess I must have thought she was at the beach," Ruth said softly. "There was no reason for her to lie to me."

"Did she make friends with any of the other models?" I asked, hoping for a close friend in whom she had confided.

"Not really," answered Mrs. Baird, adding, "She was rather involved with some boy, though, a tough looking type, tall with long blonde hair and blue eyes. Slim build."

"Harry Bascomb," I said crossly.

"I believe she did call him Harry," Mrs. Baird commented. "You know him?"

"He was murdered too," Ruth said evenly. "Only he deserved it. Obviously he was up to something. He must have known her longer than I thought. Maybe he met her at the beach last summer, and got her to model without telling me. Why he did it, why she did it, I don't know. But I wish he were still alive so I could--"

"Now, Ruth," I broke in, "That doesn't do any good."

We didn't learn anything more from Jane Baird, so we decided to go back to the Porsche. I reminded Ruth that I was taking her to lunch. She replied that she wasn't really very hungry.

"Indulge me," I countered, heading for downtown Corpus. A couple of drinks at the Oyster Street Bar, fresh seafood, a tour of the city marina, and who knows, I thought, maybe I'll see that smile again.

The Oyster Street Bar was crowded, as it usually was, and there was a loud buzz of chatter from the luncheon crowd. Ruth and I got a seat near the window and ordered daiquiris. I steered the conversation as far away from Missy and murder as I could and the combination of drinks and lighthearted gossip did bring out laughter, a little laughter, for a little while. I found that she had a charming sense of the absurd, could make amusing comments on most any subject and was surprisingly well read. She would have been a delightful lunch companion in more agreeable circumstances. I was almost sorry to see lunch end.

After I took Ruth back home, I headed back over to the high school to talk with John Watts. Unfortunately he hadn't come to school that day. I wondered if it was a coincidence or if he was avoiding me, possibly because he knew about or had something to do with what had happened to me at the roadside park. I got his home address and checked it out, but no one answered my knock or my ring.

I went back to Walter's office and found him sitting at his desk, lighting a cigarette. His feet were propped on his desk and he was studying a typewritten report.

"How are you feeling, Len?" he asked, his brown eyes looking me over, probably to see if I was still tipsy from the concussion.

"I'm feeling fine. I had lunch with Ruth Small. Have you talked with your friend in Corpus?"

"Sure have," he replied, blowing a smoke ring. "I spoke with David Beery, who was one of the guys involved with Marilyn's case. They all think she's crackers, by the way. Couldn't turn up any evidence at all. They think she is looking for attention. Publicity. A quick trip to Hollywood."

"Oh, great," I replied. "That sure puts me in the minority."

"Well, you put a pretty dame like you say she is and like they say she is in front of them and they don't always use their smarts. Particularly when they don't have any solid clues, like a bullet wound or a butcher knife. I wouldn't let it bother me. They did admit she seemed like a nice enough dame, again, their word, not mine."

"Well, thanks for calling, anyway," I said. "By the way, it was Missy who modeled at Staples. She kept it a secret from her mother, and she had a boyfriend hanging around by the name of Harry. Sound familiar?"

"Him again," Walter said. "Wonder what that was about. Think it could tie into the murders?"

"Well, it's another connection between the two of them. It's also interesting because that's where Marilyn worked."

We sat and thought in silence for a few moments, but were not blinded by any kind of inspiration. I borrowed Walter's telephone, rang the Watts' number and got no answer. I bid Walter farewell. I decided to head back to my house, check my answering machine and go back to Corpus to wade through another few names on Marilyn's feedbag list. When I arrived home I was faced by the stony cold silence of the answering machine. I picked up my address book, thumbed to the page with the name of Marilyn's beaus and pointed the nose of the Porsche towards Corpus and one Bill Winston, a shoe salesman at the mall where Marilyn modeled.

Glancing through the list of names, I found several for whom Marilyn couldn't remember a surname or address. The one which caught my eye was Harry. Could it be Harry Bascomb? Wouldn't it be interesting if Marilyn had gone out on a date with him? Of course she was a few years older, but a woman with her looks attracts all ages. I made a mental note to ask her what this Harry looked like the next time I spoke with her.

Once again I was in Corpus. If this kept up I would have to open a branch office there. I didn't mind the trip because I like the city. It is clean and it has a marina which serves as home port for hundreds of boats from tiny sailboats to large motor yachts. There is always some kind of boating activity going on at the marina. Shrimp boats come in and peddle fresh shrimp at bargain prices while tourists buy a ride on sightseeing boats which take them into the bay and up the deep water channels.

I didn't have any trouble locating Mervyn's Shoes at the mall. Happily for me Bill Winston was one of the salesmen on duty. He was short, about 5 feet, 2 inches, and balding, and what few strands of thin brown hair remained he had combed carefully to cover as much of the scalp showing through as he could. It wasn't very much. He was perhaps 40 pounds overweight, most of which hovered around his midsection and bounced when he walked. He was of a cheerful disposition and I could see where, in spite of his appearance, Marilyn might have enjoyed an evening out or a lunch with him. He had friendly brown eyes and a smile to match and wore dark horned rimmed glasses.

After introducing myself as a friend of Marilyn's family, I started to tell Winston about Marilyn's disappearance, but he stopped me short with a hand in the air.

"Whoa, buddy," he said, smiling. "Who is this Marilyn we're talking about?"

"Why, Marilyn Miller," I replied, surprised. "You know, the girl who models here at the mall. She looks like Marilyn Monroe. The sexy blonde?"

"Doesn't ring a bell with me, friend."

"I understood you took her out on a date," I said, somewhat accusingly.

"Not me, pal," he answered, holding out his left hand for my inspection. "See that ring? I'm married. I've got five kids and I don't take sexy girls out on dates. My wife would kill me and it wouldn't be pretty. You've got the wrong fellow."

He looked sincere. He sounded sincere. Of course, if I had a magnet for every time a man lied to me and looked and sounded sincere, I could attract jet airliners out of the sky.

"Look," I said, trying to sound sincere myself, "I don't know your wife. I'm just trying to do a favor for Marilyn's family. You can tell me what you know about Marilyn and it stops right here."

But it was no go. He stuck with his denial of having ever met Marilyn, much less having taken her out to dinner, even after I threatened to bring Walter into it.

"Go ahead and call the police," he said, smiling. "I don't care where you got your information, I just don't know this woman. And if you want proof, look at me. Do I look like the type she'd pick to go out with? And you call yourself a private detective!"

He chuckled heartily, spotted a new customer coming in the door and hurried off. I shook my head in confusion and departed. If Bill Winston was telling the truth, and it sure looked like he was, what was Marilyn doing? I couldn't imagine any reason she'd have to lie about a date with Winston, particularly when she had given me his name and work address. Now I had two things to ask her about, if only she'd call back.

I checked out three more names on her list, but didn't get anywhere. It was the same old "liked her, but she wasn't available" routine I was becoming increasingly familiar with. Lots of interest, not any action. I'd gone through half of the list, but I hadn't done too badly.

There was Andre Trois, with that mysterious picture, and now Bill Winston, who denied any knowledge of Marilyn. Also, the fact that Missy modeled where Marilyn did, all unknown to her mother. Not bad. Trouble is, I could not see where any of the information was likely to be of value.

I drove home the long way, down Padre Island along the beach, so I could watch the waves break and fan themselves onto the sand. It was a sunny, windy day and there were some real monsters coming in. I stopped the car for a moment, watching the white sea foam cascading down the sparkling green waters and wished the day were warm enough to go for a swim. Some people thought it was -- some people always do -- and were frolicking around in the waves. Sea gulls dove for fish and patrolled the beach for the remnants of picnic lunches, fighting here and there over a crust of bread or a bit of cheese. Out on the horizon I could spot fishing boats returning from the deep blue waters, flags hoisted high to proclaim the catch du jour. It was tempting to stay and watch the scenery for awhile, but I might have work to do at home. Reluctantly I started the car and headed for Port Aransas and the ferry boat, another way to get back to Rockport from Corpus.

No message awaited me at Chez Len so I took a steak out of my freezer, defrosted it somewhat in my microwave and put it in the broiler. I baked a potato in the microwave and threw together a quick salad. Certainly not gourmet fare, but definitely edible. Night was settling in and the stars were coming out as I gave Pokey a dish of her favorite scraps. Then I settled on my sofa, turned on a local radio station and listened to the latest in country sounds. I heard a tapping that didn't quite go with the beat of the music and realized that I had a visitor at my front door, probably Walter in search of a free beer. But no, when I spotted the silhouette on the front door, I knew it wasn't Walter. He never had that shape.

"Hi, Len," Marilyn said. "It's me!"

CHAPTER NINETEEN

Dressed in a slinky, furry pink top and tighter than tight blue jeans with high heeled white sandals, Marilyn came into my living room, looked around for the right empty chair and sat down, next to my couch.

"Champagne?" I asked, and received an enthusiastic nod in reply. I got out my very best plastic glasses, still unused even, and poured some pink blush I had bought especially for this occasion, if it ever came. And now here it was.

"I'm glad you came, Marilyn," I told her, although I was sure she could detect my enthusiasm without my uttering a word. My grin was ear to ear. "I have some questions to ask you and I really would like to have some sort of idea of how to get ahold of you if I need to."

"What do you want to ask me?" she said, her eyes watching me intently.

"Well, let's start with Bill Winston," I began. "You said you had gone out to dinner with him."

"Yes, that's right. He's the shoe salesman."

"Describe him."

"Let's see," she began, pursing those luscious red lips. "Tall, young, good looking. Blond hair, blue eyes. Sexy. A little on the wild side. Talkative. Fast. Does that describe him well enough?"

"Well enough to know that's not the Bill Winston I talked to today."

"How many Bill Winstons are there?"

I laughed. "I don't know how many there are. But there is only one who works at Mervyn's Shoes and he is middle aged, short, balding, overweight--"

"That's not my Bill Winston!"

"He does work at the right shoe store," I told her.

"I see what you mean," she replied, puzzled.

"Where did you meet this man?" I asked.

"I met him in the department store, where I was modeling," she said defensively. "I didn't ask him for an ID or anything. I never went to that shoe store. I got a discount at the department store, so that's where I bought most of my things."

"So what happened is someone gave you a false name," I said.

She shivered and took another sip of champagne. "Why would they do that?"

"Lots of reasons," I replied. "Maybe he's married, or afraid of relationships, or playing some sort of stupid joke."

"Sounds far fetched to me," Marilyn said nervously. "I don't like it."

"Where did he take you?"

"To dinner at a little Italian restaurant close to the mall. Then we went to the movies. That was all. I drove myself home."

I sighed. "Next question. What about Andre Trois?"

"Andre? He used to come by sometimes and sketch the models. He took me to a long lunch once. We had champagne and caviar at a French restaurant. He spoke French to the waiters." Marilyn giggled. "Only he used the wrong words. He ordered a shoe with cream sauce. I thought the waiter would die!" She giggled some more and I found myself laughing along with her. Was it the joke or the girl or the champagne?

"Did you ever pose for Andre?" I asked after the laughter was over and I had poured us another helping of champagne.

"Oh, no, I never even went to his studio," she assured me. "It was only the one lunch. He was never interested in painting me."

"Really? Well, I did go to his studio and hidden among his sketches is a painting of you," I told her. "I didn't let him know I had seen it. Earlier in our conversation I asked him if he had painted you and he said no."

"How odd," Marilyn commented, running her crimson nails through her short hair absentmindedly. "Why would he lie?"

"I was hoping you could tell me," I said. "Maybe he was embarrassed because he hadn't asked your permission or maybe he is obsessed with you. Could be he is some kind of kook. Did you see any signs of it?"

"You've got to be kidding!" Marilyn exclaimed. "An artist some kind of kook? What artist isn't! Their lifestyle demands it. Some are wonderfully different, some are bizarre, but to be an artist, to be talented, is by definition a much more eccentric occupation than say, a sales clerk for a discount mart."

"Come on, Marilyn. What I'm asking is did he behave in a strange manner that caught your attention, sent warning signals? Did he frighten you or did his behavior concern you in any way?"

She though for a moment, narrowing her eyes. She rubbed her forehead, as if to bring thoughts closer to the surface. Finally she said, "At the time, not really. But now that I think about him, at a distance, I recall that he did stare at me a couple of times in a funny way. Of course at the time I thought he stared like that because he was an artist and really, I am used to men staring at me. But, if I'm not imagining it now, his stare was rather intense. Disquieting. I can't be certain of anything. I was just not around him long enough to tell. Sorry." She smiled sweetly in an unnecessary apology. My heart flip-flopped and I poured myself some more champagne.

"Another question, different subject," I continued. "When you were modeling, did you meet a teenager named Melissa Small?"

87

"I saw her a couple of times, but we modeled on different days. She's the girl who was murdered, isn't she?"

"Yes, she is. She dated a guy named Harry Bascomb. Did you know him?"

"No, I never heard of him."

"How about the Harry you dated?"

"I don't remember his last name, but it wasn't Bascomb."

"Describe him."

"Oh, he was early forties, red hair, freckles," she began.

"That's enough," I interrupted. "Not Missy's Harry."

"Thank goodness," Marilyn replied. "Why, do you think there is any connection between what's been happening to me and what already did happen to Missy?"

"I don't think so, but it is a coincidence that you and she were working for the same store. Also, she hadn't told her mother about the job. She used to be a pretty good kid before she started running around with this Harry."

"She seemed like a nice kid," Marilyn said. "Poor girl. So sad to die so young."

I told Marilyn that I needed to know where she was staying so I could get in touch with her She smiled, got a pen and paper out of her purse, and started to draw me a map. It was an intricate, complicated map, requiring much furrowing of eyebrows and the tiny pink tip of her tongue between her small white teeth, but it finally got finished. She handed it to me, pointing to a large X.

I stared at the map. It looked like a nest of snakes, some of which were fighting. The X was at the very end, or the beginning, depending on which way you held the map.

"Where is this?" I asked.

"Look," she replied, pointing at three of the snakes. "There's your house. There's the island road. There's the beach road. There's Fulton. There's the other beach road. And that over there is where I'm staying." She handed the map back to me.

"If you say so," I said with a sigh. We drank some more champagne and called it a night after I reminded her to call her family and let them know she was alright. It was my good deed for the day.

Early the next morning I drove over to the high school and parked in front, hoping to catch sight of John Watts. I watched the arrival of six large yellow school buses, pulling up in front of the school and unloading the giggling, sulking or indifferent high school teenagers ready for another eight hour grind at the house of learning. Some students stayed out front to prolong the sense of freedom to the last heady minute while others rushed inside. John Watts was not among them. I saw Roy Owens on the last bus so I went over to talk to him.

"Howdy, Roy," I called loudly to get his attention. He turned quickly, dropped two books, and waved to me.

"What's up, Len?" Roy asked, after retrieving his books and glancing around, probably seeing if he could spot his red headed girlfriend.

"I've been looking for John Watts," I told him. "Do you know which bus he rides?"

"Sure. He rides my bus. He wasn't on it this morning."

"Well, that settles that," I said. "Hear anything interesting yet?"

"Not yet," he replied, spotting his girlfriend talking to several young men under a weeping willow tree. "Got to go. I'll let you know if I get something." He hurried off in the direction of the girl.

I drove over to John Watts' house and knocked on the door for a good five minutes, but there was no answer. I was beginning to worry about him. He had been a no show ever since our missed meeting when I was mugged at the roadside park. Unless he skipped it or caused it, he should have been the one to find me. Of course he could have shown up in the middle of the commotion and not wanted to get involved so he simply took off. Certainly he had not wanted to be seen with me. I assumed he had kept our meeting a secret, but possibly he had told someone about it, the same party who had clobbered me over the head. I rubbed the spot where I had been hit, and was relieved to see it wasn't near as sore.

The day was another blue sky, bright sun, warm one, so I took the top off the Porsche and enjoyed the fresh air on my way to Walter's office. I thought it'd be a good idea to see what his opinion was concerning the Watts kid being a no-show for two days.

The police station was buzzing with activity. There were uniformed cops milling around, cups of coffee in hand and cigarettes dangling from lips while desk clerks filled out forms on a number of unsavory types with hands cuffed securely behind their backs. It looked like a real successful drug bust. I weaved my way through the crowd, gave some congratulation winks to several cops and wound up in Walter's office. He was talking on the telephone and from the tone he was using it certainly wasn't his best buddy on the other end.

"Now, look, you've got it all wrong--" he began.

Ninety seconds of silence went by which Walter filled by lighting a cigarette and staring morosely at the telephone.

"No, now, you're mistaken about that—" he continued.

Ninety more seconds of silence, during which Walter performed such useful actions as tapped his pencil on his desk, folded and unfolded his newspaper twice and made a chain out of seven paper clips. After this performance, I knew quite well with whom he was speaking. It could only be Marie Fox. I hastily got up and started to slink on the door when I heard the phone banged down. Walter called my name.

"Bad time, Walter?" I asked sympathetically. "I can always come back later."

"No worse than usual," he replied, putting his feet up. "Come on in and distract me. Got any information?"

"Maybe," I said. "I was supposed to meet John Watts at the roadside park where I was attacked, so I don't have any idea now whether or not he showed up. However, he didn't show up at school yesterday or today, and he wasn't home when I called and dropped by. At least he didn't answer the door. I assumed he wasn't there."

"Have you spoken with his parents?"

"Nobody's been home."

Walter reached for his telephone and dialed a number. "Is this Rockport High School? Good. This is Walter Hughes, Rockport police. You have a student by the name of John Watts, who has been absent for two days. Have you heard from him or did you receive notification in advance that he'd be gone? No? Please let me know when he returns. Thanks for your help." He hung up, cursing. "That's what we need. Another teenage homicide. The city council will have my neck."

"That's showing a lot of sympathy for John Watts," I commented wryly.

"Come off it, Len," he said, giving me a sour look. "Well, we are probably worrying prematurely here anyway. He's probably playing hooky with a bag of marijuana and a sweet young thing and he'll be back when both of them are gone."

"That'd be my guess too," I said, wishing we knew for sure. I didn't much like the kid, but I didn't want him dead.

"How's the Marilyn case coming along?"

"It's uphill all the way, but with a client like Marilyn, you don't mind the extra time. She came by last night."

"Learn anything new?"

"Sure. But nothing that makes any sense or speeds my progress in finding out who, if anyone, is trying to do her in," I told him. "I found out where she's staying."

"Where?"

"Confidential," I replied, getting up. I wasn't about to hand him the map. He'd laugh at me. "How about dinner at Los Tres Amigos, seven o'clock?"

"Fine. See you there." He went back to his paperwork with a loud sigh.

There were four more names remaining on my list of dates Marilyn had been on during her last two weeks in Corpus. I drove the Porsche back to that city to finish my interviewing. The first two gentlemen, Barry Stevens and Jessie Grey, weren't in, but Marvin Seidelman, the holder of the third name, was. Marvin was a disc jockey for a local radio show and he was doing his show when I found him. He was nice enough to talk with me during commercials, which, since they were very frequent, allowed us quite a bit of time. He was in his late twenties with sandy blonde hair, a reddish blonde handlebar moustache, fair complexion and jade green eyes which seemed to looked right through me. He was wearing a designer tee shirt, designer jeans and several heavy gold necklaces. He hadn't reached the pierced earring stage yet.

"Good morning, Mr. Seidelman—"

"Call me Marv!"

"Okay, Marv, I'm Len," I began again, skipping the last name. He seemed like a first name sort of guy. Definitely the informal type, uninterested in long explanations or heavy involvements. Here today, gone tomorrow, yesterday long out of sight. "I'm looking for Marilyn Miller and someone told me you might know where to find her."

"Marilyn? Wish I did know where to find her. She's good people, but I haven't seen her for awhile."

"Any idea where she might be?"

Before he could answer, it was time for a commercial and he began to discuss on the air the advantages of a particular brand of dandruff shampoo. He sounded very convincing, but I noticed he had dandruff.

"Whew, man, I hate that commercial," he said emphatically when it was over and he had put another record on. "I don't like talking dirty hair. It nauseates me!"

"Yeah, Marv, right on. About Marilyn. Do you know where I might find her?"

"Naw, man, I thought we covered that."

"She's missing, Marv. Any idea who might have something to do with that?"

"Any red blooded guy who saw her. She is a babe, man."

After a few more minutes of that, and several more commercials, I gave up. This guy wouldn't be able to keep to a single subject long enough to murder someone, much less develop a strong enough feeling to want to. I crossed him off my list with a strong black mark.

The last name was Joe Selser, a veterinarian on the south side of town Marilyn had met in a pet shop. Marilyn was fond of small animals, especially cats and little furry dogs, so it was a natural for her to include a vet in her list of admirers.

Selser had a rather large practice he shared with two other doctors in an older building which looked as if it might have been a gasoline station in a previous life. It had been remodeled to accommodate a front office, a waiting room with enough square footage to separate ailing dogs and cats, and several examining rooms. There was also room in another building out back for kennels, operations and pharmaceutical items. A pretty impressive setup.

I had to wait behind two cats and one dog before I was able to speak with Dr. Selser, a mid-thirtiesh yuppy type with mod clothing and $125 tennis shoes. No white doctor's uniforms for him. He greeted me politely with a firm, no nonsense handshake with just enough pressure to let me know he was strong enough to make taking him an interesting but not guaranteed proposition, should I get the notion. I returned the pressure in kind, along with a smiling countenance. We understood each other perfectly.

"I'm a friend of Marilyn Miller's family," I told him, using that routine. I was tired of the other one. "They haven't heard from her for some time and they're concerned. Do you have any idea of where she might be?"

"None at all," Selser answered noncommittally, brushing a lock of brown hair off his wide forehead. His intelligent brown eyes studied me with curiosity. "What made them think of me? I only went out with her one time, and that was several weeks ago."

"I believe she mentioned you to them," I lied. "Do you know of anyone who might know where she is? She hasn't shown up for work in over a week and no one is at home where she lives."

"I don't know her very well," Selser said, "but she didn't seem the type to simply disappear without telling anyone, particularly her employer. She seemed rather fond of her job and anxious to do well. That is puzzling."

"Can you think of anything at all which might point me in her direction?" I didn't think he could, and of course I knew exactly where she was, but I wanted to watch his expression for any emotion which shouldn't be there. Sometimes a split second change of expression can be a dead giveaway, as revealing as a 10 page notarized confession.

"Well, I might be able to help a little," he replied slowly, "although I'm not sure. I took her out to dinner and we went dancing afterwards. When I picked her up at her apartment, I noticed a small beige foreign car pull out behind us when we left. Since the restaurant wasn't very far away, I didn't think too much of it when the car followed us there. I couldn't see who was driving. The car parked several rows away from us. The strange part is that it left the parking lot at the same time we did, and followed us at least part of the way to the nightclub where we went dancing. I didn't say anything to Marilyn because I didn't want to upset her, and then I didn't see it or any other car follow us home from the nightclub. I meant to mention it to Marilyn after we got back to her apartment, but she didn't invite me in for a nightcap and I simply forgot about it."

"Any idea what make the car was or the year?"

"Sorry, no, those foreign cars all look alike to me," Selser replied. "Really, I didn't think too much about it at the time. Only, now that Marilyn has disappeared, well, it does seem a little odd. Probably it was just a coincidence, but now I wish I had said something. Maybe she would have recognized the car, particularly if it was someone who meant to harm her."

Some excited yipping and a few menacing snarls from the front office reminded us that his waiting room was filling up, so I thanked Selser for his time and took off.

CHAPTER TWENTY

This might be the first useful piece of information to come out in Marilyn's case, but did it have to be a small beige car? There must be thousands of them on the road. Why, almost every other car that I passed on the way back to Rockport was beige and foreign, or so it seemed. Maybe Marilyn would recognize the description, vague as it was, but I could think of at least 20 people I knew who drove a car like that. If only Selser had been able to get the make and the model, or at least gotten a look at who was driving.

Traffic was light on the highway so I put the Porsche through its paces while keeping a careful eye on the radar detector. I decided to do lunch at the Rockport Dairy Queen and then test the accuracy of Marilyn's map and see if she could place the foreign car.

My timing, for once, was excellent, because Roy Owens was seated at the DQ counter downing a chocolate shake with several DQ for lunch bunch high schoolers. I motioned for him to join me at a booth after I had placed an order for a burger and fries. We shook hands solemnly.

"Good morning, Roy," I said, envying the ability of youth to feed on chocolate shakes and still stay fit and trim. "Hear anything of interest lately?"

"I've been calling you all morning, Len," Roy replied eagerly, his face beaming with excitement. "There's talk all over school that John Watts has split. Nobody has seen him in two days. They say he was in a drug deal with Harry Bascomb, and now that Bascomb is dead, he's scared it's going to happen to him too. Some kids from Corpus are in it that go by the nicknames of Shark and Barracuda. They were the suppliers for Bascomb, according to gossip."

"Good work, Roy," I praised him. "Maybe we better not be seen together until this is over. Why don't you call me if you get any more information?"

"You got it, boss," he replied, pleased. "I'll keep in touch." He picked up his milkshake and went back to the counter.

After I finished my lunch, I headed over to Marilyn's hideaway. It was a large house on the beach road, set back about a block from the street. There was a white garage separate from the house where I guessed she had hidden her Corvette. The house looked deserted, a perfect hideaway, unless, of course, she was ever spotted. Then it would be a perfectly isolated place for a murder.

There was no need for me to ring the doorbell. Marilyn had seen me drive up and opened the door as soon as I stepped onto the porch.

"Hurry," she said softly. "I don't want anyone to see me." She was dressed in a green cotton blouse and white pants, colors which set off her blonde hair and pale skin to perfection. She took my breath away, made me want to take her in my arms and... but not on a case! Reluctantly I stowed my fantasies and got down to what had brought me to Marilyn.

"Hi, good looking," I said. "I spoke with Joe Selser this morning and he told me something interesting. He said that while you were on your date with him, he noticed a car following you both when you left your apartment and after you left the restaurant. Do you know anyone who drives a beige foreign car?"

Marilyn looked at me, waiting patiently. Finally she spoke. "Well, what else? What make? What model? What year? Two door, or four? Hard top? Convertible? What was the license number?"

"Unfortunately Selser didn't get any of that. He was in your captivating company and he wasn't sure anything was wrong. All he got was what I just gave you."

"I should have gone out with a private eye that night, huh? Or a car nut, somebody who would have paid attention," she said. "Let me think. I really don't notice other people's cars, unless they're driving a sports car, like a Corvette, or a Porsche. I almost always drive myself where I'm going. I can't think of anyone I know who drives a beige car, but that doesn't mean they don't. It just means I can't think of anyone."

I sighed. Another dead end, for now. Also, there was the possibility it had nothing to do with the case. "Well, just keep it in mind," I cautioned her, getting up. "If you see a beige car parked out front, remember to be careful."

"I'll remember to be careful whether or not there's a beige car anywhere," she countered, accompanying me to the front door.

"By the way," I asked, turning, "do you need anything? Groceries, magazines, anything?"

"Thanks, but no. My friend has been taking good care of me," she replied, smiling. "I'm just getting awfully tired of sitting around. Maybe I ought to move on, go to Arizona or a little further towards Hollywood. But I hate to give up such a good job."

"Hold on a little while," I advised her. "We might get lucky and I'd much rather have you in Corpus than Arizona."

CHAPTER TWENTY ONE

The next logical place for me to hang my hat was in Walter's office. Passing on the tip about the Shark and the Barracuda seemed to be warranted, especially since we had promised to share information. Besides, he had a lot of friends on the Corpus police force and one of them might be able to lead us to those two drug dealers. I caught Walter just as he was returning from a late lunch and accompanied him down his hall and into his office.

"Sit down, Len," Walter said, giving me a searching look. "By the smirk on your eager face, I assume you have a tidbit of information to share. Spill it."

"Once again you have shown your prowess as a mighty detective in deducing the purpose of my afternoon call," I said, widening the smirk to a leer. "I recently spoke with Roy Owens, and he has heard that John Watts skipped town because he was involved in a drug deal with Harry Bascomb and he's afraid some of the concerned parties, known by the fetching names of Shark and Barracuda, are going to add him to their terminate list. The pair who favor fish nicknames, by the way, are from Corpus."

"Very interesting," Walter commented, getting out a package of cigarettes. "I'm impressed. Wonder why those kids can't open up to cops?"

"Honor among thieves, I guess. Naturally, we keep Roy's name out of this. I'd hate to see him get in any trouble, particularly with the drug types.

"No problem," Walter assured me. "You didn't even have to ask."

I stood up and walked over to his window to stretch my legs while he picked up his telephone and dialed the Corpus police station. He didn't have to look up the number because Walter has an amazing memory for telephone numbers. He can remember a number he dialed once five years ago, but he's terrible at names. He can't remember a name five seconds after he's been introduced, unless it belongs to someone young and female and shapely. I stepped out of his office and went down the hall to buy a soda. Several of Rockport's finest were arguing over who had given out the most traffic tickets in proceeding weeks, with one patrolman saying that the number of miles per hour in excess of the limit ought to count more than the number of violators caught. Another policeman scoffed and charged that it was obvious the first policeman was low on arrests and was just trying to save face. Several others joined the dispute, which began to be heated. I got my soda and beat it back to Walter's office. He was just hanging up the telephone.

"Good news, sort of," Walter informed me. "Those two are well known in, shall we say, those circles frequented by riffraff. They've been busted for selling drugs, using drugs, illegal possession of drugs, you name it, they've done it if it involves drugs. Any kind of drugs from marijuana, coke, crack, on up. Their real names are Dick Ferris, that's Shark, and Rodney Clark. He's Barracuda. Corpus has mug shots they're faxing me, when they get around to it. Sometimes they take forever. These two are on the outer fringes, wanting to get into the middle. They're a very small and expendable part of a group of drug merchants the police have been watching for a very long time. They don't have a regular address, but I have here a list of their frequent haunts and the Corpus brothers are going to have them picked up for questioning and give me a call as soon as they're seen. Want to go along?"

"You betcha," I said, practically salivating. "When might this happy event occur?"

"Who knows?" Walter replied. "These guys are in and out of town like a Greyhound bus. The fellows in Corpus know it's important to us, and they'll keep an eye out, but they're busy too. It'll happen when it happens, I guess."

I made a copy of the list of hangouts that Shark and Barracuda preferred and then told Walter I'd get the mug shots from Corpus and check the hangouts myself. I also told him about my visit with Joe Selser and the car he had seen following him on his date with Marilyn. Walter did not seem particularly interested. He probably shared the opinion of his peers in Corpus, that she was out for publicity or worse, that she was paranoid. I reminded him of our dinner plans and left.

It was a long shot, the chance that I would run into Shark and Barracuda, or Dick and Rodney, if you prefer, at one of their favorite beer joints. Once again I made my pilgrimage to the sparkling city by the sea. I arrived at the Corpus police station and went directly to the office of Harvey Rosebrock, keeper of the mug shots. He had a pretty pair of them waiting for me.

"Lookit these two," Harvey said, a big, wide smile on his large face. Harvey was constantly being warned by his supervisor for being overweight, but he was so well liked by the group that I doubt he would have been fired under any circumstance. "Kinda make you want to puke, don't they?"

I looked. Dick was small and skinny, weasel like, with deep pock marks on his face and a continuing case of adolescent acne. Rodney had dark hair, dark skin and a dark, menacing look, even in profile. Two punks with predictable futures. It was only a matter of time before they would give a Texas prison as their permanent address.

"Yes, Harvey, they're not much to look at," I agreed, putting the photos in my pocket. "Have you ever seen them in person?"

"Why, sure, Len, lots of times," Harvey said. He chuckled. "Shucks, those boys have been in and out of here more than some of our salaried workers. Lookit this here copy of their arrests." He handed me a long piece of paper with numerous arrests and bookings, mostly drug involved, with some petty thievery.

"Just nice folks," I commented.

"You watch yourself around them, Len," Harvey warned me. "Just cause they're punks, don't mean they're not dangerous. Specially that little one. Don't turn your back on him."

"I won't," I promised. "Thanks for the warning."

"Tell Walter hello for me," Harvey said, turning to go back to his desk. "Say hello to Marie too."

"They're on the outs right now, Harvey."

"Shucks, Len. It'll take you 40 minutes to get back to Rockport. They might be back together by then." He walked off.

The first name on my list of Shark and Barracuda watering holes was Jimbita's, a skuzzy little dive close to the marina. It has been no more than a little shack ever since ever since, and an occasional coat of paint has done little to improve its unimpressive appearance. Rusting beer signs hang haphazardly on the outside of the little bar. The name Jimbita is brush painted over the door in uneven strokes. Truly, not an establishment for the discriminating or the sophisticated makers and shakers of Corpus Christi. I took a deep breath and stepped inside. Taking a deep breath was a mistake. I almost choked on cigarette smoke.

The bar was dimly lit and it took a moment for my eyes to adjust. On the far corner of the main room was a pool table, over which loomed a large, dusty hanging light. In front of the pool table were several small square tables for patrons to gulp their beer and swap tales of bold adventures never taken and fading dreams never realized. To the left of the entrance was the bar, a long wooden counter behind which hung pictures of improbably endowed and unrealistically eager young women inviting the amorous attentions of unseen spectators. Seated at the bar on round backless barstools were three young men wearing motorcycle jackets, probable owners of the three bikes I had seen parked outside. They were discussing events which occurred the previous night, apparently a race in which they rode faster than anyone had ever ridden and outwitted the local police, who were as stupid as pigs. That was the general gist of the conversation, and as more beer was consumed, the riding became faster and the police became stupider.

I ordered a bottled beer, and inconspicuously wiped the mouth of the bottle on my shirt. I listened to the conversation awhile, nursing the beer.

"Man, those stupid cops--"

"Dude, I went so fast down that hill--"

"Man, those dumb cops went the other way--"

After a few minutes of that, I decided to check out the next name on my list. I paid my tab, downed the rest of the beer, and went off in search of a tavern called Same Ol Place. It was several blocks away and I would have enjoyed the walk, but I took the Porsche anyway. No use leaving it to the larcenous attention of the locals.

The Same Ol Place was similar to Jimbita's in size, state of repair and clientele. It also had a pool table, a number of square tables, a bar, and in addition, a juke box which featured country music hits. This bar had more people. There were three men, who were dressed like construction workers, seated at the bar; two older men, probably retirees, playing pool; and two young women seated at a table. There was no sign of Dick and Rodney, but I went in anyway, hoping to make my presence familiar enough to be ignored because I might be spending a lot of time at the Same Ol Place. It could be the only way I'd get the chance to meet the Shark and the Barracuda. I glanced around, wondering if maybe I should have become a dentist like my mother had wanted.

I sipped suds for about an hour and gave it up. During that time a number of people came and left, most of whom could wear the tag ruffian with no discomfort. There was no sign of the pair I sought, so I moved on to the third and final bar on my list, the Crystal Pistol. It was definitely a step up from the other two, maybe because it had a woman's touch. Owned by Crystal Dallas, a slim and handsome woman who had opened the place a couple of years earlier and was making a go of it, so far. It was located in a small shopping center and was housed in what had previously been a French restaurant. Crystal had inherited some of the French décor from the previous owner, including some large wall mirrors and several chandeliers, to which she had added silhouettes of pistol packing young ladies clad in tight fitting jeans and shape hugging tops. Glass topped tables lined a small dance floor where tipsy couples slow danced to the inevitable country music. A glass covered bar lined one wall and on the wall were shelves stocked with whiskey and fixings for mixed drinks. Definitely a step up.

I knew Crystal slightly from a previous case I had worked on which involved several burglaries in her apartment building. The thief turned out to be the guy she was dating, but I was convinced she didn't know anything about it.

'Hi, Len, come on over," Crystal invited, motioning to me with a slim hand laden with sparkling diamond rings.

I took the hand and kissed it, eying the diamonds. "Well, Crystal, business must be good," I said.

"Business is okay, but those rings are zircons. Only my jeweler knows for sure," Crystal answered merrily, her green eyes sparkling every bit as much as her fake diamonds.

I debated as to whether or not to ask Crystal to call me if the two characters I was looking for came into her place. These days you never know who is on a drug payroll and who isn't. Crystal seemed like she was a square shooter, but it had been awhile since I had seen her, and anything could have happened to change her. A pressing need for fast money or the acquisition of a demanding drug habit might have caused her to link up with suspicious characters, and the two particularly unsavory characters I was seeking might be part and parcel to the ones she joined. However, her clean cut appearance and easy, forthright manner belied any suspicions I might have, so I asked her if we could talk in private. She raised an eyebrow, grinned and led me into her private office. It was a small room elegantly furnished with a deep green rug, mahogany desk and a large green velvet couch. On either side of the couch, across from the desk, were two armchairs. I chose one and sat down, while Crystal took her place behind the desk.

"What's the deal, personal or business?" she asked, curling a long lock of auburn hair with her index finger. Her peaches and cream complexion was flawless under the soft light of a crystal chandelier and I almost said personal without thinking. With some effort, I brought myself back to the men I was after.

"Business, unfortunately," I said, settling back in my chair. "I'm on a case where it is very important for me to locate a couple of dudes who occasionally visit your tavern. Do you recognize the nicknames Shark and Barracuda? "

Crystal wrinkled her nose in distaste. "Those two? Who wouldn't! They're a mean pair of worthless bozos who drop by every couple of weeks to stir up the joint. Their idea of fun is to try and start a fight with an unsuspecting tourist. Naturally I keep a pretty tough bartender around the premises to stop trouble. These two are one of the reasons why. What are you after them for?"

"I can't tell you right now," I said, "but after I get who I'm after I'll be glad to tell all. Meanwhile, will you give me a call if they show up?"

"Glad to, if you promise to keep the trouble out of here," Crystal promised.

"Word of honor," I replied, raising my right hand.

We went back out into the tavern, where a couple of drunks at the bar were starting to trade insults.

"I am, too, stronger than you are. I'm the strongest man here," began one, hoisting his glass high. Liquid began to spill over one side.

"Naw, you aren't, neither," argued the other one. "You aren't any stronger than a newborn kitten. That's what I'm going to call you. Kitty. Here, kitty, kitty, kitty. Meow!"

"Why, I might be a kitty, alright, but if I'm a kitty, you're a dog. A real son of a--" Mercifully, at this point he broke into laughter. "Haw,

haw, haw." Having delivered that little pleasantry, he began to laugh in earnest, while his opponent drew back his fist in a slow motion effort to prove the validity of his claim. The bartender quickly separated the two men and ushered them out the front door. They were still arguing.

A quick check of my watch revealed it was time for me to get back on the road if I was going to meet Walter on time for dinner at our favorite Mexican restaurant. I got back in the Porsche and drove over to the Rockport highway, not too disappointed over the afternoon's activities. I may not have located Dick and Rodney, but I did get their mug shots and if they showed up at the Crystal Pistol, I would get an immediate telephone call.

On the north side of Corpus is a high bridge that crosses the ship channel. From the top of the bridge you can see for miles around. Today the sky was clear and I could see sailboats making their way out to sea over and through towering whitecaps. I wondered where Missy's murderer was and when was the last time he had crossed this bridge.

Walter had arrived at the restaurant ahead of me and had already ordered a cold beer. He was gloomily chewing on some tostado chips. I took a chip and dipped it into the picante sauce and grimaced.

"Too much hot pepper today, amigo," I complained, swallowing a vast quantity of water.

"So, how did it go? Any sign of our boys?" Walter asked impatiently.

"No, but if they show up at the Crystal Pistol, I'll be notified," I reassured him. "Meanwhile, take a look at their pictures." I reached into my back pocket, withdrew the mug shots and handed them to Walter. Unsurprisingly, he hadn't received the faxes yet.

"I've seen a million just like them," he said, pocketing one set of pictures and returning the extras to me. "Usually behind bars or in handcuffs where these two will be sooner or later."

The waitress came to take our order. She was a new one, not flirtaceous Juanita, and she didn't show any interest in Walter. No wonder he was glum. I ordered a Mexican plate and Walter asked for the catfish sandwich.

"Bascomb is going to be buried tomorrow," Walter said, reaching for a chip. "That'll make two of them buried while we sit around waiting for the killer to let us know who he is. I still haven't any word on John Watts. His father and mother are in California visiting relatives. They left him by himself, but that's not unusual. He is 18, almost 19, and he has family in the area to check up on him. A married sister. She doesn't know where he is."

"Running scared, no doubt," I ventured. "Probably the first smart thing he's ever done."

Across the room I saw our waitress pick up the tray with our order and head towards the table. Opposite her, coming in the front door, was a uniformed officer in search of Walter. He glanced around, saw us, and hurried over. He and the waitress arrived at the same time.

"Sorry, Walter, to interrupt your dinner, but it's important. There's another dead body at the high school."

Walter grimaced and uttered a four letter word policemen aren't supposed to say. "Who is it?"

"No identification on the body. Deceased is a tall, thin Caucasian in his late teens--"

"Losers like Watts don't know an opportunity when they see it," Walter replied. "Come on, let's go see if it's him. I may need you to identify the body, at least for my immediate information."

We got the waitress to make our dinner order a take out and followed the officer to the scene of the crime. The body was located in the same general area where Missy was found. It was covered with a white sheet which a policeman lifted as we got close. I knelt down for a good look.

"It's Watts, all right," I told Walter, getting back to my feet. "What a foolish kid."

"Not any more," he replied, gesturing for the sheet to be replaced. We went over to Walter's car and started eating our dinner. It tasted dry and bland, probably because of our mood.

"Want to go with me to see his sister?" Walter inquired. "She lives in Aransas Pass."

"Sure, I'd like to talk with her," I said, hoping the sister had been in touch with John in recent days. "Maybe she can tell us something."

We threw away most of the food we'd brought with us, got back into Walter's car and drove to Aransas Pass. John's sister lived on the south side of the city in a trailer park surrounded by live oak trees. Dozens of little children were playing on swings and slides provided by the park's management. After a brief search we found the trailer that belonged to John's sister, Tammy White. She was sitting on a little wooden porch attached to her trailer and brushing tangles out of her poodle's white hair.

"Hello, guys. What can I do for you?" she asked politely, stroking her dog's fur. The dog growled at Walter.

"I'm Walter Hughes, of the Rockport Police Department's Homicide Division, and this is an associate, Leonard Townsend," Walter said, eying the poodle warily. "We've come with some bad news. Can we go inside?"

"Is it John?" Tammy asked, getting up.

"Yes, I'm afraid it is."

We went inside and sat down in the tiny living room. Tammy waited expectantly for Walter to begin. The dog continued growling, but not loudly.

"Your brother was found today in a field in back of his high school," Walter began, searching for a tactful way to deliver the news. There was none. "He was shot through the heart. Death was instantaneous."

Tammy sighed loudly. "I guess I expected something bad. He ran around with a pretty bad crowd and when I talked to him the other day I could tell he was frightened. He wanted money to get out of town. I gave him $50. It was all I had, but you can't get very far on $50." She began to cry noisily.

We waited in uncomfortable silence for several moments for the sobs to subside. Tammy had furnished her trailer with comfortable old furniture, all centered around a small color television on a tiny wooden table. She had a much used sofa with a multi-colored paisley pattern and sagging cushions. Walter was seated on a small wooden chair a little too small for his backside but I had the best seat in the house, an old recliner with torn vinyl upholstery. We studied our surroundings while we waited for Tammy to compose herself, but as there wasn't much to see, I began looking around for a magazine.

Finally Tammy stopped sniffling and Walter offered to get her a glass of water.

"No, thank you, Mr. Hughes, I'm not thirsty," she replied, wiping her swollen eyes with a sopping tissue. "Do you know who did this to my brother?"

"Not yet. We were hoping you might be able to tell us something. Did he tell you why he was frightened or why it was necessary for him to get out of town?"

"Not really. He just said things were hot for him, that he had gotten into trouble with a real bad character and that he needed to get away until things had cooled down. I asked him what he'd done, but he wouldn't say."

"When did you last talk to him?" I asked.

"Two days ago. About three o'clock. He phoned me."

I looked at Walter. "That would have been right around the time of the little episode in the roadside park. He may have set it up and got scared."

"What happened in the roadside park?" Tammy asked in a frightened tone.

"I was supposed to meet your brother. He didn't show, but someone did. I was hit over the back of the head and got a concussion," I told her. "I don't know if your brother came or not."

"Did your brother know anyone who went by the name of Shark or Barracuda?" Walter asked.

"Once when he came to see if I would loan him some money he was with two guys. I heard him call one of them Shark. I didn't like the looks of them, and he seemed awfully nervous when he was with them."

"Did your brother use drugs?"

Tammy hesitated. She took a deep breath and looked around the room, trying to determine how much to tell us. Her delay in answering had already confirmed his use of drugs.

"I guess there is no use in trying to protect him now," the girl said. She was a tiny thing, not much more than five feet tall, with big troubles. She probably didn't weigh more than 100 pounds. Her small face had large eyes, giving her a strangely intense look. "Sure, he used drugs. He was unhappy at home, didn't get along with our father, and couldn't make many friends at school. So he hung out with the losers and began using drugs. Marijuana, coke, whatever he could afford which wasn't much because the only job he ever had was mowing lawns after school and on weekends. But he was a good brother."

I wondered what he had done to make her think he was a good brother, but she didn't say. I imagined the best part of John Watts existed only in her mind.

"How long ago was it that you saw the man he called Shark?" I asked.

"Oh, I guess it's been about a month."

"Did you notice what kind of car they were driving?"

"Yeah, it was a light colored car, sort of a cream."

Another coincidence. It was a cream colored car, which is near enough to beige, and it was a beige colored car which had followed Marilyn. Could it be the same car? Surely not. That would have been a major coincidence indeed. But, then again…

"Did you know anyone else your brother hung out with?" Walter asked.

"There were some kids at the high school. Sometimes we talked a little about them. I only knew some first names, though, like Dave and Eddie and Harry."

Walter and I looked at each other. Harry Bascomb? Probably. We knew they had some sort of drug deal going. We talked with Tammy awhile longer but got no new information. She was beginning to sniffle again, so when the young man with whom she was living arrived, we gratefully took our leave. Walter offered to call her parents in California and break the news to them, but she declined, saying it'd come better from her. A gutsy girl.

We drove back to the scene of the murder. The lab boys were doing their bit, looking for evidence in the tall weeds surrounding the body. The photographer had already finished taking pictures and left, so the photos would probably be ready by the time Walter got back to the station. A large crowd had gathered and was going in and out of the little store on the corner, buying sodas and cold beers and snacks. The scene had taken on a carnival atmosphere, especially when some of the cold beer starting taking effect. It looked like it would be a long night.

A few of the more vocal members of the crowd, recognizing Walter, came up to us and started asking questions. A hot topic was when were the crimes going to be solved. Several citizens criticized Walter soundly for not having solved the murders sooner, thus preventing the latest one. It was exceedingly unpleasant for Walter and it put him in an awkward position. Should he try to explain why the murderer had not been caught and appear inefficient or was it better not to reply to anyone and appear indifferent. He chose the latter course and began questioning the officers at the scene to see if they had come up with anything useful.

"Looks like he was shot at close range with a small caliber weapon," an officer new to the force told him. I hadn't met the officer yet, but I knew he came from Chicago and his name was Ronald Henning. We introduced ourselves quietly and shook hands. "The bullet went into his chest. No sign of the gun yet. Killer probably took it with him...so he can use it again."

"Find anything in the area?" Walter asked.

"Just the usual stuff you find around high schools. Beer bottles, soda cans, cigarette butts, papers, candy wrappers and other such items. Nothing to show that any of them belonged to the perpetrator. He picked a good place to kill somebody, because even if we find something, it could belong to any one of several hundred kids, all but one of which had nothing to do with it." Henning shook his head in disgust. "We interviewed a bunch of the kids and the neighbors, and it's the usual nobody saw anything. Course there's enough woods around to make visibility impossible. We have heard several reports of a shot, but people thought it was just hunters, which it may have been."

"Keep looking," Walter commented, keeping his eye on the crowd. "Something will turn up. Too much has happened for it not to. It's just going to take time."

A couple of reporters from the Rockport Gazette came over and took Walter's picture. They wanted to interview him about the recent crime wave, as they called it.

"Come on Walter, give us some information," cajoled Bud Harper, a veteran reporter of some 20 years. "We've got a big story here. Third kid to die in a week. Do you have any suspects?"

"We're working on it," Walter replied tersely. "We're looking at some people."

"What about motive?" the second reporter, Nat Cellar, prompted. "Is it drug related?"

"Fellows, it's too soon for me to comment on that," Walter said, sounding tired. "You said yourself it's only been a week."

"We didn't say only," Bud commented. "A week is more than only to me. A week is a long time, especially for parents who have teenagers going to Rockport High. Do you think anyone else is going to be killed?"

"I've put my best men on this case and I am spending day and night on it myself," Walter said quietly. I could see a vein on the side of his neck starting to pulse. This was a sure sign he was nervous and irritated. "I can't predict when we'll have someone in custody, but believe me when I say we're doing everything we can."

"If you don't catch him soon, do you think the Commissioner will replace you?"

Walter narrowed his eyes. "Bud, think about that question a little bit. Do you seriously believe I am going to predict my own dismissal?"

Bud chuckled. "Well, sometimes I speak before I think. It saves time. We'll let it alone for now. I know this is a tough one. C'mon Ronald, I'll buy you a beer." The two reporters put their notebooks away and walked off towards the parking lot arguing about which watering hole to head for.

"Damn, I hate that," Walter said. "This case is practically without clues so far, it involves the horrible murder of children, and I am as far as I ever was from catching whoever did it. Then, I have to talk about it with those reporters. I have to come up with things to say that will make the department look like it's not running around in the dark, which it is. What a job!"

"You could go private," I said reassuringly. "We could be partners."

Walter's eyes widened in mock horror. "You're just trying to make this job look better," he said accusingly. "I'd as soon go into partnership with a runaway train."

"You just hurt my tender ego," I said haughtily. "You'll have to buy me a beer to make up for it."

"Your tender ego? Tender like a pig's hide, but I'll buy you the beer anyway. I'm thirsty too." Walter told several policemen where he could be found and we went off in search of a cold one, being certain to avoid the establishment where the reporters had settled.

CHAPTER TWENTY TWO

"Let's pick up the Porsche and drop it off at my place," I suggested to Walter. I had left it at the restaurant where we had almost eaten and I wanted to get it safely back in my garage so I wouldn't spend the evening worrying about theft or vandalism. "We can see if I got any messages, and give Pokey her dinner."

"Fine with me, as long as you don't take all night," Walter said dryly. "I've worked up a powerful thirst."

We picked up the Porsche and then Walter followed me over to Key Allegro. The moon was big and looked like a giant glowing white wafer. It provided enough illumination to make night darkened waves visible to boaters and fishermen. I locked the Porsche in my garage and went in the back entrance to my office. The answering machine was blinking for two messages so I punched the proper buttons and sat down to await my communications.

The first inquiry was about a prospective job. I took the name and number. I was a little busy right now, but the next day I'd call and see if it could be undertaken in a week or two, providing it was the sort of job I did. Crystal's voice came through second. It was high pitched and excited.

"Hey, Len, you know those two punks you asked me about today? Well, speak of the devil, here they are at the Crystal Pistol tonight! I'll try and stall them awhile. Give me a call, and if they're still here, they're all yours."

I got out her number and fairly burned my fingertips I dialed so quickly. A deep bass voice answered. "Hello?"

"Put Crystal on please," I said.

"Who wants her?"

"Len Townsend. Make it fast, please."

In less than a minute she was on. "They just left," she said regretfully, "but they said they'd be back later. I would have offered them a free drink, but that would make them suspicious for sure."

"How long until you close?"

"About another two hours."

"I'll be there," I told her, and hung up. After feeding Pokey and getting the usual high jumps of enthusiasm, I joined Walter in his car.

"Guess what?" I asked.

"I hate it when you ask me to guess," he replied crossly.

"Okay, I'll tell you. Crystal called, and the two fish nicknamed jerks were at her place drinking beer tonight. They told her they'd be back later."

"If they are, we'll be waiting for them," Walter said, his mood brightening by about 300 degrees. He put the car in drive and headed out at a very unpolicemanlike speed. We made it to Corpus in under 20 minutes.

The music coming out of the Crystal Pistol could be heard clearly in the furthest reaches of its parking lot. Some lonesome cowboy was singing a somebody done him wrong song and the celebrators inside were stomping their feet merrily to keep time. Crystal was dancing a fast dance with a tall, lanky specimen wearing crocodile boots and leather chaps. They were whirling around to the beat of several cold beers he had consumed in the past hour. Crystal looked dead on her feet.

Walter got us a table while I strolled out onto the dance floor and cut in on Crystal and the dancing cowboy.

"Sure glad to see you, Len," Crystal said with relief. "That good ol' boy was just getting started and I have to play the good sport. My feet are killing me!"

"Why don't you come over and sit at my table awhile?" I asked her, grinning. "You can rest your pretty feet and tell me what Shark and Barracuda were up to tonight."

"That's got to be the best offer I've had all night, which isn't saying a whole lot for the quality of my offers," Crystal replied, leading me off the dance floor. The cowboy had found another, fresher partner, and they were gliding around the dance floor knocking into only about half of the other couples they passed. If he kept that up, sooner or later another fight would start.

We sat down and ordered three beers. Walter, now a free man even if it was only temporary, looked at Crystal with interest. They hadn't met before. She returned the look. I introduced them.

"Crystal, what time did our boys come in tonight?" I asked, sort of to remind the others that I was there.

Crystal reluctantly withdrew her attention away from Walter and gave it to me. "They came in a little after nine, jumpy as cats," she said. "They started drinking heavy and whispering among themselves. I went over and tried to start a conversation, but they weren't interested. They answered in monosyllables, making it pretty plain they wanted to be left alone. I was only too happy to do that. I called you, but by the time you called back they were gone. I wasn't able to get them to stay longer."

"They said they'd be back tonight," I reminded her. "Do you think they will?"

"Who knows? They're about as reliable as a $3 watch. You'll just have to hang around and see." The last was said to Walter, in the manner of an invitation.

Walter responded immediately. "Can't think of anything I'd rather do," he said grandly, with a smile that was as near to a leer as the Grand Canyon is to Arizona.

Having been well received, Crystal put her bright mind to work. She knew her time with Walter would be curtailed as soon as the Shark and the Barracuda walked in the front door, which might be immediately, so she forwent the formalities and got right down to business.

"Does your...uh...wife mind your being out this late on business?" Crystal asked, her dark eyelashes fluttering like butterflies.

"Oh, I'm not married," Walter replied, making it sound like an invitation.

Crystal upped her ante. "Well, then, I bet you have lots of girlfriends."

"I'm fresh out at the moment," Walter said. He was right about being fresh, anyway. Crystal smiled widely and took a large swallow of her beer. I felt like I was participating in the conversation through a glass wall. I could be seen but I wouldn't be heard.

Walter asked Crystal if she wanted to dance, and she must have gotten her second wind, because she hurried over to the dance floor and began a wild boogie that caught the attention of everybody in the bar, even the two drunks at the counter. Walter followed suit even though he doesn't like to fast dance. The dancing crowd moved back to give them room, whether due to admiration of their technique or in self protection I wouldn't hazard a guess. Anyway the song soon ended and a slow dance began, so I knew I'd be by myself for a little while longer if not the rest of the night.

The drinking was getting serious, because it was only about another hour until the Crystal Pistol had to close. I kept a close watch on the front door, hoping to see our elusive quarries enter, but all that came in were four thirsty cowboys and two wide eyed tourists who were getting their first taste of honky tonking. Just when I was about to give up and call it a night, the door swung wide open and in walked the Shark and the Barracuda, escorting two young ladies for whom the song about girls getting prettier at closing time most definitely had been written. I looked around for Walter but he and Crystal had disappeared.

CHAPTER TWENTY THREE

Walter's disappearance left me with a small dilemma. Should I go hunt him up? He was probably getting the house tour and could be found admiring the etchings in Crystal's office, or should I tackle the boys all by my lonesome? I decided to see if I could get them to invite me to join them and do a little undercover investigating.

The foursome picked a table near the bar and sat down, looking bored with one another. I tried to think of a way to get them into conversation, but it wasn't easy, because I normally only like to converse with someone whose IQ is larger than his shoe size. In this case, however, I was willing to make an exception.

"Where'd you get the threads, man," I said loudly, addressing Shark, who was wearing a purple shirt, a bright green vest and black leather pants, obviously a man who wanted to make a fashion statement. To me the statement said wrong. "I've been looking for some classy clothes and yours are great."

Shark looked me over, and motioned for me to join them. "All right, man, way to go! This young lady here has been putting me down about my clothes, man. Now she can see I got good taste," he said, pleased with my remarks. "Did you hear what he said, Stella?"

The petite brunette with the sour expression looked unimpressed. "Yeah, I heard him, Shark. Now there's two of you with lousy taste. I don't much like what he's wearing, either."

The other couple giggled and waited for more. Shark was only too happy to give it to them.

"Gee whiz, guys, I take this woman out, buy her drinks, take her to nice places, and she puts me down," he said in a mock complaint. "What would she do to me if I took her away for the weekend?"

The brunette looked him over with contempt. "Who said I wanted to go away with you for the weekend? With your cool, you probably want to take me to Altoona, Pa., or Montgomery, Ala., or some other big deal city."

Barracuda gave a little hoot of derision, a challenge to Shark to assert his manhood and come up with a proper put down for the young woman. Unfortunately for Shark, the attention of customers at several other tables had been caught and he had to find a remark to save the situation or be the butt of much laughter and numerous put downs.

I could see the panic building in his eyes. He nervously glanced around the room, seeking inspiration. What to do? Barracuda leaned forward in anticipation while the little brunette licked her lips, her eyes sparkling in near triumph.

"Well, uh," Shark began, holding a bottle of beer tightly, "uh, the only dames I take to big deal cities are big deal dames, and honey, you ain't no big deal dame. Why, you're just a little deal dame."

Hoots of laughter from the men mingled with gasps and boos from the women. Having won the battle of wits, at least what passed for wit at the Crystal Pistol, Shark could now appear magnanimous and make up with the little lady. However, he had hesitated a little too long as he basked in the admiring glances of his fellow drinkers and by the time he was ready to pacify his date she had already gotten up and moved halfway across the room towards the door. It would amount to a great loss of face for him to get up and go after her, so he was stuck for the rest of the evening with no feminine companionship. It was, however, an opportunity for me to get closer to him.

"No loss, man," I told him. "Dames are a dime a dozen."

"You said it, friend," he agreed, watching the door close behind her. "She blew it big time."

"Where'd you find her?" I asked him, not interested in the slightest except in the possibility of establishing where he was at the time of the shooting.

"We ran into her and the other skirt at the last joint we were in. Never saw either one before in my life. They just came in from Los Angeles, they said."

So much for an alibi. Walter and Crystal had come out of her office during the dispute between Shark and his pick up. When Walter spotted me sitting at the table with our suspects, he ducked back into the office, probably to use a phone to call the Corpus police. He could have them come out and run the two men in for questioning. My job would be to keep them talking until the police arrived, which might be a mean task because Shark was getting restless.

"Let me buy the man who knows how to deal with women a beer," I said, knowing he wouldn't be able to turn down the flattery or the free suds. I signaled a waitress to bring over another round. She went to the bar and I could see Walter whisper into her ear. Probably it would be a few minutes before our drinks arrived. Bravo, Walter.

However, I needn't have worried, because less than a moment later three uniformed patrolmen came quietly in and after a signal from Walter, surrounded our table. I noticed most of the tavern's clientele quietly leaving. Nothing empties a honky tonk quicker than the arrival of some men in blue.

"Well, hello Shark and hello Barracuda," said one cop, placing his hand on Barracuda's shoulder. "Why don't you two fellows come with us? We want to have a little chat with you."

"Excuse me," I mumbled, keeping in character. I got up and walked over to the bar. I didn't want the two suspects to know I had any involvement with the police in case I needed to talk with them another time.

"What do you want with us?" complained Barracuda. "I got plans tonight." He stroked his girl's arm. She drew back and moved her chair away slightly.

"The usual," another policeman said helpfully. "Let's go."

After the unlikely group had departed, Walter came over to me and said, "Let's go home. They're going to be pretty busy until tomorrow. Turns out they're wanted on suspicion of armed robbery too. Happened earlier this evening. This is quite a find for Corpus."

"Pretty versatile, aren't they? Drugs and armed robbery? Wonder what else they've been up to?"

"Maybe murder," Walter said, turning to say goodnight to Crystal. He promised to call her soon and I thought Marie would be fit to be tied if she found out.

CHAPTER TWENTY FOUR

Early the next morning I awakened to the shrill ringing of my telephone. I was tempted to pull the pillows over my head but it might be important so I made the great effort, threw back my covers, rolled out of bed and sprinted for the telephone. By the time I got there, the ringing had stopped and when I picked up the phone all I heard was the loud whine of the dial tone.

A shower seemed like a good idea, so I fed Pokey a dog's breakfast and microwaved a muffin for myself. I headed into the bathroom for a warm and soapy shower. I needed to remove the smokey aroma which clung to me as a not so welcome reminder of my visit to the honky tonks the day before. I went the whole route with a shower, shave, shampoo and brushing, foaming and flossing of teeth. I felt like not exactly a new man, but at least a reconditioned one.

While I was buttoning my shirt, the telephone rang again. I hurried into the kitchen and grabbed the phone on the counter on the second ring. It was Walter.

"Morning, Len. Apparently this is an early morning for you," he said, curious. "What were you up to?"

"Not up to. Out of. I was still asleep. But the time I got to the telephone you were long gone. You really ought to let it ring longer."

"Hummph. I'm in the wrong business," Walter replied grumpily. "You private types live in luxury and comfort, while I'm stuck here at the desk come rain or shine, day or night."

"Yeah, I sure have it good. Two days ago I was bopped over the head, unconscious in the park and then lying in the hospital. When was the last time a professional type like you had that happen?"

"How long has it been since I broke up with Marie?" he asked, chuckling.

"Not long enough, or too long, depending on how you look at it," I countered. "Does this call have a purpose, or did you just want to comment on my lifestyle?"

"There's a purpose, all right. When the police took that pair in last night, they made arrangements to have their car dropped off at a girlfriend's house. Guess what the car looked like?"

"Silver Rolls? Maroon Mercedes? Green BMX?"

"Try beige Toyota, 1982."

"Uh, oh. I know Tammy said that's what they drove, but I kind of figured them for the Ford pick up type."

"Or Harley motorcycle. Why don't you give Marilyn a look at the mug shots? Maybe she knows them. Maybe she's dated them."

"I was going to do that first thing this morning, but I don't think she's dated them. She likes to be taken out to dinner and they're a pair of appetite killers if ever there was any."

"I can understand that," Walter replied.

"Hey, what's the deal between you and Crystal?" I asked. "That was some pretty heavy dancing last night and I thought I saw major sparks flying between the two of you."

"She's pretty sharp, Len, and it's nice to be able to talk to a woman and not have it end up in an argument not three seconds after you get the world hello out."

"I thought you enjoyed your little arguments with Marie."

"It's not the arguments, it's the making up I enjoy. It's Marie who likes the arguments. That woman would argue over whether or not to use a straw in a glass of iced tea."

"She says the same thing about you, Walter."

"See what I mean?" he was starting to sound irritated. "Anyway, I'm going to Corpus to talk with those two dolts this morning. I guess by now they've called every lawyer in Texas and I probably won't get much out of them." He hung up, having said everything he wanted to say. I've tried to train him to say goodbye, so at least I can get the receiver away from my ear, but he's not trainable.

The sun was bright and reflecting bright diamonds over the fast moving deep green waters of Aransas Bay. I stood for a moment on my front porch, watching the sunlight dance the shimmy across the bay, anointing a fisherman with a magic yellow light. A light breeze took the sting of the heat away and replaced it with a heady smell of salt air.

Again, there was no sign of Marilyn at the house where she was staying. There was no sign of anyone, except for a black cat crossing the driveway. An omen? I didn't believe in that stuff, particularly for Marilyn. She seemed to exude an aura of good luck or maybe an aura of having been blessed. At times she didn't seem quite real.

The front door opened narrowly before I even got to the front porch. I hurried inside and took the liberty of giving Marilyn a quick kiss on the cheek. She smelled faintly like gardenias and her cheek was soft and cool to the touch.

"Hello, Marilyn. How are you doing?"

"Pretty bored, Len," she replied, pouting her lips a little. "But better bored than dead. I've been watching tv a lot, particularly the soap operas. I study the technique of the actors and actresses and then try to act out the scene myself. Want a demonstration?"

"Who could resist that?" I replied enthusiastically. "Go ahead."

Marilyn was wearing a blue tee shirt and jeans. Her hair was loosely curled, one blonde lock hanging over the right side of her forehead. Her pale skin appeared flawless, except for the mole which I hadn't yet determined was real or artificial.

114

"I'm going to do a love scene," she told me, her eyes bright with excitement. Her choice didn't surprise me. She was made for love scenes. "It's a funny scene, where this girl is trying to get this guy to admit he is in love with her. You be the guy. You just have to sort of sit there and make up an answer now and then."

"I'll do my best," I promised and sat down on the sofa to enjoy the show.

For the moment, my mind was letting all of the awfulness of the past week be bypassed by a little friendly play acting, a light hearted entertaining romp into the world of never never. There was plenty of time to bring her back to the here and now, a world inhabited by the Sharks and Barracudas and Harry Bascombs and the person or persons who were trying to kill her.

Suddenly Marilyn was a completely different entity. I could feel it. She was younger, more vulnerable and her expression became yearning, wistful. She hesitated a moment, then murmured to herself, "No, that's all wrong." She gave herself a little shake and was just as suddenly someone else. I scarcely breathed. I was spellbound; I'd never seen anything like it.

This Marilyn was a sexpot, a sparkling, curvy, smoldering volcano of a woman, earthy and knowing, all soft womanly movements and an expression in her eyes that reflected an ancient knowing of all things. The show had begun.

"Hello, Len, it's been a long time," she said in a soft, purring voice which reached out to me and fastened itself around my insides, pulling me towards her. "Why have you waited so long to come to me?"

I wasn't sure which direction she wanted me to take, but I plunged in anyhow. "I've been busy, baby," I said in a careless, offhand manner.

She lowered her eyelashes, moved seductively across the room, and turned to face me. Huskily, she replied, "I've seen your busy, sweetheart. She has red hair and alabaster skin and she drives a red Honda."

"Baby, it isn't what you think," I said, inspired. "That's my sister."

Determined, Marilyn continued, "So, what about the black haired chick who works at the Stop and Go? I've seen her in your car three times this week."

"Nothing there either, baby," I replied, enjoying myself now. "She's my accountant. She takes accounting courses at the high school at night."

Marilyn gave a throaty little growl and sat down at my feet. "But darling, you don't have any money. You're bankrupt."

"That's why I need an accountant," I replied. "To fill out the paperwork."

She tried a different tack. "Why haven't you been coming around? I've missed you, longed for you, wanted you…"

"Baby, I've been here, you just haven't been home," I countered, to see what she would do with that.

"I take lots of showers," she replied, pursing her lips. "You must have come then."

"Do you shower in your car?" I asked. "It was gone too."

"Car wash," she replied, giggling. "Oh, Len, I guess we need a script! Ad libbing isn't getting us anywhere." She was back to the Marilyn I was used to.

"Well, I really didn't come to see you perform, although I enjoyed it immensely," I told her. "What I did come to do was show you a couple of pictures."

I reached into my pocket and drew out the mug shots of Shark and Barracuda and handed them over to Marilyn. She glanced briefly at each one, her face wearing an expression of distaste, much the same expression I'd expect to see if she were looking at a large rat in her kitchen. Those two were as close to being a human equivalent of a rodent as it was possible to be.

"They look familiar, but I just can't place them," she said, sounding worried. "Who are they?"

"A couple of dudes who might be involved in the Missy Small murder," I told her, putting the pictures away. "The only thing that might possibly tie them to you is that they were driving a beige foreign car."

"That's it," she said. "That's where I've seen them. Going in and out of the parking lot at my apartment building. I don't know which apartment they live in or if they were just visiting."

"They don't have any fixed address," I told her, interested. "They were probably just visiting someone. Or, maybe they were following you. Did you get that impression?"

"I don't know. I just didn't pay any particular attention to them, didn't want to give them anything they might consider encouragement. I couldn't tell you whether they were coming or going. I just remember seeing them."

That was an interesting bit of information, as far as it went. That could be the beige car Selser had seen, following Marilyn for a lark, or with the intent to do her bodily harm, or it might not be the same car. It was too early to venture a guess. We needed to uncover more information, lots of it, and hopefully Walter would get something helpful in his interview. However, knowing the past records of that pair, it would be very difficult to get them to talk and they would have a competent lawyer sifting through everything they might have to say.

Marilyn fixed us a light brunch of an omelet and English muffin. To make it interesting, she uncorked a bottle of pink champagne and we toasted to the speedy end of her self-imposed isolation. After two glasses of the bubbly I left, feeling relaxed and refreshed.

When I got back home I called Walter, but he hadn't returned to the office yet. I went downstairs to check my answering machine. There was a message that Roy Owens had called, but he said he'd call back later, that it wasn't urgent, so I didn't make any plans to go to the high school.

While I was contemplating my next move a knock sounded at my door. It was the UPS man holding a small package. I took it, closed the door and set the package on my counter. It didn't have any return address on it, and I thought back to having been hit over the head three days earlier. Could it be a bomb? Unlikely, but why didn't it have a return address? Should I call the bomb squad in Corpus and ask them to open it? I'd risk getting a big belly laugh when it turned out to be a book on how to grow tomatoes from my mother. Or should I open it myself, and risk taking the forever trip on one gorgeous Texas day in the springtime of my life? I flipped a coin, the way I like to settle most of my major decisions. Lincoln told me to open it myself, so I gingerly picked it up, shook it a little, and set it back down. Then I heard a thunderously loud explosion which shook my windows, jiggled my dishes and blew open my door.

CHAPTER TWENTY FIVE

It was another Navy jet breaking the sound barrier. The loud blast startled me so much my knees started to shake and my teeth wanted to chatter. I wiped a thin layer of perspiration off my forehead. For a split second there I though I had bought the big one, cashed in the farm, overturned the milk bucket. It was a relief to still be standing, still be trying to decide what to do about my little brown package.

I touched it gently and moved it around in tentative circles on the counter. I put my ear next to the brown paper wrapping and listened, but there was no ticking or noise of any kind. Taking a deep breath, I tore the wrapping off the cardboard box. The box bore no markings of any kind and offered no clue as to where it had come from or what it now held. I took another deep breath and used my pocket knife to slit open the tape which held the lid to the box shut.

It contained a little black book, nestled deep in some newspaper so it would not slip around during transit. There was a note on top of the book which read "This is from a friend". I resisted the temptation to open the notebook, knowing that it might contain fingerprints. That is, I resisted the temptation to open the notebook for about 30 seconds. Then I picked up my knife, using it to open the corner and reveal the first page, which was blank. I turned another page. Bingo! It had a list of words, apparently some sort of code, followed by dates and amounts of money. The first 25 words or so were flowers, followed by another 25 colors, then 25 names of automobiles. I wish whoever had sent them to me had been friendly enough to tell me what the words meant, or to whom the notebook belonged. I slowly turned each page, but most of the pages were blank and there were no other clues. At least it was not the bomb I had feared.

The telephone rang and this time it was Roy Owens. He sounded excited and out of breath. He had probably run down to the gas station, about two blocks from his school, to make the call.

"Hi, Roy. What's up?"

"One of the kids told me who it was Harry Bascomb used to meet over on the beach at Port A," he said eagerly.

"Who was that?"

"The girl he dated before he moved to Rockport. Her name is Mary. She's a college girl, three years older than Harry. She was pretty serious about him, but he was pretty serious about drugs. She didn't take it too well when they broke up and she did some crazy things, like call him all hours during the night. His parents loved that."

"What college does she go to?"

"I don't know. I don't even know her last name. Maybe Harry's folks could tell you more about her than I can."

"Good work, Roy. Are you keeping track of your time?"

"Like a Rollex."

"Catch you later. Thanks again."

This seemed like a good time to pay a visit to Harry's parents. Maybe this Mary could tell me about the extent of Harry's involvement as a drug pusher and where he got his product. She would not have any reason to protect Harry now and maybe, for old time's sake, she would want to see his killer caught. Hopefully she was over her anger and the hurt caused by their breakup. I dialed the Bascomb number, but there was no answer.

There was no one home at the Small residence either. I guessed she had gone back to work at the little boutique over on Fifth Street, so I climbed into the Porsche and made tracks over there. Sure enough, there was Ruth's car parked on one side of the building.

Several women were coming out of the boutique carrying large packages when I went in. Ruth was helping an older lady with improbable blue hair select an outfit to wear to the yacht club that evening. She fancied a bright orange number, with which the blue hair would give her a sort of outer space alien look. I liked it. Ruth, however, was tactfully trying to steer her to a more sedate dark blue evening gown. At least it went better with the hair. The woman finally decided on green evening pants and a shimmering silver top. It wasn't bad.

"Did you come to see me, Len?" Ruth asked. "What's up?"

"I came to see if you know anything about an old girl friend of Harry's. Mary something. A college girl."

"Her! I'd forgotten all about her, that was awhile back," Ruth said, a look of annoyance on her face. She sounded angry. "When Melissa first started dating Harry, she got a few phone calls from this Mary. I can't remember her last name, but it may come to me. She tried to get Missy to stop seeing Harry, and I'll admit I agreed with Mary. It upset Missy quite a bit. Once she came over to our house, but I wasn't home. Missy told me about it. She was very unhappy and told Harry to ask Mary to leave her alone. Mary didn't bother her anymore after that. I don't know what Harry said to Mary to get her to leave Missy alone, but it worked."

"Why didn't you mention this to me before?"

"It was a long time ago," Ruth replied. "Besides, the girl had stopped causing trouble. She's probably gone through half a dozen other men by now. She couldn't do much worse than Harry."

I thanked Ruth for the information and asked her to call me if she thought of Mary's last name. As I walked out the door, a very obese woman in tight slacks entered the store. She asked to see something which would make her look thinner. I was beginning to appreciate the difficulties in Ruth's line of work.

Next to the boutique was a gasoline station which housed several pay phones. I played some coins to see if Bascomb's folks had returned home yet. I hit the jackpot. His mother answered the telephone and was willing to talk with me if I came over right away. She had another engagement that afternoon. I was only too happy to oblige.

The drive to Copano Cove was lovely. I took the beach road so I could admire the view of Copano Bay, a shallow bay which was popular for fishing in small boats which could handle shallow waters. Mrs. Bascomb was watering her rose bushes when I drove up. I took a moment to compliment her on her garden before we went inside. I also inquired as to Amos Bascomb's condition. She replied that he was doing well and had even felt well enough to return to work.

"How might I help you?" Anne Bascomb asked politely after we had seated ourselves in her living room. Her thin brown hair was swept up into a bun and her eye still had the same dark circles under them that they had the last time I saw her. "Have you found out any more about the person who killed Harry?"

"We're working on it and the police have some leads," I said noncommittally. "I have a few questions I'd like you to answer, if you will."

"Of course I will," she said emphatically. "If there is any way at all I can help I will."

"I'm glad to hear that," I said. Amazingly, not all people in a similar situation want to help.

"First, may I offer you something to drink? Some coffee, or perhaps some tea?" Her thin face looked anxious and it seemed somehow as if she were trying to please me. I thought it might make her more comfortable if she went through the soothing motions of offering refreshment, so I said iced tea would be very nice. She got up, headed for the kitchen and said she'd only be a minute. Did I want lemon and sugar?

When she got back and had given me a tall glass of light brown liquid which turned out to be surprisingly good tea, we resumed our conversation.

"Mrs. Bascomb, what can you tell me about a girl Harry used to date? Her name was Mary."

Anne Bascomb looked puzzled. "What has she to do with this?" she asked, frowning.

"Probably nothing. We just have to follow all leads and her name has come up along with several others."

"I see," she replied, settling back on her sofa. "Well, Mary was quite infatuated with Harry before he met Missy. They were introduced at some party. She was several years older than he was and I didn't care for that, but what could I do? Harry was headstrong and if I said one thing, he'd do the opposite just to show me he could. He was like that even when he was little." She paused to take a sip of her iced tea and her gaze wandered over to a portrait of a little boy.

"What is Mary's last name?" I asked, adding, "Do you know where she lives?"

"Her last name is Spaulding. I don't know where she lives," Mrs. Bascomb said, running her finger absentmindedly around the rim of her glass. "She comes from a wealthy Corpus family. I don't know what she wanted with Harry, except that maybe his wildness appealed to her. Some women are like that. They're attracted to wild men. Maybe it's because they're wild themselves."

"Is Mary wild?" I asked.

"Oh yes, she is quite wild," Mrs. Bascomb said disapprovingly. "That's why Harry liked her so much. She is a heavy drinker and probably, well, how to say it? Probably just as heavily into sex. She used to call Harry all the time, and sometimes I could tell just by talking to her on the phone she'd been drinking. She only came over to the house twice. She picked Harry up and she was driving a fancy white convertible. She was dressed both time in tight white pants and a clinging white sweater. She had curly ebony colored hair which she wore loose. It flowed down her back like so many snakes. A modern day Medusa in white spike heels. Emerald rings covered her hands and she had the longest, reddest fingernails I've ever seen. Her lipstick was the color of blood, her eyes as black as a moonless night." She paused, letting the memories return, become more vivid.

"Did you actually meet her and speak with her?" I asked curiously.

"Oh, yes, I did. I went out with Harry once when she picked him up. She didn't come to the door, but sat waiting in the car," she said, her eyes burning brightly at remembered indignities. "There she sat, in that car, with a six pack of beer on the front seat. She was drinking out of a can. Harry introduced us and she glanced at me with those horrible dark eyes and all I could feel was her contempt. She just looked at me. I asked her if she'd like to have some roses, and she laughed. If I wanted roses, she said, I'd have a florist deliver them. Then she laughed again. Harry got into the car and they drove off."

My eyes widened. Wild seemed like a pretty good word to describe that one all right. Mean might work too. I could scarcely wait to meet her. Sounded like I should take a cattle prod along, or a bull whip, or maybe just a portable bar.

"The second time I met her she was a little more civil," Mrs. Bascomb continued. "Perhaps Harry had asked her to be. Anyway, she came up to the front door and rang the doorbell. I invited her in because Harry wasn't ready. She sat down on this sofa, where I am now, and asked me about the family portrait over there on the wall, the one of the old gentleman, my great grandfather. She said he had character and she could see some resemblance in Harry. Then Harry came down and she was gone, but not before I smelled the alcohol on her breath. I could smell it all the way across the room."

"I wish I knew what she looked like," I said, thinking out loud.

"Well, why didn't you say so? I have her picture." Anne Bascomb got up, went over to an end table and opened a drawer. She took out a large pile of pictures and went through them one by one. Finally she stopped and handed a small picture to me.

"That's her," she said. "Harry took this picture early one morning in the summer."

Though not a close up, the picture was very revealing. It showed a shapely young woman with milk white skin looking challengingly at the camera, a direct, unafraid look. Her beauty was awesome, remarkable, a Snow White to Marilyn's Cinderella. She was wearing the tiniest of bikinis, so small in fact that I could not quite make out what color it was. Maybe green, maybe blue.

"What caused Harry to break up with this girl?"

"I'm not really sure," she replied. "Maybe it was the age difference. Harry was only 17, and at his age a few years is a big difference. Or maybe she was just too wild to keep up with. It could have been our move here. It was easier for him to go with local girls than to go to Corpus to see her. It happened around the time he started seeing Melissa, so maybe Melissa was part of it."

All of a sudden it happened. The calm composure Mrs. Bascomb had been maintaining dissolved like melting wax and her face crumpled into tears. I had taken her too far and her grief was too recent to allow her to talk at length about Mary Spaulding and Harry. The wretched woman pressed a large handkerchief over her face, trying to stifle the sounds of grieving. The sobbing continued unabated for a good five minutes, then showed and turned into small gasps and hiccups. Finally she lowered her handkerchief and said in a low, shaky voice, "I apologize, Mr. Townsend. I don't know why I did that, except that I do it about three times each day and twice that at night. It just happens all at once and I can't help it or stop it."

I mumbled some consoling words, the best I could come up with, and made good my departure. Mrs. Bascomb was unable to provide me with Mary's address, but said she'd ask her husband if he had anything he could add to what she had already told me. We shook hands and I left.

I stopped at the nearest pay phone, plunked in some coins, and dialed the number of a popular Corpus college, Del Mar. The woman who answered the telephone assured me there was no Mary Spaulding registered. Then I checked the number of Spauldings in the Corpus directory, but there were about 130, too many to call at this early stage, so I got back in the Porsche and beat it to Rockport.

Walter was in his office filling out paperwork and talking into the telephone while he wrote. He is very good at doing two things at once. He spoke so low I was unable to hear what he was saying even though I was only about five feet away. From the ingratiating tone of his voice I guessed it was a woman, probably the lovely Crystal of the previous night. He glanced up, saw me and ended the conversation quickly.

"I brought you a little present, Walter," I said cheerfully, putting the cardboard box and its wrapping on his desk. I had carried it on a metal tray so I wouldn't get any fingerprints on it. "Who were you talking to on the telephone just now?"

"Wrong number," Walter replied, staring curiously at the box. "What's that?"

"Something the UPS man brought me this morning. Take a look."

Walter picked up his letter opener and went through the black book, frowning at the scribbling inside. "Have any idea who it's from?"

"Sure. The note inside told me. It's from a friend."

"I see. Anonymous."

"That's right. I don't even know who it concerns, but I'd guess it's a list of customers," I told him. "A dope list. I bet somebody wants it back bad."

Walter picked up his phone, pushed the intercom button, and asked one of the desk clerks to come get the package and take it to the lab. In less than a minute the package was on its way, minus the tray I had brought it in on.

"Think this is part of the Bascomb deal?" I asked.

"Who knows? Without any more information, we may not be able to find out. Or then again, maybe we'll get lucky. Of course this could be someone you know who is trying to get back at her husband or her boyfriend or whoever in a way she can't be traced."

"How did it go with your interview in Corpus?" I asked, figuring if it had gone well he would already have told me.

Walter opened his desk drawer and got out a pack of cigarettes. He slowly unwrapped the cellophane, took out a cigarette and lit it, inhaling deeply. He blew the smoke out in a large ring, almost a perfect circle, and then gestured at it with his index finger.

"That's how it went. A big zero," he complained. "Those guys are street smart and they're used to talking to cops. They shut up and the only time they'll open their mouth is to holler for their lawyer."

"Didn't you get anything?"

"Absolutely nothing. I left a list of questions, that's all. I'm going back tomorrow. If they get ready to talk today, the interrogators

123

will use my questions, otherwise I'll do it tomorrow. I can't move them here because of that pending charge in Corpus."

"There is another angle I'm working on," I said, hoping to cheer him up. "Roy Owens told me the person Harry Bascomb used to meet at the beach was Harry's old girlfriend Mary. I'm trying to track her down. She's from Corpus and her last name is Spaulding. She used to attend college but I'm not sure if she still does or not."

Walter stubbed out his cigarette and took a swallow of coffee. "A college girl? Wasn't she a little old for him?"

"Or the other way," I replied, getting up. "Maybe he was a little young for her. His mother says she is a wild one and from her description, it sounds about right to me."

"Wonder if it's the same Mary he got the letter from?" Walter mused. Score one for Walter. I had forgotten about the steamy letters we found in Harry's drawer. "How are you going to find her?"

"I'm going to talk with Harry's father, see if he remembers anything about her. Then I guess I'll get to go through the privilege of calling all the Spauldings in the phone book and ask them if they have a daughter named Mary, or if they are Mary. Of course she may live alone and not have a listed number."

Walter conceded that might be the quickest way to locate Mary and suggested we have an early dinner so I could get started. I noticed he did not offer to take half of the names himself, but perhaps he had other things to work on. Like maybe he had plans to go crystal gazing under the stars later in the evening. The neon stars in a Corpus honky-tonk.

CHAPTER TWENTY SIX

After a fine dinner at our favorite restaurant Walter and I parted company. He continued to refuse to tell me his plans for the rest of the evening, even though I tried to make it look as if I might need to find him if I got ahold of Mary.

"You can reach me through the office," he said, smiling as he reached in his pocket for his car keys. "They always know where I am." He drove off in a hurry, running a red light, something he almost never does unless he is on official business.

I went back to Key Allegro to feed Pokey and check for messages. Pokey was barking at some ripples in the canal out back of my house. She enthusiastically welcomed the clump of dog food I put in her dish and affectionately nibbled my foot after she finished her dinner. All of Pokey's gestures involve her mouth.

There were no messages for me and no more little brown packages. I was sure the police would check with UPS to see who had sent the package but it was unlikely they would come up with a real name. I hoped the lab would find fingerprints other than mine and the UPS man's, but it was not likely.

A quick dial of a telephone number ascertained that Amos Bascomb had returned home. He answered on the second ring and said he had been waiting for my call, a sure sign he had nothing much to do because I had not told Mrs. Bascomb when I'd be calling. Apparently Harry had been more open with Mr. Bascomb about his relationship with Mary than he had with his mother, because Amos wanted to meet me at a little bar and grill later that evening. I agreed enthusiastically and we hung up. Bascomb had spoken in soft, hushed tones, and had kept the conversation short, so I assumed there was a good chance his wife was unaware of our meeting tonight. I wondered what he was hiding, or if his wife just did not like for him to frequent the local drinking establishments. At any rate, Walter would not be the only one occupied that evening.

I debated as to whether or not to start making calls to every Spaulding in the Corpus Christi telephone book, but decided to wait until after I had spoken to Amos before undertaking that project. Each call would be long distance and I did not want to waste time and money making calls if I could get the information I needed on Mary's whereabouts out of Amos.

Soon it was time to meet Amos, so I got some cash out of my wall safe, combed my hair and took off for the bright lights and night sights of Rockport. There were at least two. I recognized Amos' car from the hardware store where he worked parked at the one where we had agreed to meet. He had arrived early and so had I. Since I was at least 15 minutes early, it seemed ridiculous for us not to have made our appointment sooner. Or could it have been he was meeting someone else ahead of me?

The joint where our rendezvous was taking place was the Red Horse Tavern, a fancy name for a seedy, run down lackluster little bar. There were at least three colors of fading paint on the old building and the windows had not been washed in so long there were wash me signs on signs that had said wash me. Some of the windows were broken and the ones which didn't have cracks were missing. Several large fans whirled unevenly on the ceiling of the little bar and the linoleum on the floor was so old it no longer had a recognizable color. The booths were reupholstered in plastic which had been torn and was leaking stuffing. The tables were wooden and bore the initials of many previous patrons.

My kind of place.

The juke box played loudly while some young kid plunked quarters into its money slot and punched numbers on the buttons. He looked underage and over drunk and he seemed not to be paying any particular attention to the numbers he was punching. I couldn't wait to hear his selections. At present the song playing was about love lost gone wrong.

I walked over to the booth where Amos was sitting and shook hands with him. He was drinking a beer and eating some peanuts, not much of a diet for a man who had come close to having a heart attack a week earlier.

"How have you been, Mr. Bascomb?" I asked. "The last time I saw you, you were in an ambulance on the way to the hospital. Here it is about a week later and you're drinking beer and eating nuts."

"Aw, I'm all right," he replied, chuckling. "Call me Amos. I was on the verge of a heart attack, but they gave me some procedure where they stick some sort of balloon up my arteries to unclog them and then I'm okay again."

"Sounds good to me," I answered, signaling the waitress for a beer. Oversimplified, maybe, but it if was okay with him, it was okay with me. "Guess your wife told you I am looking for information on Mary Spaulding."

"That's right," he replied, signaling for another beer himself. "Anne was kind of hard on Mary for two reasons. One, Mary is a little rowdy, and two, Harry being her only son, she was a little protective of him. I guess any woman would be."

The waitress set two beers in front of us. Amos made a grab for his while I paid the tab. I began to wonder if he had made this appointment to see me just to have an excuse to drink beer. I also wondered if his assessment of his health was accurate. I did not want to contribute to Mrs. Bascomb's premature widowhood.

"Yes, I gathered your wife didn't approve," I told him. "She made that very clear, even in the short time I was there."

"Oh, yes, Anne is not one to keep her feelings to herself. Probably one of the reasons Harry dated Mary so long was the way Anne kept after him not to. Harry was that way," Amos said, shaking his head. "Tell him not to do something, and that'd be all the reason he needed to go ahead and do it." He took another large swallow of beer and remained silent. I was going to have to drag information out of him, if he had any.

"Do you know where Mary lives or how I can reach her?" I asked, trying to hide my impatience. "I really would like to talk to her. She might be able to help us."

Amos stared at his beer bottle. For a brief moment I wondered if he was feeling ill, but then I could see it was not that. He was wrestling something over in his mind and he had not yet made the decision of whether or not he was going to tell me. I would just have to take my time with him, gain his confidence, court his trust and hope for the best. It looked like it was going to be a long evening, a very dull evening.

I was wrong.

Finally he looked up at me and spoke. "Son, what I am about to tell you is not to be repeated to anyone. I'm not particularly proud of what I did, but I did it and I can't change it now and that's that."

He took another longer, deeper swallow of his beer, one which brought him to the bottom of the bottle and gave him an excuse to prolong the telling of something he obviously did not like to tell. He signaled for another beer and we waited in silence until it arrived. I moved my feet around under the table to keep my circulation going. I felt cramped and uncomfortable.

"Well, here's how it happened," Amos began as soon as he had beer in hand. "Anne has been a good wife, as good as a man can ask for."

Uh oh, I thought to myself. It must be confession time. There is another woman in this picture, but did it have anything to do with Mary? There was more silence, another swig of beer.

"But a man gets tempted," he continued, "by things he ought not to do."

I noticed we were no long talking about Amos or Anne, but "a man", as if Amos were trying to distance the whole episode away from himself. It did not happen to him... no, it happened to this "man".

"A man has too much to drink, he does things he wouldn't do when he's sober," Amos told me solemnly. "Or he gets to feeling old, like life is passing him by, and again he does things he doesn't mean to do. Well, that's how it was." He looked up at me for sympathy, as if I would have the slightest idea of what he was talking about.

"Yes, he does," I agreed, providing the desired sympathy and extremely curious to know what we were discussing.

He took a deep breath, burped loudly and banged his fist on the table, causing the bottles to jiggle and the other customers in the bar to look curiously our way. The waitress narrowed her eyes, but I winked at her, so she turned around and continued chatting with some roughnecks at the bar.

"What I did was wrong, but it wasn't all my fault," Amos continued. I began to wonder if he would ever get to the point. "You see, my wife and I haven't been hitting it off so well. She's pretty prim and proper if you know what I mean. She doesn't much like the physical side of marriage."

That was where I had to stop him. For sure, I did not want to hear about his sex life. Already I had been listening to him for over three beers and we had not even begun discussing Mary. It was time to change the subject, see if I could steer it back to what we had come to discuss.

"That's very interesting, Amos," I lied. "But how does that concern Mary?"

He looked up at me in surprise. "I thought I had told you," he said. "I was seeing her too."

Now it was my turn to express surprise. "You? You were having an affair with Mary?" The man was at least twice her age, maybe a lot more, and could not possibly have anything to offer her that she would want, except a similar appetite for drinking.

"Not exactly an affair," he replied hastily, taken aback. "I was seeing her. You know, meeting her. Taking her out for a beer, that sort of thing. We weren't sleeping together, though she did kiss me a time or two."

"When did you start seeing her?"

Amos scratched his head and thought a moment. "Well it was back when things began to cool down between her and Harry during the summer. Man, you should have seen her in that little bitty bikini she wore! She is something!"

"I'll bet," I said truthfully. "Did Harry know you were seeing her?"

"Oh, no," he said, shocked at the idea. "Absolutely not. She was clear about that and so was I."

"He never found out?"

"No, he never did. Neither has Anne and she's not going to because I don't see Mary anymore. Not that I don't want to. It's just that she got too busy or lost interest or something. She never said."

"What did you talk about when you were with Mary?" I asked with interest. I doubted that they had one single thing in common, but I had forgotten what it was that they did have.

"Harry," Amos answered, as if reading my thoughts. "We talked about Harry. She was hurt real bad when he started seeing someone else. We used to meet at the beach at Port Aransas, and I'd bring along a couple of six packs and we'd drink in my car. Sometimes she'd let me put my arm around her and we'd just sit. Once she cried."

That did not sound like the same girl Anne Bascomb had described earlier. I wondered which girl was the real Mary Spaulding. It reminded me of the old television game show "To Tell The Truth". Would the real Mary Spaulding please stand up? Maybe in her case all three contestants would have risen.

"Did she ask you about the girl Harry started seeing when his relationship ended, Melissa Small?"

"Yeah, we talked about her some. Missy was a nice little gal but she couldn't hold a candle to Mary. I know I shouldn't have kept seeing her like that, but I just couldn't help myself." His eyes filled and I was afraid he would start bawling right there in front of me and everybody else so I quickly changed the subject.

"Would you like another beer?" I asked. "How about some nuts?"

He took the bait and signaled the waitress. For a moment we discussed sports while he regained his composure and turned off the waterworks. It had been a near miss but my quick actions had averted disaster.

CHAPTER TWENTY SEVEN

When all danger of flooding was past, I cautiously brought up Mary's name again.

"Do you have Mary's address and telephone number?" I asked hopefully. If he did, I could call it a night and leave. If he didn't, I could grill him some more in the hope of finding a clue that would lead me to her.

"Why sure," he replied, reaching in his back pocket. He took out a small green leather wallet, well marked and torn in several places, and reached into one of the compartments. He withdrew several papers, went through them slowly, and then handed one to me. "At least, I have her phone number. I never did have her address and I don't know where she lives. She never asked me over and we always met somewhere when we got together."

"When was the last time you saw her?"

"It was a couple of months ago at the beach," Amos replied sadly. "We met where she and Harry used to meet. It seems like a long time ago and when I stopped seeing her things sure got dull. And then Harry died."

I copied Mary's phone number and then returned the paper to Amos. He hurriedly stuffed it back into his wallet as if he were afraid it might fly away.

We sat together for a few moments in silence, just drinking our beers. I don't know what was going through his mind, but mine was doing cartwheels. I could not imagine what this hot number would want with poor old Amos and it took more imagination than I had to understand what caused him to meet with her. I suppose if I could understand that, I would be a much better private detective or nuclear physicist.

"Now, you won't go and tell Anne all this, will you?" Amos asked worriedly.

"No, of course not," I replied hastily. There was nothing I was more unlikely to do than to tell Anne, initiating fireworks which would ricochet all over Rockport. Besides, that lady had been through enough grief to last her a life time and I had no desire to add to it. "Don't worry about that. We'll pretend tonight never happened. She won't hear a word of it from me."

I got up, shook his hand again, although much less enthusiastically this time, and turned to go. I spotted a couple in a small booth in the back of the bar. A familiar couple who were so absorbed in each other they did not see me. They must have come in the side entrance which was not visible from where I had been sitting. Walter and Marie!

They were deep in conversation and even deeper into a pitcher of margaritas. I walked softly on my way out, so as not to impede progress. Amos did not come with me, so I assumed he was going to keep drinking his baby bye bye.

Meanwhile, back at my house, I dialed the number Amos had given me. It rang ten times before I gave up. Looked like Mary was out, probably with Harry's replacement, whoever he might be. After an hour passed I tried again, but there was still no answer. I gave up and went to bed.

Somewhere between late last night and early tomorrow morning the telephone started ringing, interrupting my restless slumber. Amos' confession had made me uneasy and it reflected in my inability to sleep soundly. I quickly got out of bed, tripped on my bedspread, untangled myself somewhat and trailed bed covers all the way over to the telephone.

"Hello?" I said anxiously, noting the digital clock read 3:25.

"Len? Oh, Len, thank goodness you're home!" A frightened, breathless little girl voice. Who else? Marilyn.

"What's wrong?"

"Somebody's trying to get in my house. My friend's out of town. I'm all alone. I—"

"Slow down, lady," I said calmly. "Now, tell me where you are. I know you don't have a phone in that house--"

"I'm at the Circle K on the highway and I don't have my car and I don't have any money and I'm afraid!" She was right about that. The little squeaks and tremors in her voice indicated she was near hysteria.

"Hang tight, Marilyn, and count to 100. I'll be there before you finish." I hung up without waiting for a reply and grabbed my car keys. I took the front steps four at a time and put the Porsche in first gear before I had closed the door. That's 20, I said to myself, counting.

Up Bayshore, around the corner to Fulton Beach road and over the second bridge, right turn by Sandra Courts. That's 40. Onto the highway, right turn, watch out for the policeman ahead, stop light. That's 65. Got to hurry. Light changed, first, second, third, fourth gear. Now 75 seconds. Four blocks on the right and upcoming, a large Circle K sign, a small telephone booth, 95 seconds. I'm there. Great timing. Only one thing wrong. No Marilyn.

I parked at the side of the Circle K and looked around. There were several cars parked in front of the store and I could see people inside making purchases, but there was no frightened, high heeled, red lipsticked blonde sounding like she was borderline hysterical. I glanced on both sides of the Circle K, and out of the corner of my eye, where the telephones were, I could see some bushes parting cautiously. Marilyn!

She was wearing a silver robe and matching mule slippers with glittery pompoms, slightly damaged from walking outdoors. She hurried over to my car, got in, and told me, "Let's get out of here fast. He might be around somewhere!"

It was unnecessary to tell me twice. I gunned the Porsche, made a dime sized circle, and aimed us back to Key Allegro. I took the back roads to make sure no one was following. When I was absolutely positive we were alone, I drove back over the bridge, headed down Bayshore and parked us in the garage so no one could see I had a passenger. Marilyn was trembling, making the silver robe shimmer in the moonlight. I put my arm around her and guided her upstairs into the house.

"That was fast, Len," Marilyn said with relief. "I feel safe when I'm with you. In spite of the way you're dressed." She giggled.

I looked down. In the haste to get to Marilyn, I had forgotten I was only wearing my shorts. Oh well, at least they were clean. I went into my bedroom to get trousers. When I returned, Marilyn had gone over to my refrigerator in search of champagne. She was wearing a look of disappointment. "I missed my chance," she said regretfully. "I should have gotten some at the Circle K."

"Look underneath the counter," I told her. "There's a small refrigerator. That's where the champagne is."

The blonde squealed happily and brought out a bottle of pink blush. She handed it to me to open, which I agreed to do in exchange for the story on what had happened at her place earlier.

"It was awful," she began, her face sobering. "I was listening to the late, late, late show when I heard a noise outside. It was a car parking down the street. I turned out my lights so I could see better. A man got out, at least I guess it was a man, and stood by the car a few moments. I wondered what he was doing there at that time of morning. It must have been 2:30. Then he started walking toward my house. When he got to the yard he waited."

She paused while I poured the champagne. We touched glasses and sipped. She began to relax and went back to her story. "Finally he started coming towards the house, getting closer and closer. He was holding something in his hand. I couldn't tell what it was but it might have been a gun. He stopped at the front window. I slipped out the back door, and didn't even breathe until I was deep inside the woods in back of the house. I kept going until I got to the highway and called you when I reached the Circle K."

"Marilyn, there were at least 10 pay phones between the house where you were staying and that Circle K. Why didn't you call me at one of them?"

"That's the only phone that had a quarter and a dime in the coin holder," she told me.

I went over to my telephone and started dialing Walter.

"What are you doing?" Marilyn asked me, sounding panicky.

"I'm calling the police," I told her. "I want to send somebody over to your house to check it out."

"No!" she said emphatically, setting her glass of champagne down. "It wouldn't do any good. Whoever was there is gone now. That was over two hours ago. Besides, I don't want my friend involved with the police. He would be very angry about that."

I put the telephone down and looked at Marilyn. "Okay, doll. What gives? What aren't you telling me here?"

The little lady pursed her lips and narrowed her eyes. She picked up her glass and poured some more champagne into it, stalling for time. Finally she looked up at me with a sheepish expression and the little girl voice was back in full measure. "Well, Len, actually the house I've been staying in doesn't belong to a friend of mine."

"Oh?" I said coldly.

"In fact," she continued nervously, "the person who owns the house does not know I am staying there."

I looked at her. "Who exactly does it belong to?"

"I'm getting to that. It belongs to a woman who shops at Staples. Last month she bought a lot of clothes to take on a three month round the world cruise. She said she was going to just lock up her house and take off. So, when it happened that I needed a place to stay where no one would find me, I remembered her. I looked up her address in the phone book, and voila! Unfortunately she disconnected her phone while she was gone."

"Dammit, Marilyn, that's illegal!" I told her, exasperated.

"You're right, it's illegal," she conceded, "but I asked myself a question. Is it better to be doing something illegal or is it better to be dead? Illegal won out."

"Don't you realize she might have asked someone to check out the house for her? Or the neighbors might have reported seeing lights in her house if they knew she was away? Or she might have gotten seasick and come home early?"

"Well, she didn't ask anyone to check out the house. No one has been by. And the neighbors haven't called the police. Nobody likes to get involved anymore. Probably she doesn't even know the neighbors. There aren't any close ones, anyhow. And I've been very quiet and don't go out until after dark, and I keep my car hidden in the back."

"What about food?"

"She has a well stocked cupboard. I've been eating only canned food. I would kill for a pizza."

"I can't believe you pulled this stunt," I told her crossly. "Why didn't you tell me before?"

"I was afraid you'd act just the way you're acting now. Easy for you to criticize my actions, but think how it was for me. No place to go, wanting to hide where I couldn't be found, and not having much money to do it with. Having to use pay phones. Where was I going to go? A motel? Pretty easy to spot my car at a motel, even if I could afford it, and if I hid my car the manager would wonder why. The police don't believe me. Just what would you have done?"

I thought for a moment. She had a good point. A young, inexperienced woman, without adequate funds, running from an unseen, unknown enemy, and she could not trust anyone she knew. I guessed she did what she had to and after all, she had not done any harm, other than eating a few canned goods.

"I think you'd better stay with me until I decide what to do with you," I told her. "We'll get your things in the morning. Our problem now is that we don't know if that mysterious visitor you had was after you or knew that the owner of the house where you were staying was out of town and simply wanted to rob her. Of course, if he did rob her, it's going to be our fingerprints everywhere. Try to talk your way out of that one."

"Golly, I didn't think of that," she said, alarmed. "What am I going to do?"

"Get some sleep and we'll look at it in the morning," I told her. "Your room is over there, on the right. Good night."

"Len, don't be angry with me, please," she looked up at me, flashing the blue eyes appealingly.

I kissed her on the check. "I'm not mad at you, sweetheart. Just trying to get by. 'Night."

My bed was cold and empty and the covers were all jumbled. I had to make it up again. I thought of the bed in the next room and sighed. It took me a full half hour to get to sleep, even though I was dead tired.

The smell of coffee awoke me early in the morning, or later the same morning, actually. For a moment the smell confused me, and then I remembered my enigmatic guest, the lady of the mysterious enemy. Apparently she was getting good at helping herself to contents of cupboards that did not belong to her. The door to my room opened and she came in, a glamorous early morning vision carrying a steaming cup of coffee and wearing an apologetic look.

"I heard you moving around," she said, looking lovelier somehow without makeup. "I thought I'd make you some wakeup coffee so we could go and get my things."

I sat up and took the coffee. "What time is it?"

"Ten after eight," she replied. "I've already taken a shower. You're not an early riser, are you?"

"Only when I have to be," I replied, tasting the coffee. It wasn't bad. It wasn't good, either. "Okay. Let me shower and shave and then we'll get going. First I have to feed my beagle."

"I already did," Marilyn said, smiling. "She's a nice dog. What's her name?"

134

"Pokey. She's my watchdog. Didn't she bark at you?"

"Why, no, she didn't," Marilyn replied. "Was she supposed to?"

After I had showered, shaved and gotten dressed, we went down to the garage and got into the Porsche. I took the long way to the house where Marilyn had been staying to make sure there was no one tagging behind us. The house appeared exactly the same as it had the other times I had been there. Whoever had stopped by the previous night had not left any visible evidence, at least not noticeable from the front of the house. Marilyn became increasingly nervous as we got close to the house and was ready to jump out of her skin when we pulled into the driveway.

"Haven't you got a gun?" she asked nervously.

"Who am I going to shoot?" I demanded. "Do you really think whoever broke into that house is still there? If he was looking for you, you weren't there, so he left. If he wanted to rob the place, he did, so he left. If he was looking for a place to stay, like you did, he's still there. If so, do I want to shoot him?"

"I see your point," she conceded, relaxing a little. "Let's go in the back way. I left it open."

As predicted, there was no one inside. The house appeared undisturbed and the television was still on, only now there was a morning show instead of a late show. Marilyn hurriedly packed her suitcase and looked everywhere for signs of a visitor, but without success.

"I don't know whether to be relieved or terrified," she confided.

"Be relieved," I advised her. "It's easier on the nerves."

"But we don't know if he was in here," she complained. "The front door was still locked, but he could have come in the back door. It was open. I know when I last saw him he was coming up to the house. We don't know if he was after me or if he was just a peeping tom, or what. We don't even know if he came in the house or will ever come back."

Marilyn changed into her white slacks outfit and put on makeup. "I guess I'm ready to go," she said. "I'd like to buy some canned goods and put them back on the shelves. Then no one would ever know I was here."

"That's a good idea. We'll do that," I told her. "Meanwhile, turn off the tv and let's go."

I picked up the suitcase, headed towards the door and was almost outside when I heard a frightened exclamation come from the living room. I dropped the suitcase, ran back, and bumped into the hall door on my way. Marilyn's slender hands covered the lower half of her face as if she were holding her mouth to prevent a scream, and she was staring wide eyed and pale faced at the television.

"What's the matter?" I asked, putting my arm around her.

"The television!" she replied, her voice shaking. "It's on a different channel than the one I was watching last night! Someone was here watching tv after I left!"

"Are you sure?" I asked doubtfully. "After all, it was late, you were probably tired—"

"I'm sure, I'm sure!" she exclaimed "Oh, Len, he was waiting for me!"

CHAPTER TWENTY EIGHT

We drove back to my place separately, Marilyn in her Corvette and me in the Porsche. I gave Marilyn the garage and hoped no one saw her park the Corvette inside. Then I put the Porsche in front of the garage and hoped no one wondered why I was keeping my car outside in the damaging Texas sun. I sort of wondered that myself. I transferred her suitcase into the guest room and told her to make herself at home, at least temporarily.

"Just as a precaution, keep away from the windows, don't answer the telephone and stay away from the doors," I warned her.

The telephone rang. Marilyn drew back in alarm. I could see I would have to find some way to get her to relax or I would have to install thick padding on the walls of the guest room.

"Take it easy, sweetheart," I told her. "It rings all the time and it's never yet been anyone trying to hurt you. Sometimes it's even the wrong number." She grinned sheepishly.

I picked up the phone. It was Walter, on his way to interview the Shark and the Barracuda. He invited me along and I wanted to go, but I had other things to do. I asked him to let me know how it went.

"By the way, Walter, what did you do last night?" I asked innocently, remembering the cozy booth he had shared with Marie.

"Oh, a little of this and a little of that," he replied nonchalantly, hanging up before I could comment further.

"Who was that?" Marilyn asked.

"A homicide detective I know by the name of Walter Hughes," I told her. "He's with the Rockport police force."

"What'd he want?"

"Just to tell me about an interview he's conducting," I replied, wondering about her curiosity. Mention the word police and you had Marilyn's attention. It could have been because of the bad experience she had when the Corpus police refused someone was trying to kill her, or it could be some other little something she had not yet found time to tell me. I looked at her closely, but she had dropped the subject and was reading a news magazine I had on my coffee table.

I picked up the telephone and dialed Mary Spaulding's number. It rang five times so I was about ready to hang up when someone answered in a soft, interested voice.

"This is Leonard Townsend," I said as an introduction. "Am I speaking with Mary Spaulding?"

"You certainly are, but not by invitation," she replied crossly. "This number is unlisted. How did you get it?"

"A friend of yours gave it to me. I need to speak with you," I told her, hoping to sound honest and trustworthy, and not at all like I was selling something.

She was direct. "Why?"

It seemed appropriate, even inevitable, to give her an honest answer. Besides, I hadn't had time to think of a really good lie. She was holding the advantage. If she wanted to talk to me, she could, and if she wanted to hang up, she could. It was completely her decision.

"I am a private detective working on the recent murders in Rockport," I said, listening closely for any sort of response. There was none. "I understand you knew Harry Bascomb and I haven't been able to speak with anyone who knew him very well." The last was sort of true. His parents did not seem to know very much about his most recent activities and the only other one who might, Melissa Small, was dead too. Of course I had not identified any business partners, so to speak, he might have had, other than the possible Shark and Barracuda.

"Go on," she said.

"I could meet you anywhere you say and I promise not to take much of your time," I told her. "I'm quite harmless and sometimes I'm good for a laugh. I'm always good for picking up the check." The last was said in an overt attempt to entice her to go out for a drink. I had already established she liked to drink. It was about the only thing Amos and Anne Bascomb agreed on about her. A drink might loosen her tongue.

"Well…" she mused, thinking it over.

"Please. It's very important."

"All right. Meet me tonight at the Chelsea Street Tavern, 8 o'clock."

"I'll be there," I promised.

"How will I know you?" she asked.

I described myself and asked her what she'd be wearing, although that was completely unnecessary. From Anne Bascomb's detailed and intriguing description, I'd be able to pick her out of a crowd of thousands.

That left me the entire day free to do some things I should have done and undo some things I should not have done. I could interview the two men Marilyn had dated that I had missed or I could go stock the pantry which Marilyn had emptied or I could talk with the neighbors where Marilyn had been staying and see if there had been any reports of a peeping tom. I had not seen any footprints around the house but that was to be expected since there had been no rain in Rockport for weeks.

"Who were you talking with that time?" Marilyn asked, interrupting my thoughts.

"A woman named Mary Spaulding," I replied. "She knows someone in a case I'm investigating."

138

"I wonder if it's the same Mary Spaulding I know?" she said, not particularly interested. She turned a page in her magazine and stared fixedly at an automobile ad, running her index finger along the bumper.

"How do you know Mary Spaulding?"

"There was one who modeled for a couple of weeks during the summer and a few times after that," Marilyn told me, putting the magazine down and going over to the window.

"Don't stand by the window, Marilyn," I warned her. She backed off. "What did she look like?" Could yet another person connected with the case, even if only indirectly, have modeled for Staples?

"Fair skin, long black hair, dark eyes, taller than me, weighed about 118, very pretty," Marilyn replied, looking out the window from a distance.

"Sounds like the same one," I told her. "Did you ever talk with her?"

"Sometimes. She was interested in my resemblance to Marilyn Monroe. She offered to drive with me to Hollywood. She had a white sports car, too, a Mustang convertible. She wanted to get an apartment with me in Hollywood, and try her luck at the movies."

"That sounds like a good deal, Marilyn. Why didn't you go?"

"Two reasons, the first not nearly as important as the second," Marilyn replied, sitting next to me on the sofa and curling her legs up under her. "First, I want to do it by myself. It may take a little longer, but I'll know I made it on my own. Second, there is something about Mary, something I can't even define, that puts me off. I guess I'm going on some instinct in an area of my mind that doesn't translate into words. It's not that she's done anything she shouldn't, or said anything. I just have this feeling that something isn't right. Oh, I'm sorry, that isn't very helpful, is it?"

"Just the opposite, Marilyn. You seem to be a very intuitive woman and if you felt something was out of place, I'd bet you're right," I answered. "How did she take it when you said you weren't interested in going with her?"

"Not so well at first," Marilyn admitted. "In fact, she was insulted. However, I was able to smooth it over by saying I wanted to get experience as a model before I tried acting. I laid it on fairly thick, encouraged her to take someone else. There were lots of girls who wanted to go. But she lost interest and it wasn't long before she quit modeling too. I haven't talked with her since."

"Was she dating anyone?"

"There was someone she was pretty hung up on," Marilyn replied. "That's one reason she wanted to leave town. It was a way of getting over him... changing scenery and meeting new faces. At least that's how she thought of it. But then when we didn't go, she quit modeling. Maybe she went back to him and that's why she left."

"Do you know where she lived, or if she went to college?"

"She had an apartment somewhere in Corpus. She didn't say exactly where but I believe it was somewhere close to the water. She described how at nights sometimes she could see the lights of boats on their way to the Gulf of Mexico. She had gone to a college in San Antonio, Trinity, I believe she said. I don't think she planned to go back."

"Did you ever meet the man she was seeing?" I asked.

"No, but she told me a lot about him. He was like a Greek god, she said. Tall and blonde, with a fabulous body. I think the best part of him existed in her imagination, because he didn't sound too cool to me. I gathered he was a drug pusher. Good guy, all right. Good to stay away from." Marilyn gave an involuntary shudder.

I decided to go to the grocery store and get some canned goods to replace the ones Marilyn had eaten while she was staying, or rather, trespassing in the Fulton home earlier in the week. She made a list for me including the sizes and brand names. I headed out for the grocery store after repeating my warnings about staying away from windows and not answering the telephone. I knew she would be bound to get bored and the twin evils of temptation and curiosity would do their damage if she didn't have her guard in place and locked.

The local grocery store was crowded with weekend tourists and it took me longer than I had expected to fill my order. Marilyn seemed to go for canned fruit, but left meat alone. No wonder she had such a slim figure. Then, remembering Marilyn might be my guest for some days to come, I ferreted out the spiritis fermenti section and considered the merits of a number of competing champagnes. I finally settled for my favorite, the inexpensive and delectable Andre pink blush and dry varieties. I got a dozen bottles, which might last us six days if we kept busy with other things and did not spend a lot of time drinking. I also stocked up on fruit.

After I got the groceries loaded into the Porsche I rode over to the erstwhile hideout and pulled into the driveway. This time, knowing I was guilty of, while not breaking, at least entering, I was much more aware of my surroundings. There was swishing and bumping of wind through the bushes and the thumping of tree limbs on the roof. I quickly put the cans in the cupboard and thought I would have been smarter to have brought Marilyn along to show me approximately where they went. Oh, well, who remembers where they put their canned goods after three months absence? After I finished I quickly locked the door and got out.

It felt wonderful to get back on the beach road after accomplishing that little mission without finding myself behind bars. Certainly it could all be explained, but perhaps our uninformed hostess would be the type to enjoy pressing charges. The inside of a jail has never appealed to me.

When I got back to my beach house and exited the Porsche I could hear music coming from the upper story. I picked up the sack with the 12 champagne bottles inside clanging together and left the fruit in the car. The bottles were threatening to explode into a fizzing, bubbling geyser at any second. I hurried upstairs, anxious to unload the bottles. Marilyn was not exactly laying low with the radio on so loud. As I neared the front porch I heard her soft voice saying words I couldn't quite catch and then an answering voice, low and deep and male, with more unintelligible words. She hadn't been alone more than two hours and already she had broken my rule about answering the door, and it was not just any rule, it was a biggy. It looked like life with Marilyn might be like trying to balance a spinning plate on a long pole. I'd have to watch her every second.

The feminine voice, Marilyn's, sounded pleased with itself, purring, throaty and erupting into an occasional giggle, so I did not think she was in any kind of trouble. The masculine voice was boastful, show offish and pushy, not the sort to be causing trouble, but rather more like flirtatious. Brother, I thought to myself, you don't know our one-dinner and leave 'em Marilyn! Having decided the scene was not a threatening one, I clutched the bag of bottles and unlocked the front door. I nudged it open with my knee and went in, preparing to give Marilyn what for because she broke the "do not open the front door to anyone" rule. I was also pretty curious to see who the coquettish visitor was. I almost dropped the bottles when he turned and saluted me with his champagne glass. It was Walter!

CHAPTER TWENTY NINE

"Hi, Len, welcome back. Good. You've brought more champagne," Marilyn called happily. "We were almost out."

Marilyn was not the only one to be breaking rules. Walter had evidently, in his enjoyment of a new found friend, forgotten himself completely and had lit up a cigarette in my living room. This room is a non-smoking area if ever there was one, and worse still, Walter was using an empty dog food can for an ashtray. He was so far over the edge of remembrance he did not even have the good grace to look embarrassed. I should have recognized his voice when I was coming up the stairs, but the two big rule breakers were on the far side of the room and their words had sounded like low murmurs.

"Marilyn, I thought I told you not to let anyone in," I said irritably.

"Don't blame her," Walter said, giving what he must have thought was a charming smile to Marilyn, but to me it was not unlike a mule eating a clothes hanger. A little too wide and toothy. "I let myself in with that key you gave me, Len. I was going to leave you a note. I took her by surprise."

"You didn't tell me what a charmer Walter is," Marilyn said prettily. She took the bag with the champagne and put the bottles on ice. Then she sat back down, a little closer to Walter this time. "Why, we've been having such a nice talk. Walter has so many interesting stories about his work."

Yes, he does, I thought to myself, I've heard them a million times. Out loud I said, "He sure does. Does he have any interesting stories to tell about the two fellows he was supposed to be interviewing this morning?"

"That was postponed until late this afternoon," Walter said. "They're being questionned about the robbery this morning. I think the evidence is pretty solid against them."

I told him I was going to meet with Mary Spaulding that evening and see if she would give me any information about Harry Bascomb. It was even possible she had known the two men Walter was going to interview. Walter and I made plans to get together early the next morning for breakfast. I wanted to ask him if he was friends with Marie again, but since it seemed to be such a touchy subject, I held my tongue. Besides, from the way he was looking at Marilyn, Marie was not in the immediate forefront of his mind. After Walter left I made a lunch of steak and salad for Marilyn and me, which Marilyn attacked enthusiastically. With lunch over, I headed out, telling Marilyn she was on her own for the afternoon.

Having Marilyn as my temporary guest, however pleasant it might be, was spurring me on to finding out who was trying to kill her. Once the identity of her hidden antagonist was revealed and he was dealt with, she could return to her apartment and I could leave my home without worrying about her safety alone in it. It's easier to go about detecting when you're not worried about danger on the home front.

I had two names left to check out on the list Marilyn had given me. Barry Stevens and Jesse Grey. Barry worked as a pilot for an oil company and had been grounded for a temporary medical condition. This meant I would find him at the company's home office in Ingleside, a city mid-way between Corpus and Rockport on the Corpus Christi Bay. Stevens was a senior pilot even though he was in his early thirties. Apparently the bosses liked their pilots young, favoring youth over experience. A receptionist in the company's front office took me to Stevens after I presented proper identification, an unusual request for the circumstances, I thought. I followed her through a maze of institution green cubicles and click clacking word processors until we reached a back office where Barry Stevens sat with his feet propped up on a desk. One foot had a large bandage.

"C'mon in, Leonard Townsend," he said cheerfully, blowing smoke at me from an oversized cigar. He was tall and dark, with bright blue eyes and a matching smile. His frame was lean, and I assumed he smoked more than he ate. "Take a seat and rest yourself awhile. Can I get you a drink?"

The receptionist made a clicking sound with her tongue, turned abruptly and started on her way back through the maze. Stevens peered after her, his lean face wearing an amused expression, and his lips parted as if to throw a remark her way, but apparently he changed his mind and gave me his full attention.

"Don't mind it if I don't get up," he said, shrugging. "I sprained my ankle and I'm stuck here in the office until it recovers or I die of inactivity, whichever happens first." Stevens had jet black hair which was worn in natural waves and hung down almost to his collar. His piercing eyes seemed able to see through whatever they looked at. All his features combined to form movie star good looks and he and Marilyn must have been the center of attention wherever they went.

"Sorry about your ankle," I sympathized. "What did you do to it?"

"Fell over a cow," he replied, grimacing.

"Pardon me?" I said, raising an eyebrow. Maybe both eyebrows.

"Yeah, that's what happened. I drove my Rover into a field full of cattle and got a flat tire. Before I could get out of the thing, I was surrounded. By cattle. Couldn't open the door. Had the top down, so I climbed over the door and tripped across old Bossy. Sprained ankle, angry cow."

I looked at him suspiciously. We both started chuckling at the same time. "Want to try that again?" I asked.

"Fell down the steps at my apartment," he confessed. "But that just sounds so stupid."

"It happens," I said, anxious to get back on the track. "I'm here about Marilyn Miller. She's disappeared, her relatives are looking for her, and they said you might know where she is."

"If I did, I'd be there instead of here," he said wistfully. "That sister sizzles. Don't know why they put you onto me, though. We only went out one time. I took her flying. She liked it, but I couldn't get her to go out again. She has some sort of rule about one date. You only get one chance with her."

"Do you know of anyone who might want to harm her?"

"No, I don't, unless it's some crackpot who gets his one date and can't take no for an answer. Somebody who has an obsession for her. With a woman like her, anything could happen."

I questioned him some more about their date and what he knew about her, but got nowhere. Another blind lead. It was time to move on to the next and last name on the list. Last, but not least, I hoped.

Jesse Grey was a mechanic who owned his own auto repair shop not too far from the mall where Marilyn modeled. She met him when she took the white Corvette in to have the brakes checked, which he was only too glad to do for the little lady. He was short and his body was wiry and strong from lifting heavy parts and twisting and yanking and screwing them in place. He had short brown hair which grew longer in the front so it could wrap around his forehead and hang down over his eyes while he worked. He was laying halfway under a '78 Chevette when I walked in, and when he looked up at me I could see it run though his mind as to whether he could take a big guy like me. I could not read the answer.

Grey got to his feet, wiped his hands on his work pants, and asked unsmilingly with a bold, impudent gaze what I wanted. I told him I was looking for Marilyn Miller, giving him an honest look and the tired old friend of the family routine. He narrowed his eyes, snorted, and got back down under the Chevette without replying. I knelt down and repeated my question, still earnest, but with a little more forcefulness in my tone. Still no answer.

"The family is about to take their inquiries to the cops," I told him quietly. "You can talk to me now or you can talk to them. They'll probably be out later today."

Grey slowly drew himself back out from under the car and we both got to our feet, watching each other warily. "What is it you got to know?" he asked, spitting the words out like bullets. "Make it quick. I got work to do."

"Like I told you, Marilyn hasn't been seen in over a week. Not by her family, not at work. Do you know any reason she might have to

144

disappear or know anyone who might have reason to make her disappear?"

"That woman? I don't know nothing about her," he said menacingly. "Now, if that's all..."

"It's not all. What on earth did Marilyn do to you?"

"She's a tease, man. She lets you take her out for a feed, spend your money and then don't put out." He started to get back under the Chevette.

"Wait a minute, man. Did you decide to do something about it? Like go after her or fix the brakes on her car just to get even?"

He looked at me with contempt. "No, man. Why would I do that? There's just too much of it around for me to get bothered about just one piece of it." He moved back under the car, his talking for the day over.

I was not ready to cross him off my list yet, but he did not really seem to fit the part of Marilyn's attacker. He was too hot headed. I could imagine him attacking her physically all right, but even though he had the knowledge of how to do it, I could not see him tampering with her brakes. Or trying to run her off the road with a car. Or hiding behind some bushes and shooting at her. He'd be up front and personal, in her face. I went back to the Porsche and left, happy to be quit of Mr. Grey.

But I was not entirely through with Grey as I had hoped. His name kept running through my mind, over and over, as I pictured the muscular, hard body and the cruel cut of his lips. The way he spat out his words, the not so hidden contempt. His dislike of Marilyn. Maybe I was underestimating him. Maybe he was the sneak in the night, get even with the "she who done me wrong" kind. He could have borrowed a client's little beige foreign job, followed her on another date, become even more enraged. He could have waited one night, pistol in hand, for a cheap shot and having fired it, run off in fright and self-protection. It might have been his sort of poetic justice to slit a brake line, a bitter irony since she had first come to him to check her brakes. I decided to ask Marilyn her opinion. She had made no comment when she included his name on her list, whether through intentional omission or inadvertently I did not know. Skip the idea to dismiss Mr. Grey without prejudice.

Marilyn was napping when I returned home and she had slept through at least two telephone calls, as evidenced by the blinking of the answering machine in my office. One was a potential client whose name and number I wrote down for further use and the other was Anne Bascomb, requesting an immediate return call. She did not answer when I called, although I let the telephone ring over 20 times thinking she might be out in her garden. I hoped she was not calling about the little get together her husband and I had the night before. I was about to go back upstairs when the telephone rang, and thinking it might be Anne

Bascomb, I picked it up quickly. Whoever it was, it certainly wasn't Anne.

"Quit messing around in things that aren't your business," said a husky, deep voice in a threatening tone.

"Excuse me?" I replied, surprised.

"Quit messing around in things that aren't your business," the voice repeated, a little impatiently.

"Could you be a little more specific?" I asked nicely. "I've been pretty busy lately.

"You know. About the dame." Definitely impatient now and angry too.

"Which dame? Do you think I'm a monk?"

The voice was taken aback. Things weren't going the way it had planned. It was beginning to panic. "You know very well which dame! Don't mess with me!" The voice barked its last command and hung up loudly. Doubtless there was some dog somewhere getting kicked right now over this, or a woman catching hell because I had been a smart ass and he could not reach over the phone to smack me. That is, if it was a man calling. I shook my head and grinned. It sounded like I was getting close, but to what? Was the dame Marilyn, or Anne, or Missy, or Mary? Or another one I did not know about? Could it have been a wrong number? I was not kidding when I asked him to be specific.

I wished I had not turned my answering machine off because I could have recorded the call and attempted to identify the voice. I had only a hazy memory of the tone and besides, there was an obvious attempt at disguising it. However, this added a few points to the theory that Jesse Grey had a hand in Marilyn's problems, because I had left a business card in his shop with my telephone number on it. Maybe that hadn't been such a good idea.

A noise like a muffled shot sounded upstairs. I rushed up, expecting the worst, and flung myself through the door with my eyes wide open for the sight of blood, blonde hair, and a smoking gun. There was blonde hair, all right, but the shot had only been the inevitable whupp-bang of a champagne cork hitting my kitchen ceiling. Marilyn was awake and quenching her thirst.

"Oh, haven't you left yet?" she asked in surprise.

CHAPTER THIRTY

"Gone and got back," I replied, holding out a glass. "You've been asleep for hours."

She smiled and made a little purring sound deep in her throat. "I guess the combination of champagne and that soft bed kept me under. It was marvelous."

"I went to see your two buddies, Barry Stevens and Jesse Grey. Want to comment?"

She wrinkled her nose and made a face. "Barry's nice but Jesse is, ah, not so nice." She went back to her champagne, uninterested in the conversation.

I pushed. "What is not so nice about Grey?"

"Oh, I don't know. He seemed to think if he took a girl to dinner she should take him home, if you know what I mean."

"He told me what you mean."

Her eyes widened. "What did he tell you?"

"Not much, but I didn't like it. What do you think of him?"

She thought for a moment. "At first, he was very pleasant. A little rough around the edges, but very anxious to please. I wasn't all that hot to go out with him, but he persisted and I thought once wouldn't hurt. We went out to get a hamburger and he talked about motorcycles and cars. I was tired so I decided to make it any early evening. I asked him to take me home, and he tried to make it longer. We finally got into an argument, but I was able to calm him down with a lot of fast talk about not feeling well. Nobody wants to stick around someone they think might throw up. By the time he got me home he was real convinced I was sick, so he didn't give me any trouble. But he kept calling me at home for several days, getting nastier and nastier, until he finally saw it was a no go and stopped calling. That was about three weeks ago."

"How do you like him as the guy who is responsible for your brakes and the other trouble that's been going on in your life?"

"I don't think so, Len," she replied after consideration. "He's more direct than that, I think."

"How about him for the prowler last night? Same body size and shape?"

"I don't know. Could be. It was too dark to tell. Let's just say I can't rule him out, the way I can you. You're way too tall. Some men would be too heavy. Him? I don't know."

We left it at that. Keep him on the list until proven innocent. Not too democratic, but this was not democracy, it was a monarchy and I was in charge. The king. Sometimes I felt more like the court jester. We drank our champagne in companionable silence. I was mulling over the threatening call. Marilyn was probably wondering if she would ever get to go back to her apartment and start working again. I decided to tell her about the call. It might caution her to be particularly careful while she was staying alone in my home.

"I got a phone call which might interest you," I told her. "It was from a person who did not give me a name. In fact, he or she disguised his voice. I'll use the he pronoun for the sake of convenience, not necessarily for accuracy."

"It doesn't matter to me what pronoun you use," Marilyn offered. "I'm not a stickler for pronouns."

"Anyway, while you were still sleeping, someone called and threatened me," I continued, ignoring her interruption. "He told me, and I quote, 'Quit messing around in things that aren't your business.'"

"That's odd. Did he mean me?"

"I don't know. I couldn't get him to say, but he could have meant you. After all, I spoke with Barry Stevens and Jesse Grey on your behalf today. The call could have been a direct result of one of those visits or it could have been something else entirely. For the moment, let's treat it as if it involves you and be extra careful."

"I thought I was being extra careful. What have I done today that wasn't extra careful?"

"Well, er, nothing. But keep it up." I was beginning to feel a little foolish and wish I had not brought the whole thing up. Sometimes Marilyn could be very exasperating. We went on drinking our champagne and I made us a little snack of cheese and crackers. I kept my eyes open and periodically checked in front of my house to make sure we did not receive any surprise visits. I felt pretty sure my caller was only using the telephone to try and intimidate me, but the back of my head, which was still sore, warned me not to underestimate his potential.

I kept hoping Walter would call. I wanted to hear how his visit with the two men had gone and I also wanted to ask him about the black book he had sent to his lab. I knew the formalities with the interviews could take hours, so I was not surprised at the lack of information from him, only disappointed. I hoped to hear from him before I had to go meet Mary.

When it was time for dinner Marilyn decided to thaw some hamburger meat in the microwave and make tacos. We were a pretty picture of domesticity there in the kitchen, me with an apron and Marilyn with a chef's hat, getting in each other's way and bickering over how to prepare the lettuce. Marilyn maintained it was essential to use a sharp knife while I was positive the only way was to tear it with our hands. We compromised, split the head in half, and each fixed his/her own. For dessert we fried ice cream, left it in the skillet too long, and wound up with melted soggy goop. Finally it was time for me to go meet Mary, so I repeated my warnings to Marilyn once more, showed her where I kept my gun and told her to feed Pokey. I called Anne Bascomb again but there was still no answer, so I left.

The weather had changed from a bright, golden day during the afternoon to a messy, wet one at night. Rain fell out of the sky like a dam had burst and water collected in ditches, overflowed, and flooded roadways. The Porsche's removable top leaked around the edges where it came off. The leaking rivulets of water ran down the back of my neck. I swatted at them occasionally with a soggy handkerchief.

Halfway to Corpus I spotted the shape of a familiar Pontiac coming towards me. I could barely make out its green color in the foggy air, but I knew it anyway. It was Walter, heading back to Rockport after his meeting with the two drug pushers. We blinked headlights but did not pull over. Although I was interested to know how it went, I did not have enough extra time to find out. I pushed on to Corpus and arrived at the Chelsea Street Tavern only five minutes early.

I parked the car under a street light so no one could hide in the bushes and attack me the way they had at the roadside park. Of course, the bright light had its disadvantages too. It made me a well lit target. Well lit, but fast. I would have to take my chances and move quickly.

There was no one resembling Mary at Chelsea's when I walked in, so I took a corner booth and ordered a cold beer. She did not arrive for another 15 minutes, causing me to wonder if she was going to come at all. She had not seemed particularly enthusiastic when we made the date and if anything better came up in the meantime I had no illusions as to which she'd choose. Suddenly, though, there she was, all five feet ten inches of her, a tall, dark haired goddess of a girl in flaming red stretch pants and a white, glittery top with sparkles and sequins. She saw me at once, waving at her, and hurried over to my table. She glided gracefully into the booth.

"Get me a drink," she commanded, not bothering with introductions or greetings. "I'm thirsty as hell."

The waitress came over and Mary ordered a scotch on the rocks. I ordered another beer although I had not come close to finishing my first one. It seemed like the right thing to do at the time.

"So, you're Leonard Townsend, huh? I had pictured you differently," she said, looking at me curiously.

"How had you pictured me?"

"Sort of fat, balding, with a long moustache," she giggled. "I guess it was a combination of Hercule Poirot and Nero Wolfe. I've never met a private detective before."

"There's a lot of people who would say you haven't met one yet," I said.

"So, what do you want to know about Harry Bascomb?" she asked, changing the subject abruptly. Her intelligent face was as pale as ivory, and seemed paler still by the fame of jet black curls her hair made.

Her eyes were dark with an almost hypnotic power. It was hard to look away from them. Her lips were colored a bright red, the color of fresh blood, as testified to by Anne Bascomb. At once she radiated fire and ice, a line she straddled, and the slightest puff of wind could blow her to either side. Apparently Harry had brought out the fire in her; his mother, the ice.

"The police are trying to find Harry's murderer, but it's been a long, hard search," I told her, holding onto my seat so I wouldn't fall under the spell those dark witch eyes put out. "I'm helping in a limited capacity. We're trying to find out if it was a drug related crime. Now, Harry's gone and whatever comes out about his drug use or selling can't hurt him, but it might hurt his killer. Do you know anything about that and if you do, would you be willing to tell me?"

"Harry Bascomb was nothing to me," she said, taking a cigarette out of her purse and lighting it. "Why should I help?"

She took me by surprise. This was the girl who called him at all hours, hassled Melissa and cried on Amos' weak and willing shoulder? "I understand you dated him awhile back?" I ventured, poker faced.

"Casually," she answered, not looking at me. "I dated other people, too."

"Do you know if he took drugs, or if he sold drugs?"

"Sure I know. Everybody who knew Harry knew that."

"Are you willing to tell me?"

"I haven't decided yet," she answered evasively. "I don't know you from any dumb jerk narc trying to get his gold badge or monthly quota. Why should I open up to you? What makes you so special?"

This was one sharp cookie. I looked at her with some respect, in a jaded sort of way. She played her cards cautiously, much more so than the average joe with whom I dealt. Either she'd been born with smarts or she had been burned enough to know where the fire was and how to put it out.

"I'm just Mrs. Townsend's baby boy, ma'am," I replied, smiling. I was relieved to see a grin cross her face. "Let me put it to you plainly. Lots of folks have told me about your relationship with Harry. Of course, your definition of casual might be a little different than somebody else's, but that much? From what I hear, you were pretty involved with him. You would know things about him that nobody else does. You might have had enough feeling for him to want to settle the score with whoever did him in."

"Why would I want to do that?" she asked, dropping her façade. "He dumped me for that little plain jane high school girl."

"Who's to say he wasn't coming back? He hadn't been with her very long. He saved your letters. He saved your note."

A light came into those dark eyes. "I didn't know that," she admitted. "I hadn't thought of him coming back. It seemed so final at the time. Of course, I wasn't thinking clearly."

She didn't speak for a few moments, mulling it over. She absentmindedly took several swallows of her drink until only ice was left. I ordered her a refill. Her eyes narrowed briefly and I could tell she was weighing one heavy thought against another, playing some sort of chess game in her mind. When she had decided what course of action would be to her greatest advantage, we would resume our conversation. Not before. I glanced around the room. Bottles clanked across tables, wary eyes met, evaluated and accepted or rejected, stayed or left. There was a continual arriving and leaving motion while the juke box played on. Mary got her share of looks but she didn't seem to notice. She was somewhere deep inside her mind, going over old memories and stacking them up against recent events, trying to find a favorable balance.

Finally the tabulations were all in. "I'll help," she said. "I think you're right. Given time, he would have come back. What was it you wanted to know?"

"First, tell me everything you know about his involvement with drugs. What he took, what he sold. Who he sold them to. Who he brought them from. How often. How much money was involved. Everything you can remember."

The cold dark eyes glittered at me and the lips tightened. "For your ears only? You keep me out of it?"

"Cross my heart," I replied, crossing my fingers under the table. Sometimes you do what you have to do. I didn't think Harry was coming back to her, either. "Your information will stay with me. Our secret."

"Okay, I'll tell you. First, what he took," she said, sipping her drink. "He used everything, from marijuana to coke to crack to angel dust and then some. If it was available and he could get some, he used it. Where'd he get it? From a couple of dudes in Corpus named Shark and Barracuda with a rap sheet a mile long. They sold it to him to use, they sold it to him to sell. He was buyer and supplier, all wrapped up in one."

"Who'd he sell to?"

"Mostly high school kids. I don't know their names. I didn't hang around them. High school kids bore me."

Except for Harry Bascomb, I thought to myself.

She must have read my mind. Her eyes said she could. "If only I'd left Harry Bascomb alone," she complained. "He's the only high school kid I've talked to in three years and look where it got me."

"How much money did Harry make?" I asked, trying to get her off the subject of broken romance and keep her talking about Bascomb's deals.

"He was pretty much small time," she replied, "trying desperately to make it big. On a good week maybe he cleared $200, on an average week, maybe half that. Or less. Small time, like I said. I loaned him money a lot of times."

"Did he pay you back?"

"Not yet," she answered, staring somberly into her scotch.

"Who do you think killed him?" I asked her. She knew the Corpus drug scene better than I did and she might have an idea that was right on target.

"Either the Shark or the Barracuda or the guys they got their stuff from," Mary answered without hesitation. "I think a drug deal went wrong. Harry either got too greedy and tried to cheat them, or they were afraid he was using too much and was going to get careless and get caught, and lead the cops to them."

"Did you know John Watts?"

"I met him a couple of times, but like I said, I don't deal with high school kids," she said, unimpressed.

"How does he fit in?"

"He was on the rung below Harry, sort of a gopher," Mary answered. "An errand boy. Guess he got wind of something that wasn't good for him, or else they made a clean sweep."

"What about Marilyn Miller?" I threw that one in, a change in direction like a U turn.

Her head snapped up, eyes boring up into mine. Those dark irises were like looking into the barrel of a gun. I'd surprised her and it was not a pleasant surprise. Something about Marilyn upset her greatly, something made her hand shake as she lit her next cigarette.

"What's Marilyn got to do with this?" she asked, her voice trembling. A real show of nerves. She took a large swallow of scotch, either to steady herself or buy time. I couldn't figure which.

"Somebody's been trying to kill Marilyn," I said, watching closely for her reaction.

She scoffed, still all trembly. "Hah! She's got a lot of imagination, that one. She's probably looking for free publicity." She peered at me from beneath her long lashes to see if I was buying. I remained neutral, poker faced, as expressionless as a playing card. I could feel a chilling in the atmosphere, a subtle pulling away from me. What had Marilyn to do with Harry Bascomb, in anything, I wondered, or could it be that Mary was still angry at Marilyn for refusing to accompany her to Hollywood?

"Did you and Marilyn consider going to Hollywood together?"

Mary suddenly relaxed, as if a pressure had been taken off. She laughed and said, "We thought about it. But Marilyn didn't want to go yet. She wanted to stick around awhile, make some money, get some experience. I didn't mind. Going to Hollywood was only a whim. I had changed my mind, really, before she made her decision. Can you imagine the two of us in Hollywood? We'd have gone wild!" She grinned at the thought of it. Then she looked around as if to see if she recognized anyone at Chelsea's. All tension had vanished, the trace of a smile playing about her lips.

Why the sudden change? Talking about her relationship with Marilyn didn't bother her, but bringing up possible attempts on Marilyn's life made her nervous and frightened almost to the point of hysteria.

The juke box began playing Crazy, a dreamy little number by the late Patsy Cline. Mary's eyes closed as she replayed some old memory in her flighty mind and she got up and glided over to the dance floor, all by herself. She began dancing to the music, eyes staring at a never-never place nobody else in the tavern could see. Her shapely body swayed to the music as she turned and moved across the dance floor. Several cowboys considered approaching her, but when they caught the look in her eyes, drew back, and started talking amongst themselves. The crowd of couples on the dance floor stood aside to let her pass and finally all of the other dancers had moved to the edge of the floor just to watch. Mary hadn't noticed. She was still swaying gracefully to the heady sounds of the long dead singer and her mouth silently moved the words, a sorrowful expression on her face. The song ended, there was scattered applause and Mary stopped dancing. She returned to our table.

"Are you a Patsy Cline fan?" I asked, hoping to lead her into a discussion of her solo performance.

"The biggest," she said, twisting an ebony curl around her finger. Although the dancing was over the sad look was still going on.

"Excuse me, I have to go to the ladies room," she said, picking up her purse and heading towards the back of the bar.

I ordered another beer and contemplated again Mary's strange nervousness about the attempted murders of Marilyn. Could I have been reading too much in a few frightened looks and harsh words? I didn't think so. For a moment Mary had panicked, but when I changed the subject to the proposed Hollywood trip, Mary calmed down. She relaxed. The difference was like ocean air and ocean water. I decided to bring up the attacks again to see how she would handle it. I would also question her about who was Shark's boss. She might be able to give me a lead on some other characters in the melodrama.

Several women came over to ask me to dance and once I was actually tempted, but I was determined to wait for Mary and get her back on the subject that had bothered her earlier. The juke box played a few love gone wrong songs. I noticed a couple in a back booth having words and making emphatic gestures. I wondered if love was about to go wrong in that booth. Then I looked at my watch. Mary had been gone over 10 minutes. Could she have gotten sick or – horror-- murdered while she was in the ladies room? I quickly asked one of the waitresses to check on her. The waitress soon returned, whispering to another waitress and giggling on her way to my table.

"I'm sorry, sport, the lady isn't there," she said sympathetically. "The back window, which goes out to the parking lot, was open though."

"I can't believe it!" I said irritably. "I've been stood up!"

"Well, I get off in about 20 minutes," the waitress told me hopefully.

.

CHAPTER THIRTY ONE

I paid the check and made my way back to the Porsche, wondering if it was the mention of Marilyn's attacker that spooked Mary, or if she had simply gotten bored and taken the easy way out. I looked around for a sign of her white Mustang convertible, but it was long gone. I bet she had a good laugh over the dumb detective she slipped out on back at the Chelsea Street Tavern.

I debated my next move. I could head back to home or look for Mary at the local honky tonks. She'd be the kind to prefer the trendy new places with bright plastic décor and the din of loud music. The latter won out so I prowled around the young crowd's hot spots until I spotted a new white Mustang, top down, parked with one wheel over a curb. I made note of the license number in case it was hers, parked my car and went inside.

Mary was seated at a table with four laughing, leering man-about-town types. She was highly animated and talking excitedly while making wide gestures with her long, slender arms. All four were paying close attention, punctuating her remarks with sharp little yaps of laughter, and when Mary's recitation came to an abrupt close there were hoots and jeers and snickers, followed by wiping of eyes and stomping of feet. Her smoldering dark eyes roamed across the room like a huntress seeking out new game. They came to a quick halt when they spotted me standing by the door. She bent over and whispered something, unsmilingly, to the foursome, three of whom got up and quickly walked my way.

"Hey, bub, the little lady over there doesn't want you in here," said the first, a freckle faced young kid of about 19, with a skinny frame and eyes too big for his thin, somber face.

"Yeah, friend, she wants you to go," said the second, a mirror copy of the first, except without the freckles. The third fellow was built a bit more substantially, but not enough to cause me to pay close attention to them. Obviously they were out of shape, four-hour-a-night television watchers. If I couldn't out fight them, I could certainly outrun them.

"What's she told you fellows?" I inquired politely.

"She says you tried to rape her a few minutes ago in your car."

"Bull, guys," I relied in a tone somewhat between a growl and a roar to let them know how tough I was. Thank goodness my voice didn't break. "That little lady is my daughter, and she just took off without permission from a mental institution. She got put in for castrating a couple of guys from Houston with a can opener."

A unified look of horror crossed their faces. One quickly motioned to the kid who was still sitting with Mary, and they left the bar before Mary had the chance to ask them for any more little favors. I walked over to her table and sat down, and grasped her wrist tightly.

"You like the ladies room here better?" I asked coldly.

"Look, I don't owe you anything—" she began, trying to unlock my grasp.

"Settle down," I told her. "You've told me enough to make things interesting. I said it wouldn't go any further than me and I meant it. But we haven't finished our talk. If we don't finish, I might be tempted to tell somebody what I know and then you could find yourself having to deal with a whole lot of types like me wearing city uniforms."

Her eyes shot poisoned darts at me. I could almost feel cold dark venom running down my spine. Her blood red lips curled and with a violent twist, an ungirl strength, she wrenched her wrist away from me. "All right, we'll finish talking," she conceded, "but then leave me alone, for good."

"It's a deal," I agreed, not wanting to cross her path again either. I watched her eyes narrow to slits and her lips compress to a straight line. I probably wouldn't get much out of her now. "Tell me who Shark and Barracuda got their supply from."

"A dude named Frank Meyer. Ever hear of him?"

"Yeah, I've heard of him. Pretty rough character."

"You got that right. I met him once. He shook my hand and icicles fell off it. Harry was petrified of him and he wasn't too fond of Shark and Barracuda," she told me, an eager tone suddenly creeping into her voice. She was making it easy for me. Why?

"Harry was always trying to make a quick buck," she continued. "Maybe he pulled a fast one and got killed for his trouble. Him and that little high school fluff he hung around with. She was probably at the wrong place, wrong time and got hers along with him."

"Then why wouldn't they have been found together?" I asked her. Now this woman was full of theories and anxious to please, to give information, guesses and opinions. Five minutes ago she never wanted to see me again. What gives, I wondered again.

"Maybe they weren't found together so the police would be thrown off, so it wouldn't look professional."

"A good theory," I admitted. "How would John Watts fit in?"

"He knew too much," she said, as if it were a fact and not an opinion. I looked at her closely, but her face was expressionless, her dark eyes empty and cold.

I pushed farther, taking advantage of her talkativeness, no matter how temporary it might be. "What did he know?"

She turned her head, as if awakening, and stared at me. "Well, I don't know what he knew, but maybe he saw what happened to Harry. Maybe he had something that linked him to that Corpus bunch. I don't know what the little twit knew. He was a nosy sneak, a spying little crud.

He poked his nose into places it didn't belong and opened his mouth when he should have kept it shut. He got what he deserved!" The last was said with more vehemence than would normally be expected from a girl who had only met him a couple of times and did not know much about him.

"I thought you didn't know him very well," I said. Maybe his was another cradle she had robbed.

"I didn't," she murmured, a little confused at first. Her thoughts had evidently been a long way out. "But you didn't have to know him two seconds to figure him out. He was trying to hang around Harry, make himself into a big deal. Kept his eyes open so he'd know everything that was going on and could use it to his advantage. I know the type, all right."

I had spoken with him briefly twice, and while I wasn't in his fan club either, I didn't get that impression. Of course she had seen him under different circumstances than I had.

"Is that all?" she asked coldly. "Have I given you enough?"

"Is there any more to give?" I countered.

"No. I'm through." She picked up her purse as if to leave.

"One more thing," I said. "What about those attacks on Marilyn?"

Her eyes widened with fear. I was sure now. "I don't know anything. I've got to go." She clutched her purse tightly and hurried away, out into the night and freedom.

CHAPTER THIRTY TWO

What a strange creature. As changeable as the weather and just as volatile. I was thinking particularly of a storm, or a tornado, or a hurricane. She presented different faces to different people. One to Anne Bascomb, another to Harry, a third to Amos. What to Marilyn? Further, what provoked that strange reaction to discussion of Marilyn's attacker? Was it possible she knew something or could I have simply questioned her too much, kept after her when I should have backed off? No, that couldn't be it. I made a mental note to find out what she was afraid of. Maybe she was worried that someone was after her too.

It was after midnight and the drive back to Rockport, a mere 40 minutes, seemed endless. I was taking it easy because it had been a long day plus the roads were slippery from the earlier rains. The night was pitch black and spooky. Passing traffic made squishy sounds as cars drove by. Road water slung up from tires hit my windshield, covering it with a thin film of dirt and oil. Visibility was reduced by at least half. It was a good night to get home, pull the covers up and visit the land of bright dreams and easy promises.

A car behind me started to tailgate, an odd thing to do since there was no other traffic on the road. It inched closer, its headlights glaring into my rearview mirror. I slowed down, hoping my action would encourage it to pass. Didn't work. It slowed too. I sped up to get away. The car sped up too and stayed on my bumper.

Great, I thought to myself. Now I've got some nut here who wants to play chicken or some other game I don't know the rules to on a slick road in the middle of the night. I could not quite make out what kind of car it was, other than its small size and light color. Was that beige? A foreign car?

Instantly I was wide awake. Adrenaline pumped through my veins big time. Muscles tightened. I picked up my cell phone and dialed Walter's number. He wasn't at home. He wasn't at his office either, so I told the cop on duty where I was and asked for cover. He said a patrol car was twelve miles away. I said I hoped that wasn't too far. I hung up.

Ordinarily this would not have been a problem. I would have gunned the Porsche and let it do what it does best. That is, tear down the highway like a scalded hound, and that little beige job behind me would have eaten my dust in under ten seconds. However, tonight the rules were different. The roads were slick and I didn't dare speed, the Porsche being a little too light on its feet for slippery highways. I had left my gun with Marilyn, so I couldn't defend myself with any fireworks. There were no other cars to hide behind, so for the moment I was stuck where I was, heading at 65 miles an hour towards some patrol car 12 miles, make that 11 now, away and the safe harbor of Rockport.

A sudden loud noise sounded behind me. I heard the breaking of glass and the shattering of my back window. My rearview mirror revealed a small bullet hole in the glass. Now the picture was completely different. While I was assuming previously that the slick roads were more dangerous than the car behind me, that assumption was no longer valid. It had been established beyond question that the beige car was much more dangerous than the roads. I gave the Porsche the gas and left the gunman behind in a wash of road spray-- 95, 100, 105, 110-- there, that was fast enough! The tires held to the road perfectly, as if it was written in the script. I never did see the patrol car, and without me to identify the foreign car, it was a stalemate for the evening: Len, 0; beige car, 0.

After the excitement was over, I hurried back to my Rockport home, worried that the attacker might have been to my house first and found Marilyn. Since I had told her not to answer the telephone, it was no use calling her. I should have set up a signal to let her know when it was me calling, but should have wasn't going to cut it tonight.

Lights were on in my living room as I drove up and I didn't know whether to be relieved or terrified. I could hear voices when I climbed up the front steps, and it came as no surprise to find Walter and Marilyn whooping it up on my champagne when I walked in the front door.

"Where have you been parking, Walter?" I asked. "If your car was here, at least I'd have some warning about your presence."

"My car's at the marina," he replied, saluting me with a wave of his hand. "I park it there and walk here for exercise. You ought to try it."

"No need. I get plenty of exercise running away from murderers," I grumbled.

"What are you talking about?" Walter asked, suddenly serious.

"On the way home from Corpus, on that lonely little stretch between Portland and Aransas Pass, a foreign car, beige in color, started tailgating me," I said. "When I slowed down, it did the same thing. While I was happily considering my options, which I did not want to include speeding on a rain slicked road, he took a shot at me and got the rear window. Bullet's probably still in there somewhere. At least it's not in me. At that point I threw the Porsche in high gear and made good my escape."

"Why didn't you call for a patrol car?" Walter asked.

"I did. It was too far away. By now, the foreign car has blended into traffic. I couldn't identify it if my retirement depended on an identification."

"Damn!" Walter said. "Does this guy have all the luck?"

"Not all of it," I replied. "I'm here, am I not?"

Marilyn ran up to me, stood on her toes and threw her arms around my neck. She held herself close and nuzzled my shoulder. "If I thought this were my fault..."

"Hush, Marilyn," I soothed. "You weren't driving the car or aiming the gun. We're just lucky he went after me first. What if he had come after you?"

"Maybe he did," Walter said, "and heard more than one voice here or saw me walking up to the house. We have no idea who he is so we don't know who to watch for. Bat at least we know to be more careful. I'm assigning full time protection as of now for you two." He went over to the phone and made two calls: one for the promised protection and the second for the night crew to come over and go through my car for a bullet.

"So tell me about your interview this afternoon," I said to Walter after he hung up the phone.

"Guess what? We got fingerprints off the black notebook you gave us," he answered. "Shark's prints were all over it. We got at least 20 good ones."

"That's interesting. What did he have to say about it?"

"Says it's his grocery list," Walter answered. "But he's scared. Corpus has them cold on the armed robbery, with credible witnesses, fingerprints and all, but so far they aren't talking about the notebook or any possible involvement in drugs. I talked to some narcs, who confirmed they've been watching the pair and they had seen them with Bascomb on a number of occasions and even once with John Watts. Proving any involvement, that's a different thing."

"I talked with someone tonight who tied the whole bunch to Frank Meyer," I told Walter. "Said that's where the supply is coming from."

"That makes sense," Walter mused. "He's into most of the drug trafficking in that city."

"Why don't I set up a meeting with him?" I suggested. "If Shark and Barracuda were the ones who killed the three teenagers, they probably did it on their own because it was a stupid thing to do. Not with his knowledge, permission or consent. If that is the case, he might appreciate an opportunity to throw them to the wolves, us wolves. It would take some of the heat off his organization."

Walter considered it briefly. "Might work, but it's awfully risky. If they're guilty, and that's the only way we can get them, maybe okay. If they're not guilty, he might set them up. We wind up having helped frame two innocent men while the real killer gets off."

"Well, it seemed like a good idea at the time," I conceded. "We could still try it, just to see what he'd say."

"Not much use in that," Walter told me. "We couldn't believe him."

"You could tell Shark and Barracuda I was going to talk to him," I offered. "Then they would think he was going to frame them. We could see what they would come up with."

"It might make them more talkative, at that," Walter agreed. "If they're guilty, though, they won't talk regardless. I'll sleep on it and let you know what I think tomorrow. Tonight I'm too tired to think anymore. I'm going home to bed."

He bid Marilyn a fond farewell, grabbed his jacket, fumbled for a pack of cigarettes and lit up on the way down my steps. We could hear him whistling half way to the marina. The lab crew arrived as he was leaving, so he pointed them to my car and they got busy.

Marilyn, as always, looked fresh and well rested. She wanted to hear all about my meeting with Mary and I agreed to tell her. I wanted to get a woman's impression of Mary, a woman besides Anne Bascomb, who might have been prejudiced because Mary dated Anne's son Harry. I described Mary's mercurial temperament, her many personalities and her solo dance at the Chelsea Tavern. Then I told her about Mary's quick flight out the ladies room window, a description which caused Marilyn to hoot with laughter and admit she had done the same kind of thing herself on several occasions.

"How do you figure this woman, Marilyn?" I asked, pretty much baffled.

"She's quite simple, really," Marilyn said confidently, seating herself prettily on my sofa. She leaned forward and drew her legs up under her, a favorite position. "Since you're a man, you don't see it. Mary is the type of woman who becomes obsessed with one man. In her case, it's Harry Bascomb. What caused her to become obsessed with him, I don't know. Maybe it was because he was physically attractive and a renegade, or maybe because he was younger and she has some sort of hang up. When she found she couldn't control him, the obsession grew. She couldn't get enough of him. Twenty-four hours a day wouldn't have been enough. Every action she took radiated from this obsession. For example, the question of whether she was going to the beach became was Harry going to the beach, and could she go with him? He wasn't? He was going to the movies. Well, then, she wanted to go to the movies, too. Whatever he was going to do, where he was going to go, that's what she wanted. Nothing else mattered. I'll bet she nearly went wild when he stopped seeing her and started with Missy."

"Interesting theory," I commented. "Why do you think the talk about your attacker frightened her?"

"That puzzles me," Marilyn admitted. "I wonder if it made her think of a similar experience?"

"That seems too farfetched," I said. "I think I'll call her tomorrow and try to talk her into another meeting."

I picked up a newspaper. The front page was covered with stories about the murders, with pictures of the dead teenagers, interviews with their high school friends and other maudlin information the reporters were able to dig out of friends and relatives. I held up the paper and asked Marilyn if she'd read the stories.

"No, I didn't want to get depressed," she replied, "but after tonight, maybe I'd better. Hand it over."

"That's an excellent likeness of Missy and Harry," I said, pointing at a picture. The two had been photographed arm in arm on the beach one sunny day last summer.

"Harry Bascomb?" Marilyn exclaimed as she took the paper. "That's the guy who told me he was Bill Winston, the shoe salesman at Mervin's. Remember? Why would he do a thing like that?"

"Are you sure?" I asked. "Take a good look."

She looked closely and replied, "I'm positive. That's him."

"It gets deeper and deeper," I commented. "Maybe if we had the answer to why he did that we would know why somebody killed him."

"And why they were trying to kill me?" she added.

"Maybe," I replied.

CHAPTER THIRTY THREE

"Perhaps Harry did not want Missy to know he was dating you," I suggested to Marilyn as she fixed a breakfast of muffins and tea for us the next morning. I had begun to feel almost domesticated and was ready to go out and buy aprons and refrigerator magnets.

"How would she find out? I hadn't seen her since the end of summer," Marilyn pointed out. "There was no way she was going to run into the two of us together. Besides, we only went out the one time."

"Harry didn't know it was only going to be one time," I said. "But you're right about Missy. She wasn't going to find out. There must be some other reason he gave you that false name. I can't imagine what it was, though."

We said down at the table and started eating our muffins. Marilyn seemed restless, fidgeting about in her chair. She put her napkin in her lap and then put it back on the table.

"What's the matter, Marilyn?" I asked sympathetically. "Are you getting bored?"

"Oh, Len," she said dejectedly. "Just when things were going so well this had to happen. Hollywood has never seemed so far away as it does now. I can't even go outside to buy a paper."

"I know things seem bad now," I admitted. "But the person who attacked you is getting desperate. Look what chances he took last night, assuming that the one after me is the same one after you. He came after me right out in the open. He didn't know if I was armed. If I had a gun on me and got a lucky shot, I could have blown out one of his tires and called the police. Where would he have been then?"

She brightened considerably. "So now we hope he makes another move."

"Sort of," I mused. "There ought to be a way to force him to make a move, draw him out in the open."

"Set a trap, you mean?"

"Yes. He must have been following me on my rounds last night," I ventured. "He waited for an opportunity. When he saw I was in a remote spot, he made his move. It would have worked, too, if that bullet had hit me."

The phone rang, interrupting our discussion. It was Walter calling to tell me the bullet had been found. It was buried deep in the back of the headrest on my passenger set. Made a nasty little hole in the leather. It came from a small caliber pistol, big damage from a little gun.

"Thanks, Walter," I told him. "Wish the Corpus police had found the bullet from the gun which was fired at Marilyn in front of her apartment."

"That would have been helpful, wouldn't it?" he agreed. "By the way, they cleaned up the glass and taped your back window. You can get it fixed when you have the time." He hung up.

"Was that Walter?" Marilyn asked.

I told her it was, detecting a light of interest appearing in her sparkling eyes. "You two have become pretty good friends, haven't you?"

She agreed that they had. "He's a fascinating man, Len. Some of the things he's done are amazing. Did you know he used to own a bar which featured alligator wrestling?"

"Why, no," I replied, surprised.

"Or that he had an aunt who was buried in a Cord automobile along side of 30 of her favorite cats?"

"Well, no—"

"Or that he once tracked a criminal all the way across Mexico and caught him in El Salvador after a shootout in the public marketplace?"

"No, I didn't know that."

"Or that one summer he worked in a carnival hustling little children to throw baseballs at milk bottles to win teddy bears?"

"He sure gets around," I said. Marilyn had a way of getting people to open up, I had to admit. I strained back to remember what I had told her and hoped she hadn't repeated any of that nonsense to Walter.

I decided to call Anne Bascomb again to see if she was home. I let the phone ring 15 times, but there was no answer. I wished she had given me some sort of hint of what she had wanted when she left a message on my machine. Perhaps I needed to investigate Andre Trois a little more fully. He had lied to me about painting Marilyn's picture and I had caught him in a look of surprising malevolence. He could easily have been the driver of that little foreign car the night before. I could drive to his studio, check out his car, and ask him where he had been the previous evening. If he had an alibi I could eliminate him, but if he didn't, he would be much more interesting. Especially if he had a beige automobile.

"I want to come along," Marilyn said firmly when she heard where I was going.

"No, girly. You stay here. Watch tv. Eat frozen dinners. Put your hair in curlers. Do the laundry. Feed the dog. Do anything, but stay inside and don't answer the telephone."

"No way, fella," she replied in a still more determined tone. "I'm going with you, if I have to grab ahold of your little bumper and hoist myself onto your roof. I will not stay cooped up here by myself any longer. Besides, we can share the gun."

She had a point there. If I let her drive, I would be free to point and shoot in the unhappy event the attacker came after me again. Surely not in broad daylight though, not when he could be seen, license number

164

taken, driver viewed and described, maybe recognized. It seemed just as safe to take Marilyn along as it did to leave her alone where she might be a target, in spite of the occasional police drive by for protection.

"Okay, you win," I conceded. "Get dressed and we'll go pay a surprise visit to Andre. One condition, though. You have to drive."

"Oh, great!" she said, her eyes bright with enthusiasm. "I'd just love to drive that Porsche."

Misgivings started tumbling all over the place. I was fairly careful with my little car, but as there were no nicks on Marilyn's Corvette, it seemed reasonable to assume she was a good driver.

"How do you drive this thing?" Marilyn asked after she dressed and we had gone downstairs and gotten into the car. She thumped the clutch pedal with her foot. "Do you have to hold this down the whole time you're going?"

"You don't know how to drive a stick shift?" I asked incredulously.

"Nope," she replied, "but I'm willing to learn."

"I don't know if I'm willing to teach you, especially with my car," I replied uncertainly.

"Don't be such an old fuddy-duddy, Len. I'm a quick learner. You'll see. C'mon, let's get started!"

Ego overrides intelligence every time. Call me fuddy-duddy and I melt like a popsicle. I reluctantly agreed and pointed out the basics of driving a stick shift. She listened intently and soon was ready to give it a try.

The engine came smoothly to life as she twisted the key. She put it in first gear and we took off, bumping our way down the road as she let her foot off the clutch. She made the transition into second a little more smoothly but we bumped a whole lot when she went into third.

"Whoops!" she cried gleefully. "This is fun!" She turned to me to see if I was enjoying the ride as much as she was. I wasn't.

"Keep your eyes on the road," I shouted as we narrowly missed a Greyhound bus which was clinging to the far right side of the road like nylon out of a clothes dryer to avoid us. My foot was futilely stamping the passenger floor.

"Calm down, darling," she replied cheerfully, her gaze returning forward. "How on earth can you be a private detective with nerves like yours?"

Marilyn refined her technique with the clutch and the shift on the way to Andre's studio, and by the time we got there she was driving like a pro. She was a natural, very coordinated and good at following instructions. She'd rise quickly when she got to Hollywood, if I could get her out of the mess she was in before it killed us both.

There were quite a few cars in Andre's parking lot, but none were small foreign ones. The only foreign makes I saw were a Ferrari, several Mercedes and two BMWs. The rest were Cadillacs and an occasional Buick. The only beige car present wasn't really a car, it was a pick up truck and I didn't think Selser could possibly confuse a truck with a car. To make sure, though, we had to go in and ask him, and see if he had an alibi for the previous night.

Sounds of music, wining and dining were issuing from Andre's studio, and there was enthusiastic conversation interrupted by occasional ripples of laughter. A mid-morning party? An art show? I opened the door for Marilyn and we walked into a crowd of elegantly dressed well-wishers who greeted us with a mixture of surprise and amusement. We had interrupted an invitation-only affair.

"Come in dears, and help us celebrate!" Andre shouted good naturedly to us over the newly resumed din of conversation. "I've just gotten married!"

CHAPTER THIRTY FOUR

The new bride, a gorgeous young redhead with hungry green eyes and a narrow, thin mouth, hung onto Andre with nervous fingers and a possessive grasp. She looked disapprovingly at Marilyn, another woman who might have designs on her groom. Andre had obviously picked a basket of trouble.

After shaking hands all round and lifting the bubbly to newlywed toasts, Marilyn and I backed off in a corner and looked at each other in amazement.

"Kind of lets him out, huh?" Marilyn said, amused. "Can't see him carrying a torch for me when he's getting married to another woman."

"That sounds right to me," I concurred. "But just to make sure, let's find out what kind of car he drives. His fiancée too."

Marilyn gave me an exasperated look, but we mingled until we came across the best man and under the guise of wanting to know whether the groom's car was going to be gussied up in the traditional strings and tin cans way, we learned that the BMW in the parking lot was Andre's. His bride drove a Triumph sports car, which was where Triumphs sports cars spend a lot of their time, in the shop. And where was he the night before? Bachelors party, of course, at some little joint on the south side of town. It was a real blast, too, it lasted until 5 am.

Now the only real mystery about Andre was why had he lied about Marilyn's portrait. This wasn't the time, nor the place, but I decided to ask anyway. I caught him on the way to the men's room, asked for a moment of his time, and followed him to his office.

"Before I go, Andre, I must know," I began. "When I was here the other day, you said you had never painted Marilyn. Yet I saw a painting of Marilyn a few moments later under your counter. Why didn't you tell me the truth?"

Andre had drunk enough champagne not to be insulted by the question. Besides, he was in a good mood. He hesitated a moment and then answered.

"Look, when you came in, I didn't know who the hell you were. I didn't know if you were really a friend of Marilyn's or not. I didn't think it was any of your business whether I painted Marilyn. Besides, I hadn't gotten her permission, you see. I had just painted her on a whim, and before I displayed that portrait, I wanted to get her okay. Now that she's here, I'll just ask her."

We went back to the party and found Marilyn surrounded by a number of admirers, each seeking a glance of approval from the reigning beauty. Andre waded into their mist, as was his privilege as bridegroom, and took her aside, much to the disappointment of her little group and his carefully watching bride.

"Marilyn, I was so captivated by your beauty that I was unable to resist the temptation of painting your picture," Andre confessed.

"But I never posed for you," she said, surprised. "How did you do it?"

"From memory... and about three dozen photographs I borrowed from Mrs. Baird," he confessed.

"Can I see it?" Marilyn asked, delighted. "Oh, show it to me, please!" She clasped her hands together like a little child, totally irresistible.

"Well..." Andre said, looking around expectantly for others to join her so he could have a good sized, approving crowd for the unveiling of Marilyn's portrait. The new little woman, however, in her crisp while veil and knee length bridal gown, was beginning to seethe. After all, it was HER day. The crowd didn't notice her and began to gather around Andre and Marilyn, and, learning of a new toy, beseeched the artist to unveil it. After a few moments of modest resistance and sly glances, he went behind the counter, shuffled through the canvases, and withdrew the portrait. An admiring chorus of oohs and ahhs went through the group, some enthusiastic applause and a few well placed compliments followed.

Marilyn stood mesmerized before the painting. He had captured her in a wistful, waiflike dreamy state, radiating youth and innocence and trust that the future would bring fulfillment of all promises and goals. It was a painting which appealed to the dreamer, the optimist, the lover of nature and beauty. From the look on the face of Andre's bride, it was also Andre's last painting of Marilyn.

"You like? Yes?" Andre asked Marilyn.

"Oh, yes, Andre! It's wonderful," she said, still transfixed. "It's the most wonderful painting I've ever seen."

Several members of the wedding party made tentative offers to purchase the picture, but Andre, hoping to glean every last dollar out of an obviously desirable product, merely replied, "I won't sell it today. It's my wedding day. See me after the honeymoon!"

I felt we had crashed this party long enough, and we had certainly attained our objectives in coming, so I told Marilyn it was time to go and we made a hasty exit.

"I've forgotten how much fun it is to go to a party I've been out of circulation so long," Marilyn said ruefully, getting into the Porsche.

"Poor baby," I replied. "A whole week."

"Seems like a year," she commented, hunting for reverse. She found it, ground it into place and lurched us out of the parking lot, temporarily regressing in her skill as a stick shift driver. After a few exclamations and some hasty pointers from me she was back to speed and we were again on our way to Rockport.

"Let's get back to our earlier plan," Marilyn suggested, deftly maneuvering around an 18 wheel semi.

I opened my eyes. "Our earlier plan?"

"We were going to set a trap, remember?"

"Where do you get this 'we' stuff?" I answered crossly. "First you have to go along to Andre's and now you want to participate in some trap you don't even know anything about."

"I want to get this waiting over with," she said impatiently. "I'm willing to do almost anything. Besides, you're there to protect me."

"I haven't done such a hot job of protecting myself much less you," I said.

"What is your plan, anyway?"

"I don't know yet," I told her. "I just had some idea of drawing the attacker out into the open. To come after me the way he did last night, he must be getting desperate. And, we'll assume for the moment that the person after me is the same one who tried to kill you, because of the coincidence of the kind of car and also because there shouldn't be anyone trying to kill me unless it's connected with you or the Small-Bascomb-Watts murders."

"How could you get him out into the open?"

"Apparently he has been following me, at least at times," I replied. "I didn't spot him last night until he tailgated me. But he must have followed me into Corpus and waited until I was finished with Mary and was on my way back home. He took his best shot, but I lucked out. So to draw him out, I don't have to look for him. He'll look for me."

"You mean, if you drive to Corpus again at night, you think he would follow you and make another attempt to shoot you?"

"It's possible."

"Are you going to do it?"

"If I don't come up with a better idea," I replied, hedging. "I really haven't decided. I don't much like playing human decoy, but I also don't like waiting around any better than you do. I'm a target any way you look at it, so I might as well pick the time and the place and make it to my advantage."

"Sounds dangerous to me. And I haven't even paid your fee yet. In fact, you haven't told me what your fee is."

Only a real cad could charge Marilyn a fee. First, she didn't have any money. Second, I hadn't solved her problem. I hadn't told her that yet. She was a proud girl and I would have to come up with a face saver of some sort for her. Times like these I was glad I had a trust fund and could be independent.

"It's sort of foolish for me to talk about what to charge you," I told her. "I haven't done anything for you yet."

"Sure you have. You've come to my rescue in the middle of the night, housed me, fed me, and supplied enough champagne to float a boat in. You've gotten shot at and your car's taken a bullet for me. You call that not doing anything?"

"Ah shucks, ma'am," I said, lowering my head and shuffling my feet. "It tweren't nothing."

Ignoring my remark, she said, "Anyway, I'm going with you."

"You weren't invited."

"I invited myself."

I sighed and decided to let it pass for the moment. I could always sneak out the back door if I had to. She looked at me closely and her eyes narrowed with suspicion, but she said nothing. Obviously she was cooking up her own plan inside that fascinating little head of hers and I didn't have to ask. I knew it'd be a humdinger.

After we got back home we watched each other warily for a few moments while I caught up on some paperwork. The telephone rang once and I pushed the record button on my answering machine, hoping to record a threat, but it was only a wrong number.

I dialed Anne Bascomb but there was still no answer. I decided to call Amos and do some fishing. I couldn't come out and tell him his wife had called me, because she might have something to tell me that she didn't want him to know about. That's one of the many joys of being a private detective, the keeping what you know to yourself and your client, if you trust your client.

The hardware store telephone rang two times before it was picked up. I recognized Amos' voice.

"Hello?" he said, sounding hopeful.

"Good afternoon, Amos," I said. "This is Len Townsend. How are you?"

"Oh, it's you," he said, sounding disappointed now. "I'm not so good, Len."

"What's the matter?"

"I got personal problems," he replied wearily. "The other night, when we was out drinking, I stayed around for a few more beers. I guess maybe I had too many. I was drunk when I got home and said a lot of things I ought not to have said. Yesterday when I come home from work, Anne was gone."

"Uh-oh. That's too bad," I replied. "Where'd she go?"

"I don't know. She didn't even leave a note. She was just gone."

"Did she take a suitcase?" I asked, little warning bells sounding in my head.

"I don't know," he answered. "I never thought to look."

"Did you call any of her friends or relatives to see if you could find her?"

"No, I didn't want them to know she left me," he said softly. "I kept thinking she'd come back, but she hasn't." He sounded sad and tired.

"Why don't you and I meet at your house and look around? Maybe we might find something out."

"Okay. Just let me check and see if I can get some time off." He put his hand over the telephone and I could hear a muffled discussion going on in the background. Finally he came back on. "Len, I can meet you now if that's all right."

"That's fine, Amos," I told him. "I'll be right there." I hung up and found that Marilyn had gotten off the sofa and was putting her shoes on.

"Hey, wait a minute," I said. "Where are you going?"

"With you," she said, surprised.

"No way, baby. This isn't your case. I'm involve--"I began.

"Now look," she said, coming up close and throwing me a look that would melt chocolate. "You can stand there and give me lots of reasons, good reasons, why I shouldn't go with you. And I can stand here, very patient, and listen to you. I might even agree. But in the end, I'm going, and if you want to save time, you won't even bother to try to talk me out of it."

I knew when I was licked. I felt like a wimp, but I hate arguments, and besides, I would enjoy her company.

"Your trick," I conceded, "but just remember, keep your eyes open for enemy traffic, and if it were really important, you would have stayed here without argument."

She smiled, showing she knew how to be a graceful winner.

This time I drove, with Marilyn riding shotgun. She took her work seriously and kept checking all directions for any sign of a beige car or a loaded gun. She even peered out of the cracked glass in the window behind us. Twice we saw cars that fit the vague description I had been given, but the people inside seemed harmless enough, and neither car followed us. In about 20 minutes we were in front of Amos' house. He had already arrived and was waiting for us at the front door, hat in hand. His eyes almost popped out when he saw Marilyn. I had forgotten the effect on people the first sight of Marilyn often has.

"Hello, Amos," I greeted him, assuming that he was temporarily rendered speechless by the remarkable resemblance of Marilyn to the late movie star of the same name. She caught it too, so she went right up to him and offered to shake hands. "This is Marilyn Miller. She's helping me out today."

He finally found his tongue, murmured a response and invited us into his home. There was a six pack of empty beer cans on the dining room table, probably Amos' dinner the night before. A newspaper lay on the floor beside the table and some work clothes had been tossed in the hallway on the way to the bathroom. It didn't seem as if Anne had returned home yet. A vase of dying flowers sat on a counter in the kitchen.

"Does Anne normally keep flowers here?" I asked Amos, gesturing to the vase on the counter.

He looked puzzled. "No, she doesn't. That's odd. I guess she just got in a hurry to go. She must have put water in the vase and then set it down on the counter."

We went into the bedroom and Amos opened the closet door. Two suitcases stood on the top shelf. The closet was full of women's clothing.

"That's mighty funny," Amos commented. "Here's her suitcases and it doesn't look like there's any clothes missing. Maybe she doesn't mean to be gone very long."

"Is this her purse, Amos?" Marilyn asked, calling out from the living room. She was holding a brown vinyl purse which looked heavy and full.

"That's it all right," he said, worried. "What do you think happened to her? Would she go anywhere without her purse?"

"I don't know," I replied. "But I think you ought to report her disappearance to the police."

"Oh my goodness, my Anne! What has happened to Anne?" he mumbled, sitting down on an easy chair. He put his face in his hands and started sobbing, large, rasping, gulping, whoo-whoo sobs. Marilyn and I looked at each other.

"I'll call," I said, and picked up the telephone.

CHAPTER THIRTY FIVE

For once Walter was in and at his desk when I called, but he did not much welcome what I had to tell him.

"Oh, crap, not another one!" Walter said, aghast.

"Don't know yet," I said. "She's only disappeared so far. We don't know yet that she's another one, as you so crudely put it."

"A middle-aged housewife disappears overnight with no money, no clothes, no identification and leaves no note, what am I to think? You know and I know what's probably happened. It's just a matter of time until she turns up dead in someplace where there aren't any clues."

"You're overreacting, Walter," I told him. "I'll admit it looks bad, but don't forget, she may be hiding out with a neighbor. Or, if she was killed, this time there might be a clue that points to the killer. He can't be lucky forever."

"I'll send somebody over to talk to Bascomb," Walter said, ignoring my half-hearted attempt at reassurance. "Tell him to stay put until Rodger McVey gets there."

"Will do. Talk to you later." I got off the phone and passed the message on to Amos, who had stopped crying. He had gotten a beer out of the refrigerator and was staring glumly at a hole in his carpet. He nodded to show he had heard me, but otherwise made no comment. When Rodger McVey arrived, Marilyn and I left.

"That poor, sad old man," Marilyn commented, sounding close to tears herself. "First his son, now this with his wife. What do you think happened to her?"

"It doesn't look good, Marilyn," I admitted. "If I had to guess, I'd say she met with foul play. You know, she called me yesterday when I wasn't home. She left a message on my answering machine for me to call her immediately. I called, but she never answered. I wish I knew what she wanted."

"You said she had a fight with Amos the night before after he got home drunk?"

"That's what Amos told me."

"Could he have anything to do with all this?" Marilyn asked. "They have a big fight, she disappears. No signs of a break in, nothing inside the house disturbed. No signs of a struggle. Either she disappeared willingly or she left with someone she knew and didn't take her purse."

"I would imagine the police will check Amos out carefully," I ventured. "You never know. But he just didn't seem as if he were hiding a guilty secret, as if he had killed his wife the day before and disposed of her body. If he's that good an actor, to lead us around the house searching through her belongings... if he's that good, he could get away with it."

"Maybe the neighbors saw her leave," Marilyn ventured. "Maybe we should have gone from house to house and asked them."

"Sure, we could have done that. We would have made a nice target if we did. Anyone driving by could have taken aim at you or me and had at it. That's why I left the job to the cops."

We arrived back at my home and said hello to our sentry, the one Walter had so thoughtfully provided. Luckily it was at my discretion as to whether or not he went with us when we left the house. I chose to have him guard my house. He was seated on my front porch and reported that nothing of interest had happened in our absence, unless you counted the neighbor's dog getting loose and pulling down a clothesline across the road.

"Man, you should have seen it. That dog had clothes going everywhere!" he told us. "Then the dame across the street sees what's happened and starts running after her clothes. Unmentionables everywhere! It was some show." He guffawed loudly, slapping his knee. Then he noticed our silence and added that we would have had to have been there, and went back to his watch.

Inside it was warm from the rays of the afternoon sun so I switched on the air conditioner and got us each a glass of iced tea. Marilyn sat down, looking very young and fragile as she thought over the disappearance of Anne Bascomb.

The telephone rang. I hurried over to it and answered, hoping it was the caller who had previously threatened me. I had some questions for him, although he probably would not answer them. At least I'd like to have the chance to ask.

It was Walter. "Got some information you'll be interested in, Len," Walter told me. "One of the neighbors saw the Bascomb woman leave yesterday."

Finally, a break. It was overdue.

"Tell me," I said.

"About 3 pm a car pulled up and honked its horn. Mrs. Bascomb came out of her house, walked up to the car and after a moment got in. Then the car drove off."

"What kind of car?"

"Can't you guess?" Walter asked.

"This is no time-- not a beige foreign job?" I asked, disbelievingly.

"That's right, a little Honda, late eighties."

"But that car, if it's the same one, is the one that was after Marilyn, and me, because of Marilyn, at least that's what I thought."

"Rethink it, Len," Walter advised.

"Looks like there might be some connection," I mused. "I will rethink it. Real hard. Did anyone get a look at the driver?"

"Only to say that there was one. He wore a hat. That's all."

"So it could have been a woman or a man."

"Or a dog or a robot, if they could drive." Walter was making an effort at sarcasm.

"You sure about it being a Honda?" I asked.

"Yep," Walter replied. "Neighbor used to have one just like it, knows Hondas."

"At least that's something."

Walter promised to let me know if he heard any more and hung up. Marilyn pressed me for all the details on the Rockport killings that hadn't made the paper. Now that it might involve her mysterious attacker she wanted every scrap of information I could supply. I was only to happy to oblige, because I wanted to review the whole thing in my mind and find the connection. In what possible way could Marilyn be connected to the murders of Missy Small, Harry Bascomb and John Watts?

"You barely knew Missy, dated Harry once thinking he was someone else and you didn't even know John Watts," I said. "Had you ever met the Bascombs?"

"I never met Amos. I don't think I've met Anne. Her name isn't familiar, unless I could have met her while I was modeling and don't remember." She shrugged her shoulders.

"I was attacked at the roadside park the same day John Watts was killed," I said. "Could it be he was killed so he wouldn't tell me something? Then, Anne Bascomb disappears after calling me and leaving a message on my answering machine. Same question. Could she have been killed so she wouldn't talk? Then, someone takes a shot at me. What do I know that somebody is afraid of?"

Marilyn looked at me thoughtfully, her eyes looking very expectant. "Keep going," she said.

"Someone sends me the black notebook," I continued. "By itself, with almost no explanation. Therefore virtually useless, except for one thing. Was it meant as a red herring, to get me off the scent? It had Shark's fingerprints. Was it an attempt to get some drug dealers off the street so they could do a little hard time? We've been assuming that drugs and dealing played a part in the murders, but now it's time to take a closer look at that assumption."

The telephone rang, providing a neat break in our discussion. It was Walter again.

"Things are starting to happen fast," he informed me. "Mrs. Bascomb has been found. Dead. Over on some private property on Copano Bay."

"Dead? What cause?" I asked. Marilyn overheard and stood up quickly, knocking over her glass of iced tea. She hurried into the kitchen for some paper towels.

"Looks like she drowned. An autopsy will tell for sure."

"Drowned? That doesn't seem likely," I commented.

"Wait. There's more," Walter told me. "There was a note on the beach near where she was found. It's a confession."

"A confession?" I asked, shocked. "To what?"

"Wait til you hear," he said. "It says, 'I killed them. I'm sorry.'"

"Go on," I urged.

"That's all she wrote," Walter replied.

"That's it?"

"The whole thing. Some kids walking along the beach found the note under a shell with a brown scarf that belonged to Anne. The neighbor that saw her leave said she was wearing it. The kids that found it weren't supposed to be there because it was on private property. If they hadn't been trespassing, it might have been days, or weeks, or even longer, until she was found."

"Do you think it was a suicide?" I asked Walter. "After all, she didn't leave the house alone. She was in the company of someone who possibly shot at me and Marilyn earlier."

"I don't know if it is or isn't. It looks like her writing but we're sending the note to an expert in Corpus. If she wrote the note, it could be."

"I don't buy it," I said positively. "Her own son? Two other teenagers? What's the motive?"

"Come on, Len, you've seen stranger," Walter said. "Remember the Dalton case?"

My stomach turned as it always did at the mention of that name, even now, three years later. Four little boys, all killed by their loving mama, who thought she heard voices. She had seemed so normal, so grief stricken at the time. If I hadn't had a lucky break, some mismatching numbers, odd dates and times, she'd still be out there somewhere gathering sympathy from friends and relatives.

"I admit that strange things happen, but Anne Bascomb?" I said, still unbelieving. "Seems unlikely to me. What are you going to do now?"

Walter told me he was going to wait for the results of the autopsy, see if anyone saw the Honda going onto the private property and look for tire tracks. He was going to question Bascomb more closely. "I'll see if we can find any guns that belong to Mrs. Bascomb," he said morosely. "In other words, chase my tail in circles."

"I think that's exactly what you're doing if you believe that Anne Bascomb killed those people," I asserted. We said an unsatisfactory goodbye and hung up.

Marilyn was on her knees soaking up iced tea with paper towels. She glanced up at me as I replaced the telephone, her eyes alight with interest.

"Len, if she is the killer, I can go back home," she said hopefully.

"Wait a minute, sweetheart," I said. "I don't think she's the killer, not for a minute. I think it's another red herring. I think the murderer is trying to use her as a patsy, a fall guy, to take the rap. If the police buy her suicide, then they buy her as the killer and the real murderer gets away with it. Anne Bascomb doesn't have a motive."

"Maybe she does," Marilyn argued, returning to her seat. "Maybe we just don't know what it is. After all, she didn't approve of Mary. She despised her. Maybe she didn't approve of Missy either. Maybe she found out Harry was dealing--"

"Her only son?" I asked. "Kill her only son? Isn't that a little drastic?"

Marilyn thought about it. She wasn't finished yet. "She might have lost her temper in the heat of the moment," she put out. "There could have been a violent confrontation--"

"So, who's driving the beige car? A robot?" I tried not to sound too sarcastic.

"Oh, I don't know," Marilyn replied dejectedly. "Why couldn't it belong to a friend and she borrows it occasionally? Why couldn't Anne Bascomb have been the one tailgating you last night? Why couldn't she have asked the friend to pick her up... Well, it is getting farfetched."

"Probably because she was already dead last night," I said. "Even if she weren't, does it seem likely?"

"What's likely about this whole deal?" Marilyn retorted. "Three teenagers getting murdered. People shooting at each other out of automobiles. Somebody tampering with my brakes, trying to run me off the road. This whole thing isn't likely and I hate every part of it! In the past week I've been bored, lonely, frightened, terrified, trapped and had to put my lifelong dream on a long hold. When will it all end?"

"Hold tight, dear," I soothed. "I think we're getting close to the end now. Once it's proven that Mrs. Bascomb didn't commit suicide, the murderer will be even more desperate. He'll make another move, slip up and we'll get him. I'll bet on it. What would you like to bet? Air fare to Hollywood?"

This brought a smile. Marilyn countered, "First class? For the Corvette too?"

Give her an inch! I switched the subject. There had to be a clue somewhere that we'd overlooked. "What did you and Harry talk about on your date? Can you remember?" I asked.

"Let me think," she said, stretching her legs along the sofa. Long, tapering legs in deep blue stretch pants, trim hips. "Oh, yes, the braggart. He wanted to impress me with big talk. People he knew. Places he'd been. Things he'd seen. Impress the little girl from a hick town in Louisiana."

"What people?" I demanded. "What places? What things?"

Marilyn said Harry had talked about some of what he called "the rollers and shakers" of Corpus. Some of the wealthy families. He said he'd been to the ritzy country club on a number of occasions. "I thought to myself, maybe once," she said, amused. "It tickled me when he started talking to me about Mary Spaulding, because she'd never mentioned him. Of course, now I know why. He was giving me a phony name! It turns out he was the one she was so hung up on. A kid, really. Will wonders never cease!"

"What did he say about Mary?"

"He told me she was some rich girl he had dated and taken to a lot of fancy parties."

"Did he say why he quit seeing her?" I asked.

Marilyn thought about it. "Now that you mention it, yes. I thought he was exaggerating at the time, but he said something pretty strange. He said he was afraid of her."

"Afraid of her?" I repeated. "Did he say why?"

"He was sort of vague. He just implied she was dangerous, that she did strange unbalanced things. I tried to get him to say more, but he changed the subject and that was the end of it. He knew I had modeled with her."

There was nothing else of interest Marilyn could remember about her date with Harry. I was pretty amazed she had remembered that much. Obviously he had been on a talking jag to have said all that. I would have liked to have Mary's address so I could stop by and pay her a visit. I felt pretty sure that if I were to call her, she'd hang up on me, based on her parting remarks last time I saw her.

"I wish you knew where Mary lives," I said, really more thinking aloud than talking to Marilyn. "Too bad you never went there."

"We could go ask her parents," Marilyn said. "I know where they live."

I raised an eyebrow. "How do you know that?" I asked.

"They came to see her model once, and I met them. They told me to come by and see them sometime, and told me where they lived. I'm pretty sure I can find it."

"Okay, let's go," I replied. "I'm tired of sitting around here, waiting for something else to happen. Let's go see what we can find out from them. That ought to make Mary happy."

Marilyn went to freshen up. She emerged wearing a green cotton dress and pink tinted pouty lips that looked sweet and kissable. She lowered her lashes and peeked out slyly at me, gauging my reaction. Satisfied, she whirled around the room and said, "Let's go. I'm ready."

The highway was littered with tourist traffic. Marilyn kept a careful watch for potential trouble, but we had an uneventful trip into Corpus and she was finally able to relax as we crossed the high bridge into the city. The view from the bridge was spectacular. Corpus Christi Bay stretched out for miles and miles on the port side, and on the starboard side was the ship channel into the Corpus Christi harbor. Every day it seemed the view was different. Sometimes the water was rough, sometimes slick smooth. Sometimes it reflected the deep blue of the Texas sky, and other times it was cloudy grey.

"Look, Len, at the sailboats over there," Marilyn said, pointing at a number of catamarans in the distance.

"It's a race," I commented. "Looks like they're heading towards the Gulf of Mexico."

A ship was coming down the deep water channel, heavily laden with an oil cargo. A tour boat was gliding past him and sightseers were gathered to one side, starting at the ship. Life was going on as usual for the citizens of Corpus. It must be nice not to worry about getting shot at, I thought.

Marilyn directed me up the Ocean View Drive, a classy street where the heavy moneyed citizens liked to reside. Bordering the water, houses are built on a high cliff and residents can see all the way past the bay to the Gulf. Built high up, they're also protected from the high tides of hurricanes. Most people who had been able to afford a house on the coveted Ocean Drive cliffs went all the way and built a mansion, a monument to their success, at least their material success. Then came the troubles in the oil industry, and those who had put all their eggs in that basket quietly visited their real estate broker and exchanged their mansion on a cliff for a less ostentatious residence inland, the salt water having become a little too humid for their tastes, don't you know?

The Spaulding digs were about midway up the drive, Marilyn said. She looked closely at the elegant estates, trying to coax Mary's ancestral home back from memory. She had a couple of false starts, when she thought she had the right one, but each time she shook her head, seeing a fence or a statue or a fountain that was not in the recollection. Finally she pointed enthusiastically and said, "There! That's it. I'm positive."

It was a two story brick number, a little smaller than its neighbors, but still nothing to sneeze at. It was handsomely landscaped, with lots of palm trees and oleander bushes which are popular in the area due to their hardiness and love of the semi-tropical climate. A circular driveway passed the front porch, a Grecian columned affair, with a heavy brass chandelier hanging down from the porch ceiling to light the way for night callers. We stopped the Porsche in the driveway and got out. I headed for the front door and rang the doorbell. Marilyn was right behind me.

"No answer," Marilyn said. "Guess they're not at home."

"Let's go to dinner," I suggested. "We'll try again after we're finished."

We got back in the car and drove around, discussing the merits of Italian, Mexican, American, Indian and seafood. No decision was made, we just got hungrier. Finally we decided to buy some submarine sandwiches and take them to the public docks so we could watch the boats go by. This taste of freedom was pretty heady, but we kept a close eye out for beige Hondas and steel pistols, just in case.

It was seagull day at the docks, at least that's what the feathery little pests had decided when they saw our sandwiches. We sat at a picnic table and the bolder of the scavengers came up to our feet to beg. Marilyn broke off little pieces of bread and held them out until the birds came up and snatched them from her fingers. Highly pleased, she went over to a vendor and bought some popcorn to toss at the birds. Soon they had cawed an announcement of a free feed to all the other seagulls in the area and we had at least 100 birds currying Marilyn's favor, much to her delight. We finally decided to leave, the ever present cawing from 100 birds getting on our nerves.

We drove back to the Spaulding residence, but there was still no one home. I suggested a dessert, something heavy and gooey like cheesecake. We headed for Chez Moi, a fancy French restaurant which knew all about heavy desserts. They knew how to charge, too. I think they set the price of their delicacies by figuring out how many calories each contained and charging a penny per calorie.

The restaurant was located in a shopping center very close to the Spaulding residence, so I thought we could have our dessert and make another pass by Mary's familial abode before calling it an evening. The cheesecake was rich and heavy and topped with chocolate covered fresh strawberries. We followed it with two cups of expresso. After I paid the check, which would have bought dinner for a dozen people at a fast food restaurant, we went outside.

Night had fallen and the stars were out, big bucketfuls of them. I glanced sideways at Marilyn and saw that she gave off her own special glow, a sort of magical radiance lighting her alabaster skin and illuminating that sun kissed blonde hair of hers. Moon kissed now.

We got into the Porsche and drove back to the Spaulding residence. Again. I really did not expect to see anyone home. To my surprise, the home was lit brightly from top to bottom and the front porch chandeliers were burning brightly as well. There were a number of cars parked out front, probably indicating guests for cocktails or some sort of party. Then, at the same time, both Marilyn and I saw it.

"Bingo!" I said, delighted. "There's Mary's Mustang."

"What luck!" Marilyn replied. "What do we do now?"

"Well, I don't exactly want to break into that party," I told her. "Mary, being as unpredictable as she is, might make some sort of a scene. Goodness knows what she might do or say. It wouldn't surprise me for her to announce that we were white slavers out to kidnap her, or that you and I were jewelry thieves after the guests' jewelry. I think we'll wait her out."

"And do what then?" Marilyn sounded reluctant to have anything to do with Mary, now that we had her within our reach. Not that I blamed her.

"We'll follow her home to see where she lives. Probably some cave somewhere." I was only half kidding.

"Or an institution," Marilyn added. She was only half kidding too.

"Nothing about Mary would surprise me," I told her. "For all we know, she lives at a Motel 6 with a different room every night. One for each of her moods."

Marilyn was about to enter into another charming facet of detective work. This was the part where you get to sit and wait. You don't know how long you're going to wait. It could be ten minutes or it could be all night. We had not anticipated the waiting, so we had nothing with which to entertain ourselves. No books, no magazines, no wine…The problem, at least this time for me, was the close proximity to Marilyn. Sitting so close to her in the Porsche was going to be an exercise in fighting temptation. My arm kept wants to sneak around her shoulders…

The minutes crept by slowly. There wasn't enough room in the car to stretch out. My arms and legs got cramped. We were parked about a block away from the house in back of several other cars where there were no street lights and we were completely hidden in the dark. When Mary left, as she hopefully would, we would recognize her as she walked under the porch lights and got into her car.

Several people came out of the Spaulding home, chatted a few moments on the porch, split up into two groups and got into their cars. They drove off. I hoped that meant that the party was starting to break up. A short party. About 10 more minutes passed and more people exited, got in another car, and left. Shortly thereafter I recognized a familiar dark haired beauty come out alone, gaze up at the stars and go over to the white Mustang. She opened the door, got in and gunned the motor. Then she was off as fast as the pony's ponies would carry her, away into the night, a quickly disappearing target.

"Hurry, Len!" Marilyn urged, leaning forward in her seat. "Oh, hurry, or we're going to lose her!"

The Porsche leaped forward as if it were launched with rocket fuel. I held the steering wheel tightly as I whirled around corners, keeping the two red lights of the Mustang in sight, but not getting near enough to make her suspect she was being followed. I had to run several red lights but as there were no policemen around that was no problem. We headed across the city, up the bridge and over to Portland.

"I thought she lived in Corpus," I said.

Marilyn shrugged her shoulders. "I thought so too. Maybe she moved."

Our little caravan passed through Portland and kept going.

"Looks like we're on our way to Aransas Pass," I commented. "Maybe she relocated there."

We did not stop in Aransas Pass either. The red lights turned in the direction of Rockport.

"Wonder who she's going to see?" I mused. "Perhaps she is paying a sympathy call on Amos Bascomb."

She passed the turnoff to Amos' house, passed the grocery store, the service station, the shopping center and the public beach. She turned down Fulton Beach Road.

"Len, she's going to Key Allegro!"

"Looks like it, sweetheart," I commented. "Maybe she's going to my house."

CHAPTER THIRTY SIX

Like a homing pigeon, Mary made a turn onto Bayshore Drive and went up over the little bridge that connects the island of Key Allegro with the city of Rockport. It was possible that Mary was going to visit a friend on the island, but she was certainly heading in the direction of my house.

Sure enough, when she got close, the Mustang slowed. She went around the corner very slowly but did not stop. The lights were on but my car was not in the garage. For all she knew, it was in the garage. I could just barely make out the form of Walter's policeman in the shadows on the porch and I was glad he had stayed there. With Mary on the loose it was good to know there was protection available if needed. However, Mary still did not stop. She went down to the marina, turned, went past my house again and started back the way she had come. I had parked us in a neighbor's empty carport several houses down the street so she would not see my distinctly recognizable Porsche.

"What do you think she's after, Len?" asked Marilyn.

"That's an interesting question," I replied, "which I'll be sure to ask when I see her. Wonder where she's going now?"

That question was quickly answered. She stopped off at the local watering hole where Amos and I had spent an evening discussing her. Maybe she was looking for Amos. She was only there about five minutes, and when she came out she was carrying a paper sack shaped like a bottle.

"So much for Texas' open container laws," I said, referring to the fact that the state of Texas frowns on its constituents drinking at the same time they drive. Mary got back in the Mustang and headed her car in the direction of Corpus.

"Looks like we're going back to where we started," Marilyn hooted. "This is one of the silliest things I've ever done!"

Sure enough, the red taillights led us directly back to the sparkling city by the sea, resplendent with its night lights now contrasting brilliantly against the pitch black of the sleeping bay. When we were high atop the harbor bridge we could see the blinking lights of boats on their way to sea, steadily moving and bobbing up and down in the chop. A soft breeze, laden with the tangy smell of salt, blew in our windows and made me want to think of romance and sweet love, not crazy ebony haired young women likely destined for destruction and doom.

Mary drove into an apartment complex on the north side of town, a large group of brick buildings surrounding the obligatory swimming pools and exercise room. She parked in an empty space near the corner of the closest building, got out of her car and carried the bottle with her, taking a swig of whatever was inside as she disappeared through a door in the middle of the building.

"Land o'goshen, Marilyn, lookit what she parked next to," I whispered, pointing.

Marilyn turned her pretty head in the direction I had indicated and raised her eyebrows. "Do you think it's the same one?"

We were looking at a beige Honda.

"That's certainly an interesting question," I told her, wondering if Mary could be in any danger. What would be the prudent action for an up and coming private detective to take at this point? Does he risk showing his hand by going to Mary's aid? What if she doesn't need aid? What if that isn't the right beige Honda? Suppose it belongs to a visiting minister or a college kid who had nothing to do with the murders in Rockport?

Or, what if Mary is meeting that person, the one who shot at me, right now. Maybe that's why she stopped at the bar in Rockport, to make a telephone call, to ask him to meet her here. Perhaps she brought that bottle so they could share it. Or, supposing the worst, what if the person who picked Anne up, has Mary in hand right now with a similar plan for her? What to do?

"What are you going to do, Len?" Marilyn asked. I noticed it was "you" now, not "we" anymore. That was okay.

"I'm going to be very, very careful," I replied, smart alecky. "I'm going to call Mary on my cell phone to see if she needs help. After I speak with her I'll decide what to do next. Sometimes it's difficult to plan ahead." Better to tell Marilyn that than to confess I had no idea.

I dialed Mary's number and let it ring 15 times. There was no answer. "I don't like the look of this," I told Marilyn. "She could be in the shower or in the lurch."

"Let's get out of here. I'm getting the creeps," Marilyn said nervously, eying the beige car. "If that's the murderer, and Mary isn't answering her telephone, it may be too late to help her, but it's not too late to help us. Let's get the license number and get out of here. I'll call the police while you drive."

"That would be a good plan if we had more information, Marilyn," I told her patiently. "But what if we get the license number, call the police and hot foot it out of here, and it turns out Mary gets a kick out of not answering her phone past 10 pm and the beige car belongs to a salesman? I'll be getting a horse laugh from the Corpus cops for the rest of my life."

"At least you'll be alive to hear it," Marilyn countered.

"Look, Marilyn, if that's the murderer, he doesn't know we're here. Besides, we have a telephone, a car and a gun. We're perfectly safe. All we have to do is just sit here and see if he comes out. Meanwhile, though, I'm going to sneak over to the apartment building, see which apartment is Mary's by looking at the mailboxes over there, and then go very quietly to that apartment to see if I can find out anything."

Marilyn was indignant. "You mean you're going to leave me alone here? Has it slipped your mind that I hired you to protect me? So, what do you do? You drive me to within 30 feet of what may be the murder car, park and then leave me while you go and stick your neck out for no good reason."

"That's what makes me such a good private detective," I told her confidently. "I spit in the face of logic." I kissed her on the cheek for luck, put the cell phone in her hand and locked the doors. I left the gun on the floor. "You'll be safe--"

"Or you'll be sorry," she finished crossly.

I went up to the apartment building and glanced at the mailboxes. M. Spaulding's name was listed on 1B. I went inside and down the hall, walking softly with a cowboy hat pulled low over my eyes. It wasn't much of a disguise but it beat not having a disguise at all, sort of.

These were very uptown apartments. The ground floor apartments, like Mary had, came with patios, giving a second exit in case of fire. The upstairs apartments had balconies strategically placed for the optimum view of the pools. I found Mary's door and put my ear right up next to it. There was no sound, so I kept going and went back outside.

I turned the corner of the building and located Mary's apartment. There was a light on inside, so I hugged the outside wall of the apartment building until I reached Mary's window, hoping fervently that no one would see me and take me for a cat burglar or a peeping tom. I took a quick look through the window into Mary's apartment, but there was nobody visible. I could see a sofa upholstered in what appeared to be floral print fabric, an antique secretary with lots of papers piled on it, a couple of chairs, a coffee table, a gun... A gun? Why would Mary keep a gun on her coffee table? A Queen Elizabeth chair stood in the corner with about six teddy bears sitting regally on it. Mary was quite a girl. Pistols and teddy bears.

It didn't seem from my view as if she were in any immediate danger. Certainly if she were being held hostage by the unknown attacker, they would be in the living room, not somewhere in the dark. I decided to go back to the Porsche and dial her number again. If she did not answer this time, I would give Walter a call and let him call the Corpus police. Let him look foolish if nothing was wrong. That's what friends are for, right?

It took me less than two minutes to find my way back to the Porsche. I had been gone probably five minutes, six at the most, but it was more than enough time for Marilyn to disappear.

CHAPTER THIRTY SEVEN

The parking lot was empty. There was no sign of a luminous blonde in a sexy green dress anywhere. There was nothing but cars, trucks and an occasional motorcycle. I wondered fleetingly if Marilyn were playing a trick on me, but dismissed that notion immediately. She was afraid to be alone here, so she certainly would not have left the comparative safety of the car. At least I had assured her it was safe, but those words tasted pretty bitter to me now. Where could she be?

I opened the door to the Porsche. The passenger's door was unlocked. She wouldn't have left it unlocked. The cell phone was lying on the floor. She wouldn't have left the phone, nor her purse, which was right beside it. More proof that she had left against her will. What woman leaves a car and doesn't take her purse? The gun was gone!

I picked up the phone, intending to call the police, when I heard a cold voice behind me say, "Put it down, slick. That's right. Now put those hands up where I can see them or I'll shoot you into the next world before you can blink in this one." The voice was as cold as the air in the North Pole and I recognized it. Mary Spaulding. I'd found her after all.

Or, she'd found me. And she was holding a gun. Oh, swell. Looked like she had my gun. Guess the Corpus cops would get their horse laugh after all, if I got out of this one.

"Put that gun away, Mary," I said, turning around very, very slowly and smiling to show her how harmless and agreeable I was. "You know me. What do you need a gun for?"

"Shut up, Len," she replied unsmilingly. "Go over to that car there." She pointed to the beige Honda.

"Whose car is that Mary?" I asked, fearing the answer.

"Why, it's mine, of course. I use it to keep the miles off the Mustang," she replied. "Get in the front seat. We're going for a little ride."

I had now reached the car and glanced quickly inside. Marilyn was lying on the back seat, her wrists and ankles tied so she couldn't move, much less get away. Her lovely mouth was taped and there was a mark across her face where it appeared as if she had been slapped. I sure had done a great job of protecting her.

"What do you want with us, Mary?" I asked, hoping I could think of something with which to bargain.

"You're in my way, Len," she answered, sleet dripping from each word. She smiled an eerie, chilly smile. She was enjoying herself, getting her kicks out of seeing me squirm. "I'm going to take care of you. Get in front. You're going to drive."

"What if I don't?" I asked, balking.

"No big deal to me," she said. "I'll just kill you here. Starting with Marilyn."

"But you'd get caught," I argued.

"No, I wouldn't. I haven't yet, have I?"

I had underestimated Mary. I had thought her to be unbalanced, but I had not realized to what extent. She was deranged, and homicidally so, and I mentally kicked myself for not having realized it until now. Mary, the missing link between my two cases. The common thread who knew all the parties involved and who had an obsessive love for the drug dealing Harry Bascomb. Could it really be Mary who was responsible for the deaths of four people and was ready, even eager, to add two more to the list? When I stared down the barrel of the gun she was holding, I had my answer. Mary and her crazy dark eyes.

"Where are we going?" I asked.

"Drive to the docks, sweetie," she said flirtatiously. "I'll tell you where when we get there."

"A couple more drowning victims, Mary?" I taunted. "Won't that look suspicious after Anne Bascomb?"

"I doubt it," she answered with contempt. "The cops bought that one. They'll buy what I'm going to do with you, too."

She had the cocky overconfidence of the insane, an unshakable belief that in whatever she did she was so much smarter than anyone else she would never be caught. Maybe she also thought her daddy had enough money to get her out of it if she did. Probably his money had gotten her out of trouble before. I realized there was no argument I could use to convince her otherwise, so I would have to figure a way to overpower her.

"Why did you kill Harry?" I asked, partly out of curiosity and partly to distract her. If I could get her to talk maybe her grip on the pistol would loosen. Maybe I could knock it out of her hand. Maybe I could knock her out. Still, with her sitting next to Marilyn in the back seat I was a long way from the gun.

"Some detective you are," she said derisively. "That's the easy one. If I couldn't have Harry, I wanted to make sure nobody else would. The thought of him with someone else tortured me."

"But why kill Missy too?" I questioned.

"Because she was in the wrong place at the wrong time," Mary replied. "She was with Harry. Besides, she didn't deserve to live anyway. She took Harry away from me."

"If you killed them together, how come you put Harry in her grave?" It didn't take a genius to figure this out, but I wanted to hear it from her.

"I killed them both at the same time, on the beach at Port Aransas," she confessed, sounding very unrepentant. "I asked Harry to meet me there for old times' sake, but he brought her along. When he saw how angry I was, he tried to tell me she was just along to help with drug deals, but I had seen them together when they hadn't seen me and I knew the score. They had hitched a ride there and expected me to take them back in my convertible. I took them back all right, but I took them back dead."

"You stabbed them on the beach?"

"Sure did. It was dark. I was sitting next to Harry and Missy, watching the water. Harry left to go to the restroom. While he was gone, I stabbed Missy and put her in the back seat of the Mustang. When Harry got back, I stabbed him too, and put him in the trunk. Then I drove them to the high school, in case someone had seen me at the beach. When I got to the high school, I found out Harry was dead but Missy was only hurt."

"Hurt?"

"Yes, she wasn't dead yet. She was still breathing. So I strangled her. Then I picked her up and carried her into the field out back of the high school. She was easy to carry. But I was too tired to bother with Harry, so I left him in my trunk."

The strength of madness. In the heat of the moment, with all of that insane adrenalin pumping through her veins, she could most likely have picked up the Mustang and Melissa both.

"Did Harry tell you why Melissa modeled at Staples and didn't tell her Mother?" I asked, still stalling for time.

"He didn't have to tell me. That's another easy one. He wanted extra money for drugs and he knew I made good money that way. He thought I had quit working there, but he didn't know I still came by occasionally. He wouldn't let Melissa tell her mother because if her mother knew, Melissa couldn't give him the money."

"What did you stab them with?"

"My mama's butcher knife," Mary replied indifferently. "It's been in the family for years. It's back in her kitchen now. I had taken it along because I was going to kill Harry. Missy was a little like getting a bonus."

"What did you do with Harry's body from the time you killed him until you put the body into Missy's grave?"

"You're sure asking a lot of questions," Mary complained. "I would have thought you could guess that too. He stayed in the trunk of my car. Nobody had a clue. I wanted to put him in Missy's open grave. It was like poetic justice to me."

We had arrived at the docks even though I had purposely driven as slowly as I could without attracting Mary's attention. I still did not have a plan to overcome this monster. Not having a gun sure makes planning difficult.

"Drive over there," Mary commanded, pointing with her gun to a long row of boats. "Park by the Bertram with the name Charade."

In the middle of the row, sitting high in the water, was a 46 foot Bertram, white and shiny and squeaky clean, with a flying bridge and a fishing chair, all waiting right where she pointed. I parked the car and shut off the engine.

"Is that your family's boat?" I asked.

She chuckled at my ignorance. Overconfidence was consuming her now. "Not my family's. Mine. Daddy gave it to me for my birthday."

"Did he give you a captain and a crew too?"

"I can take it out myself," she scoffed. "I've been driving boats since I was ten."

Oh, good. We were going for a ride in a boat that could go anywhere it wanted... to Mexico, to Florida, to the Caribbean islands or to the end of the earth, with a woman holding a gun who was a dangerous and certifiable fruitcake. I was unarmed and harmless, out of time and out of ideas. All I could do was stall.

The dark night provided perfect cover for our little party. Mary ordered me out of the car. She followed me onto the boat and made me go up the ladder onto the flying bridge. She had brought along some rope and was smart enough to stay far enough away so as not to give me a shot at grabbing the gun. Even if I was able to get away, I couldn't leave Marilyn.

"Tie yourself up," she snarled, "or I'll shoot you right where you stand. It doesn't matter to me."

I wrapped the ropes around my ankles, holding them a little apart to give me maneuvering room. Then I wrapped my wrists, again, a little loose. When I finished, Mary took another rope, motioned me over to a seat, and tied me securely to it. Still holding the gun, she took another rope and tied my ankles, keeping far enough away so I could not kick out and knock her down. Finally, after make a few little adjustments here and there, she stood back to admire her work. She seemed satisfied, turned around and disappeared back down the ladder. I heard a car door open, some muffled sighs and Mary returned, carrying a limp Marilyn loosely over her shoulder as if Marilyn were some little fur wrap she was wearing. She climbed slowly up the ladder and dropped Marilyn onto the seat by me. Mary sighed, shaking her head as if she were tired of being inconvenienced.

"Why her?" I asked. "Why do you want to kill Marilyn? She hasn't done anything to you!"

Mary looked at me with her eyes opened wide in surprise. "She dated Harry. He was involved with her too."

"She didn't date Harry," I said.

"Course she did. I saw them together at a restaurant. They didn't see me. I made up my mind then and there she was a goner."

"So what did you do?"

189

"I fixed her brakes, of course," she said, talking slowly as if explaining something to a child. "That didn't work. I tried to run her off the road, but she didn't die then, either. I guess I'm not very good at arranging accidents or else she's pretty hard to kill."

"So you took a shot at her outside her apartment?"

"Yep. I missed her then, too. Of all the bad luck," Mary said regretfully, eying Marilyn with distaste. Meanwhile, she was busily readying the boat for our night voyage. Turning dials, flicking switches, starting engines. This boat had everything to make it easy for her. Bow thrusters, auto pilot. Radar.

"After I killed Harry, I didn't try to kill Marilyn anymore," Mary commented. "She was no longer a threat. It's too bad you had to bring her along tonight."

Very ironical. Marilyn could have gone home days ago and been safe, but instead she stayed with me for protection and put herself in terminal danger. The man she had seen outside her window was probably some harmless bum looking for an empty house in which to spend the night.

Mary went downstairs to untie the ropes which held Charade to her pilings. All was in place for the trip to the forever land, at least for Marilyn and me.

A few moments later she returned, a glass of wine in her hand.

"Let's see," I began. "Red for meat, white for fish. What color for murder?"

"Either or both," she replied. "Whatever suits your mood." She pushed the throttles forward, easing Charade out of her slip. She pointed the bow towards the channel which led to open water. Soon we had left the twinkling lights of the marina far behind. We were going slowly, and as there was only a light sea, we were moving smoothly through the obscure black waters. Mary's maniacal dark eyes were illuminated eerily by the reflection of lighted dials on the instrument panel. She was watching the water intently, looking for channel buoys as they appeared ahead of her. She set a course for the Port Aransas jetties and beyond them, the open Gulf of Mexico.

"What did you have against John Watts?" I asked. "Surely he wasn't dating Harry too?"

She gave me an exasperated look. "You'll clown to the very end, won't you? John Watts had seen my car at the cemetery, where I dumped Harry. Nice touch, wasn't it? Harry wanted to be with that tramp? Well, that's where I put him. Too bad he couldn't say how he liked it. Anyway, Watts saw my car, and later, when Harry's body was found, Watts put two and two together. He wanted money to keep quiet. I got it and met him after school in the Honda. When he was near my car, a kid called him over and asked him what time he was meeting you. After the kid left, Watts got in my car and I made him tell me who you were. It was easy to figure out that he had lost his nerve and was going to blow the whole deal for me and then skip town after getting the money. So I shot him. I've had enough dead bodies in my car lately to need a permit as a hearse."

"Then, you met me instead of Watts," I commented.

"That was me all right, and if you didn't have such a hard head, you'd be dead, too," she told me. "I thought if I varied my killing methods the police would not be as likely to suspect they were done by the same person." She looked at me crossly. "You're hard to kill, too. After I left you the night we hit the bars, I changed cars and hurried after you. I took a shot at you but you got away."

The yacht picked up a little speed. Mary had adjusted the throttles, apparently bored with the conversation. She wanted to get down to her business and send us on our final voyage to the bottom of the deep black sea.

Soon the lights of Port Aransas appeared. I could see ferry boats crossing the channel in the distance, the headlights of cars bobbing gently as the ferries moved them slowly through the water. On shore I could see lights in houses and apartments shining through the dark night. Colorful neon lights glowed in the distance, calling thirsty travelers to friendly, welcoming taverns. Oh, to heed that call!

"I guess about the only thing you weren't involved in lately is sending me a little black notebook," I said to Mary.

She smiled. "That's very funny. You're some detective. I certainly did send you that notebook. I gave the Shark a ride home one night after he'd gotten himself very drunk. Barracuda was off chasing some girl. The next day, while Shark was gone, I broke into his place to see what I could use. I wanted to throw suspicion on him as Harry's murderer. I found that notebook. It worked, didn't it?"

"Did you also make a threatening call to me?" I demanded.

She replied, in the same muted tone she had used on the phone to me, "Yes, that was me. It didn't back you off, though."

We had gone past the jetties and were in the Gulf of Mexico now. The seas were a little heavier and the Bertram slowed as it went through the low chop. Mary narrowed her eyes at the totality of the surrounding darkness, apparently intimidated by the feeling of powerless the darkened sea had forced onto her. She seemed confused for a moment and then pushed the throttles forward a little further, probably to get the deed over with a little sooner so she could return to the safety of the harbor.

"That leaves Harry's mother Anne," I said. "What did she do to you?"

"Amos came home drunk the other night and they got into a terrible, knock-down, drag-out fight," Mary said. "After he went to bed, she went through his wallet because she suspected he had been seeing another woman. She found my name and phone number on a piece of paper."

"So she called you?" I questioned.

"After he left for work the next day, she called me. I didn't know what she wanted. I thought she must have suspected I killed Harry," she said. "She said she wanted to see me but she wouldn't say what about. I drove to her house and waited at the curb until she came out to talk to me. I got her to get in the car and I took her a private spot I know on the beach. We talked. I got her to write a note and then held her underwater until she drowned. I thought the police would think it was suicide."

"Last I heard, they weren't sure," I admitted.

"Hah! You see, I will get away with it," Mary said confidently. A completely remorseless killer. "Anne told me she had called you, but that was a lie."

"It wasn't a lie. I just wasn't home. What did she want with me?" I asked.

"I don't know. I think maybe she wanted to fuss at you for taking her husband drinking or to ask you if her husband was seeing me. I would have been fixed for sure if you had been home and she told you I was coming to see her."

"So, why did you kill her?" I continued. "She only thought you were having an affair with her husband."

"I didn't know that when I got there. Unfortunately I let something slip and she guessed I killed Harry. Then I had to kill her. She knew too much."

I was near to running out of questions. I still had one important one. "Why me?"

"You were getting too close. You almost found out about me from John Watts. You even brought me into it. I couldn't take any chances you'd pull all the loose ends together into a neat little package."

"So what about--"

"Enough talking! Let me think," she commanded, staring straight ahead. The wind had come up and the seas were much heavier. The bow of the Bertram was raising way up over the horizon, or where the horizon would have been if we could see it, and dipping deeply into the trough between the waves. Perhaps a squall out in the distance that was producing streaks of lightning had contributed to the size of the waves.

"All right, here's what we're going to do," Mary said, a wild look in her eyes. "I'm going to untie your ankles and free you from the seat so you can go down the ladder. Then I'll let you go over the side of the boat. It's your only chance. If you can somehow make it the 15 miles back to shore, so be it. Otherwise, you can take a bullet right here, right now. Which is it going to be?"

"You call going over the side with my hands tied in the middle of the night in shark infested waters with heavy seas 15 miles from shore a chance?" I asked skeptically.

"Compared to a bullet close range in the head, I do," she answered, amused. "Oh, well, all right. I'll loosen your hands a little. I'd rather you drown than wash up on shore with a bullet in you. Plus, if I loosen them, the ropes will at some point come off. It'd be suspicious if someone found you on the beach, dead, with tied hands." She came over and loosened them a millimeter or two.

"Okay, it's a deal," I said, not particularly enthusiastically. Mary bent down and took all the ropes off my ankles. Then she removed the ropes holding me to my seat. I stood up and stretched. Mary put the controls on autopilot and motioned to the ladder, gun in hand.

"Down, boy," she said. "I'll follow you just to make sure you don't get any big ideas about going into the stateroom instead of the deep. Marilyn will be along in a moment."

I went down first, leaning into the ladder so I wouldn't slip off. Be a shame to fall off and get hurt, right? When I got to the deck I stood back and waited politely as she came down face forward, pistol aimed at my head.

"Now, dear, over the side and swim for it!" she urged, eyes reflecting brightly from a light inside the cabin. Her dark coal colored eyes were frenzied now, and I don't know if the coal had at long last been pressured to change, or if the light's reflection was in them, but I was looking into the sparkling depth of deadly diamonds... Mary's wild, crazy eyes.

It was my last chance, all right, but I wasn't going to take the chance she thought I was. Instead of going meekly over the side, I turned and gathered all the force and power I could in the short deck space available. I quickly aimed my 205 pounds at her, meaning to push us both over the side before she could move her index finger an inch and send me to the end of the life line. At least if we both went over I'd have saved Marilyn. I hit her full force and prepared to feel the cool, salty water as we both toppled over the side. I did feel it, too, at least my head and shoulders felt it, but my leg got wedged tightly in the swim ladder on the stern of the boat, and I was dragged like a rag doll through the swirling, frothy waters of Charade's wake.

By grabbing onto the swim platform, a sturdy wooden support suspended off the stern of the boat near the water's edge, I was able to move myself backwards until my leg was free. I worked the ropes off my wrists, climbed up the ladder onto the deck, and stared out into the dark water. Mary was long since out of sight, somewhere in the distance riding the up and down seas, taking the same chance she had offered me moments earlier. At least her hands were free. Assuming she hadn't fallen under one of Charade's propellers.

I rushed back up to the flying bridge and untied Marilyn, making sure she was all right. She was terrified, angry, confused and seasick. Then she became calmer, happy to feel the heady taste of freedom again. I took the wheel and turned the boat around slowly, starting a careful search for Mary, the deranged madwoman of the deep. I turned on the search light, but all I could see ahead were dark and turbulent waters and in the far, far distance the lights of Port Aransas. I radioed the Coast Guard for assistance and they said they'd be right out, but I heard the doubt in their voices about Mary. It was unlikely we'd find her, but maybe that was just as well.

A boat was rapidly approaching us from the direction of Port Aransas.

"Maybe that's Walter," Marilyn said.

I looked at her sharply. "Are you okay?" I asked, concerned that she might have suffered a head injury. Why else would she look for Walter out here?

"I called Walter on the cell phone while you were looking for Mary's apartment," Marilyn explained. "He told me that the autopsy showed that Anne Bascomb had drowned all right, but that she had bruises on her shoulders from where she had been held down while she drowned. I gave him the license number of the Honda. He ran a quick check and found it was registered in Mary's name. He decided to come immediately and talk with her."

"So by the time he got there, the Honda was gone and so were we," I said. "But the Porsche was still there. He must have gone to her neighbors, or called her parents. He found out she had a boat and checked the marina. The boat was gone, and there was the Honda parked by its slip." Finally, I was detecting.

I heard Walter's voice coming over the marine radio. I picked up the mike and acknowledged his call. He had alerted the Coast Guard even before they got our call and was on their first boat to reach us.

"Are you all right?" he asked. "Is Marilyn okay? What's going on?"

"We're all right," I reassured him. "But you got here a little late this time, amigo."

"Better late than never," he replied, and clicked off.

BRINGING BACK KAY-KAY